Dreams of the Night

JOYCE HARRINGTON

Reprinted by arrangement with St. Martin's Press

ISBN: 1-55547-291-5

Manufactured in the United States of America

FOR CHRIS AND EVAN

1

DREEMZ. The letters were fat and round, 3-D, magenta shaded with lime green. The boy who called himself Dreemz stood back and admired his work in the dim light of the subway yard. It was good. It was the best piece he'd ever done. Almost as good as Caine, or Dondi, or the Fab Five, heroes of the golden age of graffiti writing. DREEMZ blazed on the side of the subway car, over a background of faded lesser tags. Toy writers, taking up space on the cars with their ugly scrawls. Anything to get their tags up. They'd never be real graffiti artists. Their tags didn't *mean* anything. They didn't practice the way he did, testing out new pieces in his sketchbook, trying out new color combinations, writing DREEMZ, DREEMZ, DREEMZ on page after page, in book after book. They didn't know the history of graffiti, study the art, collect other writers' pieces. They didn't take any risks, like going into the yards and lay-ups late at night, evading the transit cops, tearing clothes and sometimes skin on the vicious razor wire. All they did was throw up their stupid tags on trains standing in stations when there wasn't anybody around. Bombing the inside of a whole car between one station and the next at three in the morning. Chicken-shit stuff.

Toys were the cause of all the uproar and crackdown against graffiti. The outside world didn't understand the difference between toy writing and the real thing, the masterpieces. All they saw was train after train, car after car, covered with unreadable black scrawls, with every once in a while a really beautiful piece, like the legendary Christmas train done in 1977 by Lee and Mono and Doc and Slave, four of the Fabulous Five. That one didn't last very long. There wasn't a trace of it left. Buffed years ago. Or the time he'd done Vaughn Bodé's Belinda Bumps on a No. 4 train to celebrate his fifteenth birthday. A year and a half later, you could still catch Belinda shooting up and down the Lexington Avenue line, her mammoth tits aimed at the passengers getting on through the center door. She was faded now, and her name and her frame had been gone over by the toys. But when she was new—oh God—she was something else!

That was before he'd become Dreemz. In those days, he'd signed himself Stoke because he was practically living on grass. Now, he'd given up the herb totally and meditated instead to concentrate his mind, but he was still flunking out of high school—not because he was stupid but because it was all so boring. Reading was okay, especially when they let him read stuff about guys turning into cockroaches. He could really get off on that. But the rest of Kafka wasn't nearly so weird. They didn't like it when he brought *Zippy the Pinhead* comics to school or tried to turn the class onto Carlos Castaneda. Fuck them. If they didn't want to listen to what he had to say, he wouldn't listen to them. And forget about art class. Doing pretty pastel drawings of still lifes or jerk-off posters for the senior play. When he'd handed in his best piecing book as an independent project, they'd given him an F. "Not fulfilling the requirements," the asshole teacher had written on the first page in red ink.

What did she know? She thought art died after Michelangelo. He'd had to tear out that first page. He'd been so mad, he'd almost torn up the whole book. Instead, he'd wasted time arguing with her. If it was okay to paint the ceiling of a church, for Christ's sake, why wasn't it okay to paint the sides of subway cars?

"Because those cars are public property," she'd said. "Nobody asked you to paint them."

"Well, isn't a church public property?"

"That's not the point. The ceiling of the Sistine Chapel is art. Graffiti isn't. It's that simple."

"Norman Mailer says it is. I got his book right here."

"Norman Mailer says a lot of things."

"Are you giving me an F because you hate graffiti?"

"I'm giving you an F because that's all that garbage deserves."

The yard was quiet and deserted and cold. It was after midnight. Dreemz knew that at this hour the guards would be huddled in their work car, wallowing in the fug of their own cigarette smoke and stale breath. He studied the side of the car he'd been working on. The piece was perfect, almost dry now, but it only took up half the car. Should he repeat it on the other half with variations? Or do one of his atomic holocaust pieces? He could repeat his DREEMZ in maybe an hour, but a full-scale atomic piece with an evil Uncle Sam and a mushroom cloud and dead babies, even on half a car, would take him until dawn. He crawled under the car and lay down on the track to study his piecing book by the light of a flashlight. He wore woolen gloves with the tips of the fingers cut off, to keep his hands warm but leave his fingers free for the delicate work of giving the spray can buttons just the right amount of pressure. Too heavy and the whole thing dripped and ran, too light and the result was uneven.

3

The smell under the train was funky and weird, like a graveyard or a battlefield. Dead rats maybe, and the cold smell of old train grease. And rotting garbage. It was the smell of the world, the world he wanted to change. People were such pigs. Maybe they didn't deserve to be saved from the bombs that would turn the whole planet into a dead wasteland. But that's what his DREEMZ was all about. Dream, you guys. Dream up a better world than this. Stop all the Star Wars shit before it's too late. I don't want to be nuked. You don't want to be nuked. Well, let's do something about it instead of rattling bombs at each other. The world could be a beautiful place. Kids should be able to grow up without worrying over whether they're going to be fried or stumble around puking nuke juice.

Dreemz flipped the pages of his piecing book, skimming past the visions of destruction that filled his mind and poured out of the chiseled tips of his marking pens. Somewhere toward the back of the book, he'd done some pieces that showed what he wanted the world to be. Flowers and white fluffy clouds, a girl dancing and a boy meditating, naked but not raunchy. Things like that. Rainbows. His mother said they were pretty, but he was a dreamer. A left-over hippie and how did he ever get that way? His mother said he ought to try to get into art school if he ever finished high school before he was fifty years old. Why couldn't he paint on canvas the way a regular artist should? There was money in art. Look at Andy Warhol. Not that she wanted him to be like that. But, at least, she didn't try to make him stop. She knew she couldn't

He'd shown his piecing books to his father only once. That was enough.

He found the piece he called ADAM AND EVE II. No snakes in this garden. No traps set up by the big guy in the sky. No fucking fig leaves to make people ashamed of what they were. ADAM was a black dude and EVE was white. Some people still couldn't hack that. His father for one. Up at one side of the piece he'd written the message in bubble-letters inside a cloud. NO GOD. NO SNAKES. NO NUKES. JUST US. And then he'd signed his graffiti name. DREEMZ.

It was a new piece, something he'd sketched out in algebra class—remedial of course—the week before while the teacher had been droning on about X equals blah, blah, blah, and filled in later at home while his father and mother argued over what to watch on television. He wasn't sure he had all the colors he needed, but he'd just have to use what he had. The more he looked at it, the more he felt this was the piece he had to do tonight. He wished he had some of his friends with him, Juice or Zebra, to help him get it up. They could have done the filling in and some of the shading after he'd got the design outlined. But after the fight he'd had with Juice last week, he didn't feel right about asking him to go bombing, and Zebra was getting into computers as if they were kings of the world and he was some kind of brain-slave to them. No time for anything else. He never even came around the storefront anymore. Well, this wasn't the first time he'd gone out alone and it wouldn't be the last.

Dreemz stared at his ADAM AND EVE II piece, memorizing all its form and shadings so he could get it up without looking at the book. He couldn't use the flashlight while he was working. Someone would see it and crash down on him. He would be practically painting in the dark. The yard had bright worklights here and there, but he'd chosen a car well away from any of them. If the guards patrolled, he'd be able to see them before they saw him. And he'd worked in the dark so much, he sometimes thought he was getting cat's eyes. Graffiti eyes. Next step on the evolutionary ladder. He'd liked it when they talked about Darwin in school. Darwin was cool. He saw things nobody else could see. Evolution made monsters understandable, mistakes along the way, and held out hope for something better. Eventually. But it took so fucking long. That was one thing old Darwin didn't take into account. That we'd blow ourselves off the face of the earth before we had a chance to evolve into something better. It wasn't Darwin's fault. He didn't invent it. He just figured it out. It was up to us to cool things out before there was nothing left but sizzled bones.

Dreemz turned off his flashlight and rolled out from under the train. The smell was intoxicating. It turned him on. Better than grass. It gave him visions. Up and down the tracks on either side of him, darkened subway cars slept. He flashed on what they'd be doing in just a few hours, racing through the tunnels, screeching into the stations, bulging with people pushing to get on and off. He felt almost as if the cars were monolithic creatures enslaved to the people they carted around the city. Sometimes, when he was painting a car, he practically sensed it breathing and sighing with delight, knowing it was being made beautiful, and that people would stare and get the message that it carried. He put his piecing book away in his backpack and got out a half-dozen cans of spray paint to get started with. Quickly, he sketched in ADAM, tall and strong, with muscle bumps like Conan the Barbarian, and then the smooth round figure of EVE, with her arms spread out to love the world.

He hummed a tuneless small sound while he worked, close to his mantra but not quite, just enough to keep his mind concentrated on what he was doing. The vision of his piece stayed before his eyes as it took shape on the side of the subway car. This one was going to be good, his best work ever, a real burner. Later, he'd wait for it at the Brooklyn Bridge station. That was the only way to get a good look at what he'd done.

2

Alex Carlson slammed his fist down onto the alarm clock and recoiled with pain. "Dammit!" he muttered and rolled over, burying his head and his aching hand under the pillow.

The ringing continued. He ignored it as long as he could. When he couldn't stand it any longer, he sat bolt upright in bed and blinked into the darkness. It wasn't the clock at all. It was the phone. And where was the phone? Last week, he'd put a new long cord on it so he could take it anywhere in the apartment, and now he could never remember where he'd left it.

He got out of bed, naked and shivering, and stumbled across the room. He remembered talking to Edie last night before he went to bed, but he'd made himself a sandwich while he was talking to her and couldn't remember if he'd left the phone in the kitchen or put it someplace else. One of these days he'd have to get himself a lamp to put next to the bed so he wouldn't have to do this groping around in the dark. Maybe next payday he'd have enough money left over to buy one. He reached the wall and flipped on the light switch. One good thing about a studio apartment, you couldn't really lose anything for good. The phone was sitting on top of the stove in the tiny kitchen alcove, right where he'd left it, ringing its head off.

He snatched up the receiver, ready to blast the lunatic who had the nerve to wake him up in the middle of the night. "Hello!" he shouted into it. "And it better not be a wrong number!"

"Alex? Is that you?" It was his mother, sounding worried. But that was nothing new. She sounded worried a lot lately.

"Yeah, Ma. What's up?" He softened his voice. Sometimes, she really had things to worry about.

"Nothing, really. What's the matter with you?"

"Well, Ma. To tell you the truth, I was sleeping and I wasn't expecting to hear from you. Is something the matter or did you just call to see if I was behaving myself?"

"It's morning, Alex. It's time to get up."

Alex squinted at the window where dim gray light showed between the slats of the venetian blinds. "I didn't ask for a wake-up call, did I?" The alarm clock showed six-thirty. Another half-hour was all he wanted. He could have slept until seven and still got to the Academy on time, if he was lucky and the trains weren't screwed up this morning.

"No. No. It's not that. Is Paulie with you?"

"No. Isn't he there?"

There was a long silence, and then her voice came through again, whispering as if she was afraid someone would hear her. "Would I be calling you if he was? He didn't come home last night. I'm worried about him, Alex. I don't want your father to know he's not here."

"It's not the first time, is it? He probably stayed with one of his friends. Don't worry, Ma. The kid's sixteen. He's a big boy now. He can take care of himself."

"He's not that big, Alex. And don't tell me about his friends. I know about his friends. They're nothing but trouble. And I know where he's been. Out doing that graffiti on the trains. Can't you talk to him, Alex? Make him stop? He'll listen to you."

"No, he won't, Ma. We've been through all that before. Just give him time. There aren't any middle-aged graffiti writers. They all get serious and stop after a while. Paulie'll stop too, but not if you keep after him about it." Alex carried the phone across the room and got back into bed. The sheets were cold, but he pulled the blankets up around his naked shoulders and his shivering subsided. The radiators had begun to hiss, but the warmth hadn't yet penetrated the early morning chill. He knew from experience that there was no way to turn his mother off until she'd finished saying everything she had on her mind. He might as well be comfortable while he listened.

"The thing that worries me," she went on, "is what your father might do when he finds out. The last time Paulie stayed out all night, there was a terrible scene. You're lucky you weren't here. The two of them were like wild animals. Neither one of them would give an inch. I thought I was going to have to call the police."

"Don't do that, Ma. Don't ever do that. There's not much the police can do about family quarrels."

"Not even if they start swinging at each other?"

"Did they do that? My God, Ma! Why didn't you call me?"

"They didn't, but it was close. I'm afraid the next time, they will. Your father has a temper and Paulie's so hard-headed. He won't even lie about what he does. Sometimes, I wish he would, just to keep the peace. But no, he just gets that look on his face that drives Theo crazy."

"If it'll do any good, you can tell Pop that Paulie spent the night here. Tell him we went to a movie and it was late when we got out."

9

"I can try, but I don't know if he'll buy that. He knows you two don't hang out much together. Listen, I've got to go now. He'll be coming downstairs any minute. I don't want him to catch me on the phone. He'll want to know who I was talking to and what about and so forth."

"Don't let him push you around, Ma."

"Oh, it's all right. I know how to handle him. Just don't make him mad. Thanks, Alex. It always makes me feel better, just talking to you. Goodbye."

Alex said, "Don't worry, Ma." But she was gone.

The phone was resting on his chest. He left it there and closed his eyes. Too early to call Edie, but in a little while he would. In the meantime, he could just lie back and think about the weekend. It would be great if they could go off to Puerto Rico or the Virgin Islands, not just for the weekend but for a whole week. February was the lousiest month of the year, cold and gloomy. Nothing good ever happened in February. If it was up to him, they could just erase it from the calendar.

He let his mind drift to a sandy beach, a bright blue ocean lapping gently just inches away from his toes, and a searing sun blazing down on him out of a cloudless sky. And Edie, lying there beside him, both of them tan and happy, without a worry in the world. But none of that could happen for at least another three months, not until after graduation, and who knows what they'd be doing then.

When the ringing started again, he jerked awake in a panic. The phone fell off his chest, and he heard a tiny voice saying, "Hello? Hello?" The face of the alarm clock remorselessly showed seven-thirty. He'd overslept.

He fumbled the receiver to his ear and muttered, "Edie?"

Her voice came bright and clear, with that little tinge of Texas that he loved and loved to tease her about. "I'm leaving now, but you didn't call so I thought I'd better call you and make sure you were up. You're up, aren't you?"

10

"Uh, yeah. No. Not exactly. Thanks, Edie."

"The sergeant's got it in for you already. If you're late one more time, you're in deep trouble."

"I know. I know. I'm in the shower already."

"See you later."

"Edie?"

"Yeah?"

"If we lived together, you could wake me up every morning."

She didn't answer, but he could hear her breathing, considering her reply.

"If we lived together," he pursued, "I'd get more sleep because I wouldn't have to get up in the middle of the night and come home."

He heard exasperation in her sigh, and hoped she was smiling. She said, "If we lived together, neither one of us would ever get any sleep. Bye. I'll see you at roll call."

Alex hung up the phone and shoved it under the bed. He took two minutes in the shower, the last thirty seconds of it ice cold to make sure he was awake, and then five minutes to shave. Carefully. No point in showing up with less than a good, close shave. The sergeant was a stickler about things like that. Alex's uniform still held a fairly decent press. Thank God he'd hung it up the night before. And his shoes, under a layer of city dust, were still shiny. He gave them a quick swipe with his damp towel and put them on. No time for breakfast, but he slugged down a glass of milk and promised himself a good lunch at the coffee shop near the Academy. In fifteen minutes, he was ready to leave. In his old down jacket, with his black police recruit's satchel bumping against his legs, he ran down the stairs and out into the chilly gray morning.

The Brooklyn streets were thronged with people heading for the subway station at Grand Army Plaza. Alex hurried along, half running and threading his way among the

11

slower-moving civilians. At a deli a few blocks from the station, he dashed in for a cup of coffee to drink on the train.

Waiting on the platform, Alex finally allowed his mind to edge toward the problem of his kid brother. Paulie was a brat, a little vandal, a weedhead, and a rip-off artist. His hair was longer than most girls' and he went around in rags that no self-respecting bum would be caught dead in. He was too young to have much of a beard or he'd have that, too. But worst of all, he was a graffiti freak. He lived, breathed, ate, slept, and pissed graffiti. Sure, Alex knew where Paulie'd been last night. Out writing on the trains. Where else would he be? And his mother knew that, too. So why did she have to call him up at the crack of dawn to ask him? Did she expect him to do something about it? Not that he hadn't tried. He'd talked to Paulie and talked to Paulie. Didn't do any good. Paulie just smiled in that goofy way of his and said, "You gotta talk that way, bro. You're a cop, and cops are down on graffiti automatically. You won't even let yourself think about it."

As a crowded No. 2 train pulled in, Alex scanned each passing car for evidence of Paulie's night out. All of the cars were marked with graffiti, but most of it was the kind that Paulie called "toy writing," ugly scrawls that must have meant something to the kids who put it there but nothing to the people who rode the trains, except to irritate them. At least what Paulie did had some thought behind it; he was always going on about some cause or other. Lately, it had been Star Wars and nuclear disaster. He spent a lot of time drawing in his sketchbooks, designing the pictures he painted on the trains. Still and all, it was vandalism, and it was dangerous. Alex wished there were some way to reach Paulie and make him see that he was wasting his time and giving their mother a lot of grief.

On the car that stopped in front of him, Alex thought he saw Paulie's old tag, STOKE, but he couldn't be sure. It was faded and marked over, hard to read. And there were so many tags that started with the letter S. SEEN and SNAKE and SEX and SLICK and probably hundreds more. Paulie said the graffiti writers liked S because it was curvy and juicy and quick to write.

He managed to get aboard the train. When the pushing and shoving was over and the doors closed, he found himself wedged into a knot of people clinging to one of the center poles. Too bad he'd have to do it all over again at the Nevins Street stop, but this was the Seventh Avenue line and he'd have to change to the Lex to get to Union Square.

The train ground its way through the tunnel, and the herd aboard it rode patiently. Sometimes, Alex used his subway time to study, but this morning the train was too crowded for him to open his satchel and get out a book. It was strange, being back in school after two or three years of being out, and trying to settle into a job that gave him any kind of satisfaction at all. There was so much about the Academy that grated on him. The regimentation, the instinctive feeling that when he finally got out on the streets he'd find out that it was all very different, and he'd never use most of the things they had to learn. Worst of all, most of the guys in his class were three or four years younger than he. The girls, too. Only you'd better not call them girls. They were Women with a capital W. There were a few recruits who were older; one guy was at least thirty, but he was a police officer in another state and was just going through the Academy to learn how New York City trained its "Finest" and then take the experience back home. Everything was easy for him, and he loved to tell stories about how much better they did things in the rinky-dink town he came from. He wasn't a popular guy.

But it was better than the last job he'd had, managing the office of a bicycle messenger service. He'd had to deal all day long with the crazies who rode the killer bikes all over the city and with the customers that the crazies drove crazy who thought they had perfectly good reasons not to pay their bills. It sure wasn't the kind of job he'd spent four years at Brooklyn College for, but it was all he could find at the time he had needed it most. It had given him the courage and the cash to leave home and get his own apartment.

The train pulled into the Nevins Street station just as a No. 4 train across the platform was about to close its doors. Alex and about half of the other people in his car surged through the narrow door and raced in a flying wedge for the other train, the ones in front holding the doors open while the conductor yelled, "Let go the doors! There's another train right behind this one!"

Alex, at the rear of the crowd, was determined to get on the train. There might or might not be another train behind this one, but he didn't have time to wait for it. He'd been late too many times already, and he'd been warned. Once more and there'd be disciplinary action. He didn't know what that meant, but he didn't want to risk being kicked out. He shoved against the people blocking the door, trying to gain a foothold inside the train and squeeze himself and his satchel aboard. The woman blocking his way glared at him and shoved back. He was about to say something, plead with her to make room, when a patch of bright blue on the side of the train caught his eye. He backed off and stared at it. It was one of Paulie's pieces.

The doors closed and Alex stepped back a few more paces to see the whole car before it disappeared down the line. It was Paulie, all right. On one half of the car, a huge DREEMZ, magenta and green, screamed at him. The other half was covered with one of Paulie's scenes. Blue sky,

14

clouds, two figures covering up the windows. Man and woman. Black and white. Paulie's idea of heaven on earth. And over on one side, a cloud outlined in black with one of his goofball messages written inside it. Alex tried to read the message, but the train was starting to move. He ran along beside it. There was something wrong with the message. He read, "NO GOD. NO SNAKES. NO" and that was all. The message wasn't finished. It wasn't signed. There was no DREEMZ to finish it off. The train picked up speed and racketed past him. Alex stood on the platform and watched the twinkling red lights as the last car dwindled away into the tunnel. Something had happened. Paulie hadn't finished his piece. That was like God deciding on the fifth day that He'd done enough, He wasn't going to finish the job. Maybe he'd got busted. That was the best thing that could have happened to him. A night in jail might straighten him out if nothing else could.

Another train pulled in, crowded as all the trains in the morning rush hour were, but Alex managed to jam his way aboard. With Paulie's latest graffiti piece still vivid in his mind, he decided he'd try one more time to talk to the kid. Something had to be done. Someday he might find himself having to arrest his own brother. Ma wouldn't know how to deal with that one, and Pop would have a shit fit. Paulie had already been arrested a couple of times, once for jumping a turnstile and once for spray painting on the wall at the Canal Street station. Both times they'd let him off with a lecture, but that wouldn't last forever.

The thing was, Paulie could really be somebody if he just tried. The kid was smart, a whole lot smarter than Alex ever was in school. You had to give him credit for that, but not for the way he just wouldn't use the intelligence he had. And he was good-looking, if he'd just clean himself up and get a haircut. And he could talk his way into or out of any-

15

thing. Not like Alex, who even at twenty-four still some-times got too excited and talked too much, or got swamped in shyness and couldn't say a word. Alex knew he'd spent most of his younger years being jealous of Paulie, the baby who'd come along when he was eight years old and used to being the only kid in the family. But there was nothing to be jealous about anymore. Now that Alex had made it into the Police Academy and Paulie was the one who was fuck-ing up with his graffiti mania.

The train jerked to a halt, and an angry-sounding voice shouted a garbled message over the loudspeaker.

"What'd he say?" someone asked.

No one bothered to answer. Subway passengers were used to the trains stopping between stations for no apparent reason. It was just another indignity they had to put up with.

Alex put his satchel down on the floor between his feet. It could be a long wait. The people around him stood pa-tiently, reading newspapers or magazines or just staring blankly at the advertising cards that fought for wall space with the graffiti that covered the interior of the car. Alex studied their faces, wondering what kind of lives they had, what jobs they were going to, and what their dreams were. He imagined what they would do if they were suddenly given a chance to do something illegal that would make them rich, and they were guaranteed not to be caught.

These were the people he would one day be sworn to protect. Put that way, the idea sounded wimpy, and he'd never say it to any of his classmates. But he took it seri-ously. Sure, there was a little larceny in all of us, but he thought most people were pretty honest. They were too scared to be otherwise. But they weren't scared enough. Most of them had no idea of the danger there was all around them. Right here, on this train, he thought he could pick out two, maybe three, basically criminal types. Nothing serious, just your average New York City dirtbags, and they weren't doing anything but standing there looking innocent. But meet up with any one of them at the wrong moment and you'd be minus a wallet or a gold chain. Alex stood just a little taller than his six foot two and tried to make his face look stern and serious. If this train would ever get going, and if he didn't get thrown out of the Academy for being late this morning, then soon, in a few months, he would graduate and become a real cop. And he'd be a good one. He was sure of that.

The train jerked into motion and from the far end of the car a voice sang out, "Praise the Lord! Jesus is here on this Lex express right now, this minute, and wants you to come to Him. He maketh the sun to rise and the moon to rise and he maketh the trains to roll. He just don't maketh mankind to see the true path of salvation. You got to do that for yourself. But He's waiting. He's here and He's waiting. Don't keep Him waiting too long. This train's going to glory! Praise the Lord!"

3

The work crew trudged through the yard, lugging their cleaning equipment and complaining: the weather; the Islanders; their wives; Mayor Koch; their hangovers; the women who were trying to get into the union and take their jobs away; how much they hated their jobs anyway and maybe they ought to all quit and go on welfare and let the bitches take over and see how they liked it. Ernesto Fuentes listened and nodded but didn't say very much except, "Yeah, man," and "No, man," just to be agreeable. He didn't even understand most of what they were talking about.

Ernesto was glad to have his job. He didn't like it or not like it. It was okay. He got paid. Cleaning subway cars wasn't his idea of the good life in *Nueva Yorqui,* but it was better than slow starvation in the streets of Barranquilla. The frigid early morning air sliced through his sweater and windbreaker and, like a snake of ice, coiled itself around his chest. Next payday, after he gave Lena the housekeeping money, maybe he could buy himself a pair of long johns and a new pair of gloves. These he was wearing were falling apart and wouldn't last through the next few months of cold weather. His fingers were already frozen and the day

18

had hardly begun. Even after three years, Ernesto could not get used to the winters in this terrible city. It never got warm enough, not even in the heat of August. There was always the memory of snow.

The men crossed the yard slowly, stepping high each time they came to an electrified third rail. No need to hurry. The day's quota of cars to be cleaned was waiting for them. Tomorrow there'd be more. And the day after that. It was endless. The job was impossible. They could never get the inside of the cars really clean. The bigger yards had cleaning machines that scrubbed the outside, but even they couldn't remove every trace of graffiti. On the inside, no matter what they used, traces of marker ink and spray paint remained on the doors and walls. The best they could do was to scrub it all down to a faint shadow of itself, then wait for that car to come around again with a new layer of paint for them to scrub off.

Ernesto thought some of the big pictures on the outsides of the trains were pretty. The bright colors made his eyes happy and sometimes reminded him of a picture that used to hang on the wall of his mother's house when he was a child. It was a strange picture, not religious like the pictures in other houses in his village, but his mother didn't go to church like the other women. Not after his father had been killed and robbed by the *bandidos* when he was coming back from selling a load of fish in the city. After that, his mother had become an *espiritualista,* selling little bottles of purple and blue and green sugar water with a little rum in it, and killing chickens at midnight behind the house, muttering and singing in her hoarse, sad voice. The picture on the wall was something she'd torn out of a magazine. It was, to the young Ernesto, both frightening and peaceful, and he used to stare at it by the hour, puzzling over the figure of the sleeping man in his brightly striped clothes whose face was

19

darker than his own, and the lion who stood over him. Ernesto could never figure out if the lion was guarding the man or was about to eat him up. Sometimes, he thought the man was his dead father. After they'd moved into Barranquilla, he'd never seen the picture again, but it stayed in his mind as a remembrance of a time when skies were almost always blue and the great ocean was just outside his house for him to play in. He thought he was about seven years old when they left the village.

"Hey, Ernie!" The voice of the crew boss blasted into his reverie. "Time to wake up. You go on down and start in on that end car. I'll send somebody down later to give you a hand."

Ernesto nodded and gazed down the line of cars. The end car looked miles away. Most of the time, the crew boss sent him off to work by himself. He thought it was because the other men didn't like him and didn't want to work with him, but he didn't mind. He could think his own thoughts, sing his own songs, and not have to talk so much in the strange *inglés* language that he was still struggling to learn and understand. Ernesto plodded away toward the end of the line of cars, carrying his bucket and brushes and rags and the heavy can of cleaning solvent, hoping that the low gray sky would not unload any snow that day or the next, not until he could get himself a good pair of boots to keep his feet warm and dry. It took so much money to keep Lena and the two *niños* and his mother in clothes and food and pay the rent, and his mother was always after him to get a car so she could see the *norteamericano* mountains and the seashore that she'd only heard about. Go on the subway, he would tell her, go to Coney Island. But she wouldn't. She was afraid.

The end car wasn't painted with one of the pretty pictures, and the inside of all the cars was never anything but a

20

jumble of hard black lines that made him feel sad and a little crazy. He wondered if that was how the bad boys who painted the lines felt. He put his cleaning gear down near the door at the end of the car and climbed up to open it with his precious key. To Ernesto, the key was a symbol of the importance of his work. With it he could open any subway car on the line. The boss had warned them all that the graffiti boys liked to steal the keys so they could get inside the cars and do their damage.

Standing in the open doorway of the car, Ernesto stretched his arms toward the sky, getting his muscles ready for the hard work ahead of him. On a good day, he could clean an entire car in less than an hour. He always hoped that the boss would notice that he was such a good worker, so fast, and his cars were always the cleanest. But that never happened. It was as if the boss didn't care whether the cars got clean or not. But Ernesto cared. What good was work if you couldn't take pride in what you had done? He gazed out across the yard. The empty track beyond his car snaked away toward the distant fence along with all the other tracks that made a dull gray shine like the ocean on a stormy day. And like the ocean, there was something breaking the slick surface not too far away. If it were really the ocean, it would be a rock or the back of a big fish. Ernesto sighed for the lost happiness of his childhood and got to work.

Once he'd been scrubbing for a while, the cold didn't seem so bad. He even began to work up a sweat. But the fumes of the paint solvent made his eyes water and his nose run. When it got so bad he couldn't see what he was doing, he stopped scrubbing and got out the torn piece of sheet he used for a handkerchief. Every morning Lena gave him a clean piece of sheet and every evening he gave it back to her, streaked with paint and the water from his eyes. He refused to call it tears. A man didn't cry when he had work to do.

After wiping his eyes and blowing his nose, Ernesto went back to the open door and stretched his muscles once again. It was good to feel his arms so strong, but all the stretching and bending and scrubbing made his back hurt. His mother had given Lena some salve to rub on his back, but Lena was so busy with the children and with the cooking, and the housecleaning, he didn't like to ask her to rub his back. She'd been so pretty, Lena, when he'd married her, but now she was starting to look skinny and hurt. Not so pretty any-more. She didn't talk about it much, but Ernesto thought she was sorry they'd left Colombia to come here. She was a mountain girl, and he knew she didn't like living in the city. There wasn't anything he could do about that right now. Maybe later, in a few years, if he could hang onto this good job, if he could win a little something in the lottery, they could move out to Yonkers or even out to the real country where she could keep a few chickens and plant a garden. She might look pretty again if they could do that.

With his arms stretched above his head, Ernesto gazed out across the sea of tracks. The dark lump was still there, rising above the gray steel surface. Ernesto wondered what it was. If it was truly a rock, put there by some of those bad boys who came in the night and painted on the cars, it could cause some damage to the trains when they were brought into the yard. It could even cause a train to go off the rails and somebody could get hurt. He didn't like to leave his work, even for a minute, even to relieve himself between the cars as the other men did. He had promised himself never to give the crew boss any reason to criticize him. But he could be criticized for not reporting a rock on the track, especially if it caused an accident and he was the only one close enough to have seen it. He thought about calling one

22

of the other men to go look at it with him, but they were all hard at work and no one had come to work with him. He decided to scrub one more section of his car and think it over.

But even as he worked, his thoughts kept straying down the track. If it was a rock, it was a pretty big one. From where he'd seen it, it seemed to fill up the whole area between the two rails. Where had it come from? It must be heavy. How could boys, even those bad boys, have carried it into the yard, over the fence, or through it if they'd cut a hole, and why had they put it just there? If it wasn't a rock, what was it?

Ernesto threw down his scrubbing brush and went back to the door. The rock, or whatever it was, lay several tracks and about four subway car lengths away from him. Too far for him to come to any conclusion about it. He jumped down from the car and crossed to the track upon which it lay, looking over his shoulder and hoping that the boss would not see him deserting his work. Still, he could not decide what it was. He walked along the ties, blinking and squinting, trying to figure it out. As he drew closer, the lump began to look less and less like a rock, more and more like a big soft pillow. But who would put a pillow on the track? And why?

He walked closer and closer. When he was about twenty feet away, he noticed another smaller lump at one side of the track. That was strange. This other lump was not as dark as the big one and it looked as if it was covered with hair. Some kind of animal? The ground around the small lump looked sticky as if somebody had spilled some paint. Dark red paint. Closer, and he could see buttons glinting on the big lump. Closer, and there was a pair of dirty sneakers. Closer, a hand with the fingers sticking out of a glove with no fingertips. Closer.

23

"Ay, Jesús!" Ernesto thought he had screamed, but he'd only made a whimper that was lost in his throat. He turned and ran, crazy-legged, back up the track. He stumbled on a tie and fell to his knees. The pain and the sight he had seen churned in his stomach. Up came the good breakfast Lena had made for him. He shook his head and splattered himself with vomit. Still retching, he scrambled to his feet and ran again. The men, the work crew, seemed a thousand miles away. He shouted, but his voice choked on the sour residue in his throat. He coughed and spat and ran and shouted again.

A man peered out at him from the nearest car. Ernesto could see the dull boredom of work graven on his face.

"Ayuda!" he screamed. *"Hay un muerto!"*

The man jumped down from his car but just stood there, looking annoyed.

Ernesto ran up to him and fell again, clutching at his feet. Pleading, screaming, shouting in a wild mix of Spanish and unfamiliar English, he begged for help, God's mercy, a doctor, the police, and to go back to Colombia where such horrors didn't happen.

The man kicked him away and muttered, "Crazy spic."

"No. No. No," Ernesto panted. "Is true. Go look. A dead one. On the track. I don't go back there. You go. I swear to God. On my dead father. It has the head off." He drew the edge of his hand across his throat in an unmistakable gesture.

"You're kidding," the man said.

"No. I don't kid. Is there. *Hay tanto sangre."* And as he said the awful word, blood, in his native tongue, the smell of it lurking in his throat clutched at his stomach and he vomited again.

"Hey! Hey!" said the man. "Watch out for the shoes." But he looked down the track in the direction from which

24

Ernesto had come running. "There's something down there, all right. I'll get the boss."

As the man hurried away, Ernesto tried to pull himself together. It wouldn't do for the boss to see him puking and crawling around on the ground. He squatted on the gravel in the way of the people of his village and tried to remember that distant cluster of tiny houses, the peaceful shore, the ocean lapping gently on the sand. But he kept seeing his own sons, grown a little older in this hard, unforgiving city, fallen onto a subway track and a train rushing down on them. Tears, for them, for Lena, for himself, for the *muerto* with its head cut off, spurted from his eyes. He folded his arms across his knees and rested his head on them. Maybe this job wasn't such a good one after all.

4

Alex ran all the way from Union Square, five short blocks and three and a half long ones, his satchel banging against his legs, each indrawn breath of dank February air searing his throat and piercing his lungs with its chill. And still he was late.

He tried to tiptoe into the roll-call room and squeeze invisibly into a space next to his buddy, Maldonado, but his hard black police shoes sounded thunk, thunk against the hardness of the worn vinyl tile floor. The sergeant's eyes flicked against his face, flickered, and moved on.

"This is it," Alex told himself. "Show no mercy. Take no prisoners. The execution by extreme verbal abuse of Police Recruit Alex Carlson is about to take place. Please don't bleed on the floor." He looked for Edie and found her in the front row, standing smartly at attention, her long thick chestnut hair primly bound into a knot at the back of her neck. Last night, it had flowed across his face and chest, faintly smelling of something green and fresh, springtime maybe. Better not think of that now.

Beside him, Maldonado sniffled and stifled a cough. "He's really on the warpath this morning," he whispered.

Alex nodded stiffly and glanced down. His shoes were

26

dusty again. They'd been clean when he left the house, shining like black diamonds, but the damned city was so filthy you couldn't go anywhere without getting some of it on you. But his shirt was clean, his tie was knotted correctly, and his trousers still held a reasonable press. He was proud of his uniform. It set him apart from the rest of the world—the civilians—and filled him with a sense of dedication. He'd only been a little kid in the sixties, but he'd heard the older guys in the neighborhood calling policemen pigs. As he grew older, he'd heard stories of police brutality. And he'd believed them, and done some name-calling himself. It was just something you did because everyone else was doing it. It had never occurred to him that he would one day want nothing more than to be one of the despised men in blue.

Even now, he couldn't quite put his finger on what exactly had brought him to the decision. There'd been so much disorder in the world, and in his own family, his father out of work for so long until just last year, his mother going off and getting a job after years of just being there in the house, and his brother not quite a criminal but not exactly Mr. Straight Arrow either. And his own ambitions taking quite a slide after he got out of college and found out that the world was full of college grads and not so full of jobs for them. Everything was upside-down, out of sync. The first president he could really remember had turned out to be a liar and a crook. Vietnam had been a distant war he'd never understood, but pictures of destroyed villages and naked, screaming children had come home to him on television. He'd grown up with chaos all around him, and there wasn't much he could do about it. Except maybe become a cop. He didn't think of himself as being particularly idealistic, but he did want to help people, and he yearned to make things orderly. It had been a slow realization rather

27

than a deep conviction that had prompted him to take the police exam.

His father hated the idea, but then his father found something wrong with anything Alex tried to do. It was a hard thing to live with, but Alex did his best to keep on an even keel with the old man. It wasn't always so; they'd had some terrible fights in the past, but that was all over now. When he visited his parents, it was safe to talk about baseball, football, and television and that's what he stuck to. Forget about politics, women, Paulie's escapades, and the NYPD. No way could he ever tell his father how much he wanted to be a cop, what it meant to him, or how devastated he would be if he failed.

If he failed. Today could be the day. He stood stiff and straight, waiting for his name to be called, waiting for the sergeant to blast him for being two minutes late.

Beside him, Maldonado sneezed. He'd had a cold and a sore throat since last week and couldn't seem to shake it. Jim Beatty, another recruit whose father owned a drugstore in Jackson Heights, had brought him all kinds of cold pills and throat lozenges, but nothing seemed to help. Of course, Maldonado got even less sleep than Alex did. When he wasn't fighting with that wife of his, he was out searching the bars in his neighborhood trying to find her. She swore she wasn't in the life anymore, but just had to get out and have some fun. She said Maldonado wasn't any fun anymore; he was always at the Academy or wanted to stay home and study. Maldonado's troubles were a daily topic among the little group of recruits who had lunch together.

Beatty's troubles were different. He just couldn't resist the police groupies, the girls who hung around outside the Academy and tried to come onto the recruits because they had some kind of thing about uniforms. He flirted with them and he'd even gone out with one of them once. She

28

couldn't wait to get him up to her apartment and begged him to handcuff her to the bed. Sicko. Beatty said he didn't mind that so much, but she was dirty. He had to make her take a bath before he would touch her, and even then he worried for days after about whether he'd got herpes or something worse.

The sergeant was working his way up and down the lines of recruits, chewing out one guy for a smudge on his name badge, another one because he'd forgotten his memo book, a cardinal sin. When he got to Maldonado, he'd worked himself into an evil frame of mind.

"Is that snot I see dripping from your nose?"

Maldonado sniffed and muttered, "Yes, sir."

Alex could feel the tremors that shook his friend's body. Maldonado wasn't a coward, but he was obviously feeling lousy, and the sergeant could make the toughest and healthiest of them tremble.

"Didn't your mother ever teach you how to blow your nose?"

"Yes, sir."

"Your eyes look like two piss holes in the snow. What's the matter with you, Maldonado? You on drugs or something? You craving a fix?"

"No, sir. It's only, I got a cold."

"Oh. You only got a cold. I suppose you want to share the wealth."

Maldonado stared at him, miserable and uncomprehending.

The sergeant reached out to touch his forehead. Maldonado flinched and sneezed at the same time, spraying the sergeant's hand.

At first, Alex thought the sergeant was going to haul off and hit him. Evidently, Maldonado did, too. He raised both hands to protect his face. Instead, the sergeant got a handkerchief out of his pocket and deliberately wiped his hand. Then he handed the handkerchief to Maldonado and said, "Pretend I'm your mother. Blow your nose."

While Maldonado was doing that, the sergeant pressed the tips of his fingers to Maldonado's forehead. Then he felt the back of his neck. The recruits remained at attention, but all eyes and ears were trying to follow the action. The room was utterly silent, except for the whisper of hushed breathing.

"You're sick, man," the sergeant barked. "What the hell are you doing here?"

"I didn't want to miss anything," Maldonado mumbled.

"Oh, you didn't want to miss anything. You want all the rest of us to get whatever creeping crud it is you're carrying around. Don't you know you're burning up with fever? Or are you too dumb to figure that out?"

He backed off from Maldonado and surveyed the entire roll-call line-up. "Here's a lesson for you guys. Girls included. If you're sick, stay home. How would it be if an entire precinct came down with galloping pneumonia? Or measles? Don't laugh. It could happen. I don't mean stay home if you got a hangnail or the monthlies. We don't like malingerers. But if you're sick, we don't want you around. You won't be able to perform, and if you're out on the street, somebody could get hurt. You or your buddy. Just because you thought it was sissy to stay home and take care of yourself. Enough said."

He bore down on Maldonado again. "And you. Get the hell out of here. Go see the doctor and tell him I sent you. And you better do what he tells you, because I'm gonna ask him. I don't want to see you around here until you get that snotnose dried up. Understand?"

"Yes, sir." Maldonado stood, undecided.

"What are you waiting for?"

30

Maldonado held out the used handkerchief in both hands like a peace offering. "What do you want me to do with this?"

"Stuff it, for Christ's sake!" the sergeant roared. "Take it home. Give it to your wife. Make her wash it and iron it. Give her something to do. Keep her off the streets."

Maldonado backed out of the room. Alex, not daring to turn, heard his dragging footsteps quicken to a run once he'd reached the corridor outside. He braced himself to face the sergeant next.

But the sergeant only looked him in the eyes and said, "Carlson?"

"Yes, sir."

"What's next on your schedule?"

"Exam, sir. Arrest procedure."

"Right. Well, skip that. You can make it up later. I want to see you in my office."

"Yes, sir."

The sergeant moved off down the line, leaving Alex stunned and disbelieving. He'd prepared himself for a royal reaming out before the entire group, but this was ten times worse. A hundred times worse. A private audience could only mean he was about to get the ax.

The sergeant finished his inspection and dismissed them. Alex stood rooted to the spot while the uniformed recruits hurried past him on their way to the first class of the day. Edie came up to him and put a hand on his arm.

"What was that all about?" she asked.

Alex shook his head. "I wish I knew," he said. "If it's too awful for him to yell at me at roll call, it must be pretty bad. Worse than being two minutes late. But I don't think I've done anything that terrible."

"How would you know?" said Jim Beatty, coming up behind him. "With King Kong, it doesn't have to be terri-

31

ble. He just has to think it's terrible. He was right about Maldonado, though. It might be just a cold, but it might be something worse. A lot of really bad contagious things start out like that. Meningitis. Or scarlet fever. God, I hope I don't get it, whatever it is."

"It's only a cold," said Alex. "You worry too much."

"And you don't," said Edie. "Let me know what he says. I'd stick around and wait, but he didn't offer me a chance to make up the exam later."

"Hey!" said Beatty. "It can't be the end of the world if you get to take the exam on a make-up. At least, that means you'll still be here."

"Yeah," said Alex dolefully. "Maybe he was just being nice and trying to soften the blow."

"Since when has our beloved Genghis Cop been in the business of being nice?" Beatty asked. "No. He's got something in that Evil Empire he calls a mind, but I don't think it's the doom and destruction of one puny recruit. He'd do that loud and clear in front of all of us, so we could all benefit from it. Let me know what happens. I gotta run now." Beatty followed the last stragglers out of the room, leaving Alex and Edie alone.

"I've got to go, too, Alex," she said, "but whatever it is, don't let him hassle you. Hey, maybe it's not bad news. Maybe they want you to take some kind of special training. Weren't you asking about hostage negotiation the other day? Wouldn't that be great? If they wanted to put you in a special class?"

Alex smiled at her eager face. "Edie, be sensible," he said. "They don't give advanced training to people who haven't even finished the Academy yet. No matter how brilliant they are, and I'm not exactly a star student."

"Maybe not. But you've got a lot more going for you than most of these kids. I just wish you wouldn't always

32

put yourself down. Do you think I'd hang out with a numb brain? I gotta go now." She kissed him swiftly on the cheek. "See you for lunch?"

"Okay."

She ran out the door, her long legs in their blue trousers stretching the sturdy fabric as she moved. Alex followed slowly and watched her racing down the corridor. Then he turned in the other direction and trudged toward whatever awaited him in the sergeant's office.

When he got there and looked in the open door, the sergeant was tilted back in his swivel chair facing the window with his feet propped up on the windowsill, talking on the phone. Alex waited in the doorway for a moment but then, to avoid the appearance of eavesdropping, went across the hall and sat down in one of the battered chairs placed there for the convenience of the doomed awaiting the sergeant's displeasure. To keep himself from dwelling on the possible forms that displeasure might take this morning, he tried to think of some way of reaching out to Paulie, to convince him that there was more to life than graffiti.

The kid was wasting the best years of his life, missing school the way he did, staying out all night, hanging out with all kinds of creeps. For a while, it was Rastafarians over in Bed-Stuy, that time he'd come home with his long hair braided into dreadlocks and trying to talk like they did. That didn't last long, but while it lasted all he could talk about was Bob Marley and Haile Selassie and ganja, man, ganja. Lately, he'd been spending a lot of time sitting cross-legged on the floor with his eyes closed, singing some weird kind of song, over and over and over. Meditating, he said. Getting himself centered, whatever that meant. But at least, when he was doing that, you knew where he was and what he was doing. It seemed dopey but harmless. Not like the time he'd gone off with the Moonies for a week and Ma

33

was ready to call out the police, the FBI, and the Army to find him. But Alex had found him. Paulie had dropped a few hints about a bus that was going to pick him up in midtown on a Sunday afternoon. Alex had put that fact together with the fact that the Moonie headquarters was near Madison Avenue in the forties, and with Paulie's susceptibility for any offbeat religion that spouted peace and harmony. He'd gone to the Moonie shop and squatted there, politely making a nuisance of himself until they told him where Paulie was, at one of their camps upstate. He'd taken the car, over his father's objections, and gone up there and hauled the dumb kid home. Give him credit, though. He said he'd only gone because they promised him the use of an art studio, which was true enough, but they never left him enough time to use it, with all their singing together and working together and doing everything together. Too much together, and Paulie liked doing his own thing. He was really pissed at Alex for coming to get him, even though he was planning to leave in a few days anyway.

And through it all, there was graffiti. Paulie'd been doing it since he was about ten or eleven years old. More than five years. If he'd ever hurt himself or come close to a bad accident, he wasn't talking about it. That, by itself, was enough to make you worry about him. But beyond that, beyond the danger, it was a waste of time. What could you do with it? There weren't any middle-aged graffiti writers. Most of them gave it up by the time they were fifteen or so. Here, Paulie was almost seventeen and still at it. Oh, sure, some of them managed to get their work shown in art galleries. But that didn't make them artists. It was just a fad. Here today and gone tomorrow. The people who knew how to make money were ripping off the graffiti style and using it on everything from wallpaper to sleazy dresses that sold for a couple of hundred dollars. Guys like Paulie didn't make a cent from it, but try to tell him that. He didn't seem to care.

"Carlson? That you out there?"

The sergeant's voice ripped into his thoughts and he sprang to his feet. "Yes, sir!" he shouted.

"Don't shout. I can hear you. Come on in."

The invitation sounded friendly enough, but Alex walked warily into the den of the dragon. It wasn't much of an office, scarcely bigger than a closet and thick with the institutional reek of disinfectant, old cigars, and overbrewed coffee. The sergeant sat hunched behind a dented steel desk piled high with file folders, regulation books, and stacks of circulars. A copy of the morning's *Daily News* was folded open to the sports section and a mug of the sergeant's infamous coffee sat beside it. Alex glanced at the coffee pot resting on a hot plate on the windowsill and hoped it was empty. One of the worst threats a recruit could face was to be offered a cup of the sergeant's coffee. You couldn't turn it down, but to drink it meant heartburn for the rest of the day.

"Sit down, Alex. Sit down."

Alex looked around for a place to sit and settled on a rickety standard issue green chair with the stuffing poking through its torn vinyl cover. There wasn't anything else that wasn't piled high with office debris. The sergeant sounded strange. For one thing, he wasn't barking or roaring. But he wasn't exactly jovial, either. Something between mournful and pissed off but not knowing what to do about it. Alex sat and forced himself to lock eyes with his tormentor.

The sergeant's eyes shifted down to his desk, then lifted with inspiration. "Cup of coffee?" he asked.

"Ah, thank you, sir."

Alex waited, wondering, while the sergeant heaved himself to his feet and rummaged on the windowsill until he found a mug that was clean on the outside but heavily stained brown within.

"Haven't got any milk," he said. "You want some sugar?"

"No, thanks." Alex planned to drink as little of the coffee as possible. His stomach was already knotting up without it. All this fussing around with cups and sugar was giving him a bad case of nerves.

"How about a shot of whiskey in it?" The sergeant was staring at him as if he were some strange specimen of life never before seen on earth.

Alex didn't know what to say. The regulations were specific. No drinking on duty. And here was the sergeant offering him a drink. Was it some kind of test? Was he supposed to say yes or no? If he said yes, would he be kicked out? If he said no, would the sergeant think he was turning down a friendly gesture? As a compromise, he shrugged and shook his head at the same time, trying to indicate that he'd like to but didn't think he ought to.

The sergeant said, "Ah, well. Maybe later." He handed Alex the mug, filled to the brim with inky black coffee. "Drink some," he said. "It'll do you good." And he sat down again behind his desk with his own mug refilled.

"Now then," he said. "It seems I got a phone call this morning. Before you got here. You were late." He paused.

Alex waited. This was it. But why drag it out like this? If he was going to get booted out, let's get it over with.

The sergeant stared at the ceiling. He cleared his throat. He closed his eyes. And then he sat forward suddenly and looked straight at Alex.

"It seems they want you to go over to the morgue."

Alex felt himself turning numb. "The morgue?" he echoed. "I've been to the morgue."

Part of their training had been a tour of the Medical Examiner's Office, complete with autopsy. He hadn't liked it much. The body had been that of a young gay guy who'd

36

got his head bashed in, but the ME had done the whole job on him, cut him open and weighed up all his insides. Alex had come away feeling very small and fragile.

"It seems," the sergeant went on, "they want you to meet your parents there."

"My parents?" Alex felt the panic rising in his throat. It tasted worse than the sergeant's coffee.

"It seems you have a brother."

"Paulie?" If only he would stop saying it seems, it seems, it seems.

"It seems Paulie's had an accident."

Alex could find nothing to say.

The sergeant passed him a pint bottle of Four Roses. "Drink some of that," he said. "Go ahead. Don't bother putting it in the coffee. Take it straight."

Alex put the bottle to his mouth and drank. The harsh whiskey slid down his throat and seemed to flow hotly from his eyes.

"It's okay, kid," he heard the sergeant saying. "Don't mind me. Cry if you want to. But then get yourself together and get on over there. Your mother's gonna need you. There's a car waiting for you. I'll go with you if you want me to."

Alex shook his head. He handed the bottle back and wiped his eyes with the back of his hand. From a desk drawer, the sergeant produced another clean handkerchief. "I don't know why you guys can't get it in the habit of carrying your own. Do you know how many hankies I give away every week?"

"Thanks," Alex muttered. "Where's the car?"

"Waiting out in front."

"I'll be back."

"Take the rest of the day off. Tomorrow, too."

"I'll be back."

5

From the outside, the Medical Examiner's building on First Avenue looked ordinary enough, a six-story afterthought fronted in blue-glazed brick, bathroom modern. Alex sat looking out the window of the police car, numb to what came next.

"You gettin' out or what?" the driver asked him.

The old cop's eyes, glazed blue marbles embedded in mottled red flesh gone soft and streaked with broken veins, had seen it all. Delivering Alex to the morgue was just another boring job to be done and forgotten. His glory days were over, drowned in an ocean of beer. Alex wondered if in twenty years he'd be the same—burnt out, boozed out, and empty uniform. Twenty years. At least, he still had twenty years to look forward to. Paulie had zero, zip, sweet fuckall. The rage swept through him like a flame thrower, heating his body from scalp to toenails. Every cell and organ burned with the desire for vengeance. But on who? For what? The sergeant had said "accident." Alex shook his head and felt the sweat trickling down out of his hair.

"Hey, thanks," he muttered to the driver and yanked open the car door. Cold air rushed into the car, shocking him out of his funk.

"Want me to wait around?" the driver asked.

Alex knew the man was hoping for an hour or so to coop out in the car, sleeping the rest of his life away, or to duck into a local deli for a sneaky six-pack. But he couldn't bear the thought of that ruined, indifferent face waiting for him when he came out. "No, thanks," he said. "I don't know how long this'll take. I can walk back from here."

"Suit yourself."

The car began rolling even before Alex had both feet on the pavement. He slammed the door and watched the blue and white shoulder into the uptown stream of traffic.

He considered the blue building, sitting there, waiting for him to enter. On one side, Bellevue, immense and old, a dirty red brick catchall for the city's sick, crazed, wounded, helpless multitude. Behind him taxis and buses whizzed by, mothers pushed baby carriages, bag ladies pushed shopping carts loaded with junk, ambulances shrieked, and clean young doctors in white coats ran dodging traffic for a quick cup of coffee and a moment's calm. The city was normal. Only he was not. He walked on legs that seemed as long and unpredictable as stilts. The whiskey he'd gulped in the sergeant's office sent stale fumes up his throat, and he was shamed by the ravenous hunger that chewed like a cancer at his stomach. "How can you think of food at a time like this?" he asked himself as his wobbly stilt legs carried him through the door.

He saw his mother standing alone near the wall in the lobby. Dorothy Carlson stood straight, bundled into her new stormcoat—the one she'd got at the after-Christmas sales and was so proud of—gloves on her hands, facing him but not seeing him. She looked gone, out of it, spacey. He'd never seen her look like that before.

Alex groaned and walked toward her. She saw him before he reached her. One gloved hand moved, as if it

39

wanted to touch him, but dropped again to dangle at her side. Her mouth worked, trying for a word, but nothing came.

He took her hand, then didn't know what to do with it. It had been a long time since he'd held his mother's hand, and then it had been she, mother, holding onto him, little kid, to protect him. Now it was the other way around.

"Ma," he said, "I'm here."

"I see you, Alex. I see you."

"Don't you want to sit down?"

She looked into his face as if she'd never heard of chairs or sitting or anything but standing there in the lobby of the morgue, waiting for the inevitable. He put an arm around her shoulder and guided her toward a bench a few feet away.

"Sit down, Ma." He felt old, telling her what to do. Old and bitter. She shouldn't have to go through this.

She sat, still with her back straight, as if by stiffening her spine she could find the strength she needed. Where he'd expected softness when he touched her, he'd felt, beneath the layer of the coat, shoulders that would not yield.

"I don't believe it, Alex," she murmured. "I just don't believe it." She looked at him. Her eyes had come alive with questions.

"What happened?" he asked her. "Who brought you here?"

"I don't know what happened." Her voice was low, a monotone without feeling. "Two cops came. A man and a woman. A black woman. She was very nice, very decent about it. I was just leaving for work. Your father'd left already. They stood there, on the front porch, and told me. Paulie." She stopped and her eyes went distant again.

"What did they tell you? How did they know it was Paulie?" He had to keep her talking, keep that dead look out

40

of her eyes, otherwise she might drift away and never come back.

"They had one of his sketchbooks, you know, with that DREEMZ all over it. It had his name and address in it. They said it was found near the . . ." She paused for a moment, steeling herself for the word. And then she said it. "Body."

Alex sat back and looked around the lobby. It was empty except for a gray-haired woman sitting behind the reception desk.

"Where's Pop?" he asked. "Is he here?"

"He's coming. He couldn't leave right away, but he'll be here."

"You talked to him?"

She nodded. "I called him from here. He'd just got to the shop and they had to unload a truckload of beef. He said he'd come as soon as he could."

The hunger gnawed at Alex. He remembered the old story of the Spartan boy who hid a fox in his tunic. It felt like that, an animal eating away at his guts. "Can I get you something?" he asked. "Some coffee?"

She shook her head. "I have some," she said. "My thermos." She looked down at the tote bag in her lap. "I don't know why I brought this. I had it in my hand when they came. My lunch." She handed him the bag. "I don't want it. You have it."

How did she always know? It was uncanny. Ever since he could remember, she'd always known what was going on inside his head. At first, he'd accepted it as something mothers did. When he was real little, he believed she could see through walls, read minds. Later, he'd resented it and done everything he could to thwart her knowledge of his secret self. She'd known that, too, and gone along with it, only indicating now and then that she was onto him. Now,

41

he was grateful for her keen sight and the offhand way she used it. He unscrewed the top of the thermos and poured himself a dose of hot milky coffee. "Want some?" he asked, holding out the plastic cup.

She took it, sipped, and handed it back to him. "There's a sandwich in there, too."

He rummaged in the bag and pulled out the sandwich wrapped in a plastic bag. The first bite of leftover meatloaf brought back all the childhood dinners when she'd coaxed the two of them to eat. "Come on, boys, eat your meat-love." That's what she used to call it. Meatlove. "It'll make you big and strong and all the girls will love you." And Paulie, dropping his on the floor for the dog to scarf up. And Pop getting so mad down at his end of the table. "That's not dog food!" he would yell. "That's choice beef. I ground it myself."

Alex wolfed down the sandwich, hardly bothering to chew, but it did little to ease the pain in his stomach. His mother sat watching him eat, a faint sad smile on her face. At one point, she patted his knee to let him know it was okay with her. He was just starting in on an apple when his father stalked through the door.

He spotted them right away and lumbered over to them. Theo Carlson was as tall as his son, but where Alex was lean and muscular, Theo was burly with the weight that years of heavy eating and drinking had added to his frame. He wore an ancient navy peacoat over his work clothes, and his balding head was covered with a black wool watch cap.

Alex had never seen his father scared, and he wondered if that was what he was seeing now. Theo's mouth looked small and sunken; his eyes flitted to this and that around the lobby, but never connected with their faces.

"What the hell, Dottie!" he shouted. "What is all this? I can't stay long. Today's a busy day. We're shorthanded. The boss didn't like it one bit."

"It won't take long," Dorothy said. "We just have to look at him and say if it's him."

"That's all? Don't they know that already?"

"Sign some papers, I guess."

"Well, couldn't you have done that without dragging me down here?"

"Yes. I guess we could have." The distant look was creeping back into her eyes.

"Oh, Pop," said Alex, "you look at dead meat every day. Don't tell me you're afraid to look at your own son."

"Shut your big mouth. Look at you. Your own brother, and all you can do is stuff your face. How can you even think of eating at a time like this?"

"Leave him alone, Theo. He's hungry. It takes some people that way."

"I wouldn't know about that. I'd have thought he'd be a little more respectful."

Alex, stifling the childish urge to hurl the half-eaten apple across the lobby and stalk out, dropped the remainder back into the bag and stood up. "I'm respectful," he said. "All this arguing doesn't help anything."

His father backed off a few paces and looked around the lobby impatiently. "Let's get this show on the road," he said. "What are we waiting for?"

Dorothy said, "Go tell the lady at the desk we're all here." She stood up and reached for Alex's hand. Her grip was painfully strong.

"Ma," he whispered as his father walked away from them, "you don't have to do this. It's enough if Pop and I do it."

"I have to, Alex," she said. "He's my Paulie, my baby. I watched him being born and I'll see him now. Don't mind what your father says. He doesn't mean it. It's just that he's not real good at saying what's really on his mind."

"Bullshit!" said Alex. "He's always looking for a fight

43

and you know it. It took me a long time to figure it out, but now I'm wise to him. He can't get to me anymore. But he could still do it to Paulie. If he wasn't all the time picking on him, maybe this wouldn't have happened."

"Don't even think it," said his mother. "Don't you think I'm trying not to blame myself? If we all start blaming each other, we'll be in a fine mess. We have to stick together now, and be nice to each other."

"Nice!" said Alex. "Okay. I'll be nice. But he's got to be nice, too. And I don't think he knows how to do that."

"Hush."

Three police officers were coming toward them. Dorothy recognized the two who'd broken the news to her and nodded to them. The third was a lean, dark man who looked more like a *mafioso* than a cop. All three gave Alex the once-over, instantly cataloging him as one of their own.

"How are you doing?" said the lean one whose name badge read Meyerson. "We're ready for you now."

The other two clustered around Dorothy. "We have to go now," said the black woman. "Take it easy. I know it's not easy, but you have to find a way to keep on going."

"Yeah," said her partner. "There's a chapel here if you want that. I don't know. Sometimes it helps."

"Thank you," said Dorothy. "Thank you both."

The black woman officer bent suddenly and kissed Dorothy's cheek. "God bless," she murmured softly.

Theo bustled up. "What's going on here?" he demanded. "Haven't we been waiting long enough? My wife's in a state of shock."

"Theo, please," Dorothy protested.

Alex stared at the floor.

"We're ready now, Mr. Carlson," said Meyerson. "We didn't want to start without you. Follow me."

He led them through a door and down a corridor. Theo

44

Carlson took his wife's arm. To Alex, walking behind them, it seemed that his father was leaning on his mother instead of the other way around. But maybe he was imagining it; maybe that's the way he wanted it to be—his father weak and his mother strong. There were so many things he was just beginning to understand, things he'd never thought much about before. Being around Edie had opened his eyes, and his mind, to what really went on between people. Like, for instance, how loving someone meant a whole lot more than just jumping into bed. Like how, despite all the teasing and squabbling they'd done through the years, he really loved Paulie. No other word for it. And now there was no way he could ever let him know it.

Maybe when they got there, when they got a good look, they'd find out it wasn't Paulie after all. Some other graffiti writer. He felt ashamed of himself for wishing it onto some other kid, but if only it could be not Paulie, he'd make it up to him for all the times he'd punched him around and called him shithead and worse. But how did they know it was Paulie? He was always lending his sketchbooks to his graffiti buddies. They did pieces in each other's books. It could be someone else.

And how did it happen? Nobody'd told him that yet. He wondered if his mother knew, but he couldn't ask her now, not with his father looking so weirded out just by being in the morgue. He hadn't even seen anything yet, and he looked like he was about to barf. Alex felt a sudden pang of sympathy for the old man. He acted so tough, but he wasn't really tough at all.

Alex tried to think of something else, and for a moment he panicked at the thought of his parents walking past the long ranks of little refrigerator doors where the corpses were kept and into the bright autopsy room where they would see Paulie bare and dead on a table, ready for the

45

knife. But no. That was what he had seen, he and his class-mates. All that was down below, on the lower level, where the sharp smell of chemicals mingled with the sweet odor of death. They wouldn't have to see any of that or inhale the unmistakable reek of bodies opened under the probing knife. He remembered that they'd been shown a small room on the main floor, removed from the real work of the place. It had chairs and a glass panel that separated those who came to view from what they had come to see. He glanced at his mother to see how she was holding up. Okay, so far.

She marched along behind Meyerson, practically drag-ging his father along with her. Meyerson led them into the little room. It was lit, but not brightly, and the space behind the glass panel was dark. Alex strained to see what lay there, but the darkness was complete.

"All right, now," Meyerson began explaining, "what I'm going to do is this. Whenever you're ready, I'm going to lower the lights in here and raise the lights in there." He nodded toward the glass. "You can sit down if you want to."

"Sit down, Dottie," said Theo. "I don't want you keeling over on us." He pushed her toward a chair.

She ignored the chair and walked up close to the glass. "Is this how I see him?" she asked. "No closer? I can't touch him?"

"It's better this way," said Meyerson.

"Better for who?" she asked.

"Don't make trouble, Dottie." Theo tried to pull her away from the glass, but she shook him off.

"Better for us," said Meyerson. "We have to determine the cause of death. If we allowed direct contact, the autopsy results could be questionable."

"They told me he was run over by a train. Isn't that enough?"

46

Alex drew a deep breath and thought of Paulie scrambling to get out of the way. And not making it.

"We have to examine the body," said Meyerson.

"You mean you're going to cut him up? My baby? My Paulie?"

"Dottie! Cut it out! Don't get hysterical!"

"Damn it, Theo! I'm not hysterical. I want to know. I'm his mother. I've got a right to know."

"Ma," Alex called out softly from the opposite end of the glass panel, "they have to do it. It's the law."

"Ah, the law," his mother said, and nodded. "The law. We have to let the law have its day. Now. When it's too late. Tell me, Alex. Why is the law always too late?"

Alex had no answer for her. He didn't think she really wanted one. But if he were to try to answer her, he would probably have to say that he was trying to make it not always be too late. That's why he was becoming a cop. But that sounded stupid and swell-headed. He was only one guy. It was all of them together. All the cops. And there were never enough of them.

"Okay," his mother was saying. "I'm ready."

"Everybody ready?" Meyerson asked.

His father grunted, and Alex nodded. Meyerson went to the wall switch. Gradually the lights in the room dimmed and as they did, the area behind the glass began to glow. A shape became visible, long and oddly flat, covered in white up to its chin. As the light grew stronger, Alex saw at one end, near where his mother stood, a head. At his end, a raised mound under white cloth. Paulie had big feet. Size twelves.

"That's not my Paulie."

Alex stared at his mother. What was she talking about? His father had inched up to the window. "Dottie. Don't talk crazy. That's him. Don't you know your own kid?"

47

"That's him, but it's not him." She spoke slowly, trying to figure out what she wanted to say. "Paulie's not in there. Paulie's in here." She struck herself in the chest. "And in here." She put her hand to her head. She turned to Meyerson. "It doesn't matter what you do to him now. You can't hurt him."

"Let's get out of here." Theo Carlson flung himself away from the glass panel and lurched to a halt near the door.

"There's no hurry," said Dorothy. "There's all the time in the world. Look how beautiful he is. He was always a beautiful kid."

Alex went to her end of the window for a closer look at his brother's face. Somebody must have washed him off and brushed his hair. Paulie wasn't the cleanest guy in the world and his long hair was usually snarled and tangled. Now it lay beside his cheek in a shining golden sheaf. Yes, he was beautiful, all right. Almost as pretty as a girl. You couldn't tell by just looking at his face what had happened to him. Alex wondered if the white sheet covered up some awful injury. Run over by a train, but he didn't look it. There was something funny about the top of his head, though. Alex craned for a better look. A darkish spot staining the dark gold hair. Funny.

"I don't want to rush you," Meyerson said.

"I'm ready to go," said Dorothy Carlson.

The lights behind the window went out abruptly and the room lights came up. Alex blinked. His brother would go now into that big white tile room. He didn't want to think about it, but the image of the perforated steel tables, the scales and knives, the saw for cutting through the skull, the gross black stitches when everything was finished, refused to leave his mind. He walked with his mother to the door.

"We can do the rest of it in the office," said Meyerson.

"I hope they got a men's room in this place," said Theo.

48

Alex glanced at his father. He'd never before seen anyone look green. He wanted to reach out and touch his father's hand. Hug him. But he didn't dare.

"Near the office." Meyerson opened the door and pointed the way.

Theo ran.

Alex wondered when his mother would cry. If she would. He couldn't remember ever seeing her cry. But she must, sometime. It wasn't healthy not to. He'd cried already today and couldn't be sure he wouldn't do it again. He'd come close, in that room, until he'd become interested in trying to figure out exactly how Paulie had died. He still didn't know, except for that funny mark on his head, and not knowing bothered him. Maybe if he stuck around after his folks left, Meyerson would tell him something. After all, wasn't he almost a cop himself?

6

It was all over the evening news. The late edition of the *Post* ran banner headlines. "GRAFFITI WRITER WRITTEN OFF." Television stations resurrected old footage of graffitied subway cars, toys as well as masterpieces, but none of Paulie's DREEMZ tags. An enterprising TV reporter had located an older, retired writer and interviewed him about the dangers of graffiti. "How did it feel," she bleated, "when your paint cans exploded and you were suddenly on fire?"

"Shit, man, it was hot!" The rest of his answer was bleeped.

Alex, sucking on a beer can, had to laugh. Serve her right for asking stupid questions.

Another graffiti writer was looking solemn for the camera and saying, "Dreemz, he was bad. Real bad, despite he wasn't a brother. He could rack up the paint by the ton. He wore these parachute pants, see, with the big pockets. He started out a toy. I remember him when he was little, always hanging out, bugging out over the kings like Lee and Seen, biting their pieces until he learned his own style. He got political lately. That's when he started writing Dreemz and going on about nukes. You suppose the CIA took him out?" He laughed. "I mean the other CIA. Not the Crazy Inside Artists."

The tube flashed over to the reporter, who smiled with all her big white teeth and said, "I think we need a translation. What our anonymous graffiti writer said, I think, was that Dreemz, young Paul Carlson, who died accidentally last night under the wheels of a subway train, was a fine graffiti artist despite being Caucasian. He was adept at stealing spray paint and learned his art by imitating acknowledged graffiti masters. We'll be back with a few words from Dreemz's mother. And now this."

As the television jolted into a commercial, Alex finished off his beer and called out, "Hey, Ma. You're on next."

Dorothy Carlson drifted into the living room, drying her hands on a dishtowel. "Turn it off, Alex. You don't need to see that." But she stood watching the screen until the commercial was over and the familiar front of their house appeared. An urgent male voice said, "This is the house where Dreemz lived, an ordinary house on an ordinary strect in Flatbush. But Dreemz was not an ordinary boy. Like many teenagers, he craved adventure. Unlike most, he found it late at night in the city's subway yards. Last night, at Gun Hill Road, Dreemz met his destiny."

A yellow taxi pulled into the picture and suddenly there was Dorothy Carlson getting out of the backseat. In the background, across the street, neighbors stood watching and children waved and pranced for the camera. Another woman reporter appeared. "Mrs. Carlson, did you know your son was a graffiti artist?" She shoved the microphone into Dorothy's face.

"Of course I knew. How could I not know?"

Alex, watching his mother's television face, saw the sorrow and despair she managed to conceal in his presence. She hurried along the walk toward the front porch, trying to evade the reporter. The camera lurched along beside her and the reporter followed.

"Couldn't you have stopped him?"

"No."

"Did you try?"

Dorothy ignored the question.

"Have you any advice for other mothers whose sons do graffiti?"

Alex saw his mother turn and square off at the reporter. Her lips moved, but he couldn't hear what she said. Suddenly, the scene was gone and the reporter was back in the studio.

"Understandably," she said, "Mrs. Carlson was too distraught to say more than that. Sixteen-year-old Paul Carlson killed under the wheels of a train sometime last night or early this morning in a Bronx subway yard."

Alex switched the set off. "What did you tell her, Ma? Must have been good, the way they cut you off."

"Never mind. I shouldn't have got mad at her, but they shouldn't come around bothering people. It's not decent."

"Looked like the whole neighborhood was out there, trying to get on TV."

"Mrs. Cardozo brought over some baked ziti. Can you stay for dinner?"

"I'll stay as long as you want me to. Where's Pop?"

"I don't know. He said he was going back to work, but I called the shop and he never got there. If he doesn't turn up soon, we'll go ahead and eat."

The phone rang. Alex saw his mother wince. "You answer it," she said. "I don't want to talk to anybody."

Alex went out into the hall where the phone had its own little niche under the stairs. He sat down on the spindly chair and stared at the phone through three rings before picking it up. Anybody who called now would probably want to talk about Paulie. He wasn't sure what he should tell them.

He picked up the phone and said, "Hello?"

A man's voice came on, hoarse and slurred. "Damn kid got what was coming to him. All them graffiti bums should be shot. Line 'em up and shoot 'em down. Be glad to do it myself."

Alex slammed the phone down. The rage flared up in him again. How could anybody be so stupid as to make a call like that? Suppose his mother had answered the phone?

"Who was it?" she called from the kitchen.

"Wrong number," he shouted back.

She came into the hall and leaned wearily against the newel post. "Crank call?" she asked.

Alex nodded.

"There've been a few of those."

"We shouldn't answer the phone at all. Unplug it."

"No," she said. "Most people are okay. It's just a few loonies. I should have warned you."

"Paulie . . ." he began.

"Not now," she cut him short. "I can't talk about it now. Let's just get through tonight without too much talk."

"You want to go bed? You look tired."

She shook her head. "I don't know what I want to do. For the first time in my life, it doesn't make sense to *do* something." She sighed. "I guess I'll go make some tea."

The phone rang again as she was drifting back toward the kitchen. Alex saw her hesitate and then move on. He picked up the receiver, ready to blast the next person who said anything out of line.

"Hey," came a soft voice, "this Dreemz's place?"

"Yes," said Alex, "who's this?"

"You see me up, you see me down, you see me all

53

around the town. Name's Juice. I just want to say, it's a real scuz thing what happened to Dreemz."

"You're a friend of his?"

"Friend! Man, we was partners in crime! Real tight, Dreemz and me. We went bombing together. He asked me to go last night, but I didn't. I got this chick, you understand. All that takes time. But now I got to thinking, if I'd of been with him maybe he wouldn't of got wasted. Maybe I would of. Who did it to him? Do you know?"

"It was an accident."

"Yeah. Sure. That's what *they* say. Dreemz didn't have accidents. He was so careful. So fast. No, man. Somebody took him out. Hey, who's this I'm talking to?"

"His brother."

"The one wants to be a cop?"

"No other."

"Well, cop. Listen to what I say. It's the only way. Think it through and you know it's true. If it was my brother, I wouldn't listen to that accident noise. They just saying that so they don't have to do anything about it. Just another graffiti writer. Wouldn't surprise me if they offed him theirselves."

"Who? The cops?"

"Remember Michael Stewart. They picking us off, man. One by one."

"That's crazy."

"Okay. Okay. Stay cool. But think about it. It's your brother. I could tell you some things."

"What could you tell me?"

The phone clicked dead. Alex thoughtfully replaced the receiver. This could mean something, or it could be just some smartass kid trying to make himself important.

Think about it. He had thought about it. He didn't need Juice or the graffiti writer on TV to put the thought into his head. Somebody had killed his brother.

He'd stayed at the morgue after his mother and father had left and convinced Meyerson to let him see the body uncovered, up close, without the glass between to keep him at a safe distance. Because he was a recruit, nearly a cop, and Paulie's brother, Meyerson had taken him behind the scenes. He'd been devastated by the damage Paulie had suffered, but he hadn't let it show. Paulie's head had been completely severed. That was why they'd covered him up to the chin. And one of his hands, still in its cut-off glove, was hanging by a thread of skin. There were bruises and lacerations all over his chest and back. No telling yet if any bones were broken, but one of his legs was bloody and looked peculiar, as if it could bend both ways. And then there was that dark spot on the top of his head.

"Is that blood?" Alex asked.

"Yes. We cleaned most of it off before the identification, but we couldn't get it all out of his hair."

"Could it be a bullet wound? Like maybe somebody was shooting at him?"

Meyerson had shrugged. "Why would anybody be shooting at him?"

"I don't know. I just thought, maybe it wasn't an accident."

"If it wasn't, they'll find out."

And that was all he'd been able to get. He'd walked back toward the Academy, but a block away decided he couldn't face the rest of his classes and didn't want to have to explain things to anyone, not even to Edie. He didn't want sympathy. He wanted to find out who did it to Paulie and take him apart with his bare hands. He wanted to gouge eyeballs and crack neck bones and stomp ribs. He wanted revenge.

Instead, he kept on walking. All the way downtown to the Brooklyn Bridge, passing through Little Italy, Chinatown, City Hall Park, without noticing anything along the way. Then over the bridge, impervious to the icy wind that funneled up the East River from the bay. One foot after the other, he walked on and on, until at last his mind went numb and vengeance became a tiny seed tucked away in a secret place, not to be forgotten, but only put to rest until its time for flowering arrived.

He walked through Brooklyn, remembering places he and Paulie had been together, things they'd done. Going to the esplanade in Brooklyn Heights to see the tall ships of the Bicentennial and then down to the piers where they'd gone aboard one of the clippers. Paulie'd been about six or seven years old and climbed all over that ship like a demented monkey. Other times, sneaking off to buy firecrackers for the Fourth of July, down around the waterfront where they came in on cargo ships from all over the world. They'd had some good times together, despite the fights they'd had almost every other day, up until the time Alex moved out. Flying kites in Prospect Park, hiking through snowdrifts after a blizzard just for the hell of it, the time Paulie was missing for half a day when Alex was supposed to be taking care of him. The rotten kid had gone off to a movie without telling him.

And now it was all over. There'd be no more fights or good times. Now he'd have to take care of his mother and help her get through this terrible time, and probably his father, too. The old man didn't look too swift there at the morgue, dazed, sort of, and sick. Like maybe he was going to have a heart attack. He'd spent a lot of time in the men's room, and looked pale and empty when he came back. Who would he yell at now that Paulie was gone?

Without really thinking about it, Alex found himself in the old neighborhood. He stood across the street from the house, his parents' house, the only home he'd ever known until he'd gotten his own place. It was almost dark, but the porch light hadn't been turned on yet. The dark windows stared back at him, blank and uninviting. But he'd come this far and he was tired and cold, numb inside and out. He didn't want to see Edie just yet, and if he went to his own place, she'd be sure to call and want to come over. And face it, he wanted to be *home,* among the old familiar rooms and furniture; he wanted the sights and smells and feelings of home. He wanted his mother. Who knows, maybe she wanted him.

He walked around to the back of the house, up the driveway, past the tiny single-car garage, the little plot of lawn, shriveled and brown-spotted from the rigors of winter. He opened the back door with the key he still kept on his key ring and walked into the kitchen.

A gasp came at him out of the darkness and then a voice. "Oh, it's you."

He switched on the light and in its bright overhead glare saw his mother sitting at the kitchen table, an untouched cup of tea before her. She closed her eyes, then shaded them with her hand and blinked. Her eyes were red-rimmed and bloodshot. Her face was blotchy, ashen white and angry red. He couldn't bear her hurt gaze.

He did what he could to bring life to the house, turning on lights all over the place, turning on the television, searching in the refrigerator for a beer and something to eat. He told her about his long, cold walk home. He didn't talk about Paulie at all.

But later, after the television news and his conversation with Juice on the phone, he was bursting with the need to talk over his ideas about his brother's death. Only not with her. It would be cruel to add to her punishment with words like murder.

She'd set the table for dinner. The familiar blue-rimmed dishes were in their usual places. Three places. Paulie's place was set, but not his own. He'd have to sit in Paulie's place and not make an issue of it. She'd done it out of habit.

She was standing by the kitchen sink staring out the window into the dark backyard. Another cup of tea was growing cold on the counter beside her.

"Who was that on the phone?" she asked.

"Some friend of Paulie's," he said. "Heard the news."

"Oh," she said. "That's nice."

She wasn't there. She wasn't listening. She was off somewhere in a dream, denying what had happened. Alex wanted to shake her and make her listen. But what good would that do? Maybe she was better off this way. Maybe she was remembering better days, just as he had through all those miles he'd walked to get here.

"I think I'll lie down," she said. "Just for a while. The ziti's in the oven keeping warm. Help yourself."

"Don't you want to eat?"

"Maybe later."

She went away and he heard her slow footsteps going up the stairs. Then the door of the bedroom closed behind her.

Alex wandered through the house. Nothing had changed. He'd been gone for two years, visiting sometimes on Sundays and for holidays, and everything was still the way it was when he'd left. The furniture a little shabbier, the wallpaper a little dingier. She always talked a lot about redecorating the place, but she never got around to it.

He went back to the phone and tried to think of someone to call. Someone he could trust to listen to him and not think he was crazy. There were relatives, but since that business with his uncle's butcher shop years ago, they hadn't been too friendly. His cousins were a lot older than he was and they'd all got married and moved out to New Jersey. He hadn't seen them in years. His grandparents were dead except for his mother's mother and she was in a nearby nursing home, practically senile. His friends from college were mostly scattered, off working in places like Dallas or Seattle, and those who were left didn't want a police recruit for a friend. They were afraid he might do something about their penny-ante drug dealing. He'd found that out the hard way.

That left his Academy buddies, but Maldonado was sick and Beatty lived way the hell out in Queens, too far to travel. He needed to talk to someone face to face. On the phone, you couldn't see what the other person was thinking.

Edie, then. Edie would be at her place, wondering what the hell had happened to him, waiting for him to call. She'd probably got the news by now. They all would have the news by now. They'd be all over him tomorrow, sad-eyed and saying how terrible it was. And that was just what he didn't want—sympathy, phony or real. He wanted someone to help him get a hard, cold look at the suspicions that were boiling in his brain and making him want to scour the city until he found the killer and then . . . And then, what? That's what he needed to figure out. Or if he was just dreaming up a phantom killer out of his own need to make some kind of sense out of Paulie's death.

So—Edie, then. She could be tough. He'd seen her in action and heard her rip up a couple of macho recruits who still thought women should stay home and make babies.

He picked up the phone and dialed her number. She answered on the first ring, not even waiting for him to speak.

"Alex! Where are you? I've been ringing your place very five minutes."

"Take it easy. I'm at home. With my mother."

"How is she? God, what a thing to happen!"

"Not too good. She's in bed now, but she's been acting strange, like she's not even here."

"Is she sleeping?"

"I don't know. I hope so. Listen, Edie, can I come over for a little while? I won't stay long."

"Sure. You don't even have to ask. You can stay all night if you want to."

"Thanks, but I don't think I should. I'll probably be staying here for a few days. At least until things calm down."

"Did you eat yet?"

"No, but there's food here. I can eat before I come over."

"Don't bother. I couldn't think of anything else to do, so I started cooking, just in case you turned up. I figured you'd be starving. You like home-cooked Chinese food? I'm trying out my new wok."

"Anything. It doesn't matter. I just want to talk to you."

"I'm here. See you soon."

"Thanks, Edie."

He hung up the phone and ran upstairs. At the door to the bedroom, he hesitated. If she was sleeping, he didn't want to wake her up. But she might get worried if she woke up and didn't know where he was. He eased the door open and poked his head into the room.

She was lying in bed, clutching the blankets under her chin. Her eyes were closed and she was breathing evenly. Her tousled dark hair, shot with gray, lay in straggly curls on the pillow. Even in sleep, she looked old, older than Alex had ever seen her look. There were lines in her face he'd never seen before. No point in waking her up.

He withdrew his head and started to ease the door shut when he heard her speak. She whispered his name.

"Yeah, Ma. I didn't mean to wake you up."

"I wasn't sleeping, just lying here with my eyes closed. You want something?"

"No. But I'm going out for a while. I wanted to let you know."

"Is your father home yet?"

"No. I'll be back. I won't be gone long. You'll be okay?"

"Fine. I'll be fine."

"I won't go if you want me to stay."

"No. You go. I'm not very good company tonight."

"It's not that, Ma. It's my girlfriend. She's been trying to get hold of me."

"I didn't know you had one."

"Yeah, I do. Her name is Edith Summers. She lives near me in the Slope. I met her at the Academy. She's a recruit, too."

"Your girlfriend is a cop?" She sat up in bed and smiled at him. "Alex, Alex, I hope she's not a bruiser like the one who came here this morning. She was sweet, though. As nice as she could be. Is your girlfriend big?"

"She's tall, Ma. Almost as tall as I am. And she's strong. You should see her lift weights. But she's not fat, if that's what you mean." Alex was glad to see his mother smiling and taking an interest in something.

"Is she pretty?"

"I think so. She's got long brown hair, almost red when the sun shines on it, and she's got freckles all over."

"Is that anything to tell your mother?"

Alex laughed. It was good to hear her making a joke, however feeble. "She's from Texas, but a long time ago, when she was a baby. Her folks went back a few years ago, but she stayed here."

"So, what are you waiting for? Go see your Texas lady cop. When do I get to meet her?"

"Soon, Ma. Only don't get any ideas about you-know-what."

"What?"

"Love and marriage and a baby carriage."

61

"Oh, that. Furthest thing from my mind. Doesn't she want to get married?"

"We both don't. Not yet. There's plenty of time."

His mother sighed. "Sometimes, there's plenty of time. Sometimes there isn't."

"Ma, I'm sorry. I didn't mean to remind you."

"It's all right, Alex. I don't need reminding. It's not something you forget. But I'm glad you told me about Edith. It'll give me something else to think about."

"She likes to be called Edie. I'm going now."

"Okay. I'll stay in bed until your father gets home. If I know him, he's over at Hurley's with his cronies. I hope he doesn't get in any trouble."

Trouble. That was her word for getting bombed, smashed, drunk out of his nut. "Want me to stop by and send him home?"

"No. He'll come when he's good and ready. Tonight, I don't blame him. If I was a drinking person, I'd probably tie one on myself."

"Okay, then. I'll see you later."

Alex ran downstairs, grabbed his jacket and let himself out the back door. The night had turned colder and there were heavy clouds that looked like snow. He could get to Edie's by subway, but the thought of getting on a train, possibly the one that had rolled over Paulie, revolted him. He could walk through Prospect Park, but that wasn't too smart after dark, especially in the middle of winter when it would be pretty much deserted. The buses were slow, and he'd have to transfer. He swung open the garage door and gazed at his father's car. It was an old Pontiac sedan, still in pretty good shape, probably because his father treated it like the crown jewels. He never let anyone else drive it, and he never drove it into Manhattan, taking the subway back and forth to the upper east side butcher shop where he worked.

Way in the back of the garage, crammed in between the car and a jumble of garden tools, he spotted Paulie's bike. He dragged it out and got on it. It'd been a while since he'd done any bike-riding, but that was something you never forgot. He closed the garage door, God forbid he should leave it open. The old man would have a fit. And then he pedaled away down the driveway and into the street. Edie was waiting for him. Between the two of them, they ought to be able to figure out how he could find the scumbag who killed his brother.

7

"So what, really, do you have to go on?" Edie asked.

The wok was empty, and Alex was full of Edie's no-name Chinese invention. Shrimp and chicken and celery and onions, some very strange looking mushrooms, and some very, very hot red peppers, all in a rich brown sauce that would clear up anybody's sinus trouble. Alex reached for the jug of cold white wine and poured himself another glass.

"Nothing much, I guess," he admitted. "It's just a gut feeling I have. Paulie wouldn't have got himself killed by accident. He was too smart and too fast. He didn't take any chances."

Edie put a bowl of apples and oranges on the table for dessert. "Accidents happen even to the smartest and the fastest," she said. "That's why they're called accidents. He took chances just by going into the yards."

"But he'd been doing it for years. He knew all the moves. Even his friend Juice, his writing partner, doesn't believe it was an accident."

Edie said, "Huh! What's in it for him for you to think it was murder? Don't let him use you, Alex. It sounds to me like he's got some kind of grudge against the police."

"I know. They probably all do, all the graffiti writers. Paulie didn't, though. Each time he got busted, he took it kind of philosophically. Just laughed it off. I miss him, Edie. I can't help thinking he would have got his shit together sooner or later and really done something great with his life. And somebody had to do this to him, before he even had a chance."

"Look at it this way," Edie said. "You're trying to deny the accident. Wipe it out. What you're really trying to do is make Paulie be alive. Changing the accident to a homicide isn't going to bring him back."

"I took that course, too, you know. Maybe I'm not as good at psychology as you are, but I'm pretty certain I'm not trying to kid myself. I saw the mark on his head. It looked like a bullet wound to me."

"Will you at least wait until the autopsy report comes in before you do anything? And whatever you do, I'm in it with you."

"No."

"No, what? You won't wait, or I'm not in it?"

"Both. How do I know how long the autopsy report'll take, or even if they'll let me know what it says? And you stay out of it. If what I think is true, it could get dangerous."

"Oh, right," said Edie. "I forgot about that. I thought police work was nice and safe, just cruising around the city and smiling at all the fine, law-abiding citizens. Don't try to be a hero, Alex. You're not the Lone Ranger."

"Can we listen to some Willie?"

"And don't change the subject." But she got up and put a Willie Nelson tape on her cassette player. As the wise, nasal voice sang about sad, bad love, she walked around behind Alex's chair and put her arms around his shoulders. "If you

65

leave me out," she whispered in his ear, "I think we'll be in for some big trouble, you and me."

"Edie, don't blackmail me. I don't even know yet what I'm going to do."

She kissed the soft place behind his ear. "I'm just telling you. If you're going off on some kind of wacky crusade, then I'm going with you, and we'll both get ourselves kicked out of the Academy. Then we can ride off into the sunset together all the way to Austin, Texas. You can hear plenty of Willie there. I'm so glad you like country music. Can you ride a horse? You'd be great in a posse rounding up rustlers."

"Edie, cut it out. I'm serious."

"So am I. But I'm not gonna argue about it anymore. Have an orange. I'll even peel it for you." She sat down again, across the table from him.

"Thanks, but I think I'd better be going. I don't like to leave my mother alone too long. By the way, she wants to meet you."

"You told her about us?"

"I'm glad I did. It woke her up a little, got her interested."

"I thought we weren't telling anybody until after graduation, until we knew where we were going. I don't want to have to deal with pressure, from your folks or mine. I've been through all that and it's a killer."

"This is different, Edie. She needed something to hold onto. It was all I could think of. I told her not to start thinking about us getting married."

"That's fine. But she's a mother, and mothers can't help doing that. At least, mine can't."

"You'll like her, Edie. She's okay."

"Yeah. But will she like me?"

"Of course she will. But even if she doesn't, she won't

66

make an issue of it. She's not that way. My father's something else. He doesn't like anybody."

"Oh, great!"

"Just don't take anything he says personally. Ever since I've been in the Academy, he's developed a bad case of police phobia. According to him, all cops are corrupt or stupid, or both, and we'd be better off without them. Just declare martial law and turn the city over to the Army. They'd clean it up in no time. It doesn't mean anything. He just likes to hear himself talk."

"I don't know if I'm ready for this." She'd been peeling the orange, and now she handed half of it to Alex.

"It won't be tomorrow. Maybe in a few days, when she's feeling better." He bit into the orange, and juice squirted across the table and hit Edie in the eye.

"Wow!" she cried. "You really have a way of making a point." She wiped her eye with her napkin. "Next thing, you'll be mashing me in the face with a grapefruit. If your aim with a pistol was as good as it is with an orange, I wouldn't care if you Rambo'd your way to fame and glory all by yourself."

"Don't rub it in, sharpshooter. Just becasue *your* father is a gun nut doesn't give you license to rank on me. If I'd been popping off since I was four years old, I'd be pretty good, too. They should have you giving the gun training."

Edie smiled and ducked her head. "It could happen," she murmured. "The instructor spoke to me about it last week when we were at Rodman's Neck. I'm not sure I want that, though. At least, not right away. I don't want to be treated any differently than any other rookie. I want to learn everything, and the only way I can do that is to start at the bottom." She got up and started clearing the table.

Alex got up, too. "Let me help you with that."

Together, they stacked the dishes on the counter in Edie's tiny kitchenette. Edie washed and Alex dried.

"Getting back to your problem, and be careful with those," Edie remarked as she rinsed the wine glasses and stacked them in the draining rack, "what'll you do when they come to your house and start questioning your mother?"

"What!"

"Ha! You didn't think of that one, did you? Whenever there's a murder, who are the first people they talk to? The family, right? That's where it always starts. Sometimes, that's where it ends."

"I don't want them bothering my mother. They can talk to me."

"Oh, they'll do that, too. They'll talk to all of you. Your father included. The neighbors. Your brother's teachers and the kids at his school. Come on, Alex. You know that's the way it's done. Don't be so shocked. It's all talking and asking questions until they come up with some answers. Nobody's immune. Not even you."

Alex hung the dishtowel up and grabbed for his jacket. "Edie, everything you said is one hundred percent correct. I should stay out of it. I should let the big boys take care of it. But, goddammit, I can't. Right now, I'm thinking I should never have left my mother alone. They could be there, this minute, raking her over the coals. So, good-bye, and thanks for the meal. I guess it was delicious."

"It was, Alex, it was. Will I see you tomorrow?"

"I don't know. I just don't know anything yet."

She unlocked the door for him, all three locks, and held her face up for him to kiss. He brushed her lips quickly and ran down the stairs.

When he got outside, he looked up at the front of the brownstone. She was there, leaning out of her third floor window despite the cold. "Take care," she called down to him. "Take care of yourself. You're the only cop boyfriend I have."

He waved to her and bent to unlock the chain that moored Paulie's bike to the iron fence surrounding the small planted area in front of the house. Then, without looking back, he mounted the bike and pedaled away up the street toward Prospect Park and the shortcut home. If there were any muggers or bike thieves in the park tonight, they'd be taking a real chance if they tried anything on him.

8

"I think you ought to quit that cop school and get yourself a decent job." Theo Carlson sat slumped in his armchair staring at the television screen.

"Pop, it's decent. What's not decent about it?" Alex didn't feel like arguing with his father, but he couldn't let the remark go by without a protest. All of the determination he'd brought back with him from Edie's place had dissipated when he'd found his father sleepless and antagonistic, looking for a fight.

"It stinks. The police department in this city is a joke. They're crooked, they're stupid, and they're never around when you need them. Where were they all the times Paulie was sneaking around at night, scribbling on the trains? They could have stopped him."

"Pop, I've heard all that before. If you don't mind, I'd like to get some sleep."

"If the police were any good, your brother wouldn't be lying dead in the morgue tonight. It's an insult to his memory for you to want to be one of them."

Alex slumped down onto the couch. "Okay, let's talk about it. Do you mind if I turn the television off?"

"Leave it on. It makes more sense than you do. Why

70

couldn't you have made him stop? You were the older one. Eight years older. You should have done something."

"Like what? You yelled at him enough for both of us. Anyway, I did talk to him. He wasn't into listening. To me or anybody else. You know how he was. Is there any beer left?"

"Yeah. I think so. Bring me one, too, will you?"

Alex walked out into the darkened kitchen. The light on the oven dial glowed in the dark, and there was a warm, spicy smell of overcooked Italian food. He turned on the overhead light and opened the oven. Half of Mrs. Cardozo's baked ziti lay shriveled in its pan. He turned the oven off and, remembering at the last minute to use pot holders, he lifted the pan out and carried it over to the sink. In the sink, there was one dirty plate, one fork, and three empty beer cans. That meant his mother hadn't gotten up to dish up dinner for the old man. Good. She needed her sleep more than he needed to be waited on. He put the hot pan down on the counter next to the sink. He'd clean everything up before he went to bed. After he'd had a beer and tried to listen to his father without getting into an argument.

In the refrigerator, he found half a six-pack of Bud. He took two and hid the remaining can behind a bottle of apple juice. Paulie was the only one who ever drank apple juice, and his father looked as if he'd had enough beer for one night. He popped open the cans and carried them back into the living room.

The television was still on, rumbling away in the middle of an old war movie, something his father might have seen when he was a kid, but the old man was sprawled in his chair with his eyes closed, snoring softly. Alex put one of the beer cans down on the little table next to the chair, where an overflowing ashtray and an empty glass stein told him his father had spent most of the night just sitting there.

71

He turned the TV off and started for the stairs. He'd be sleeping in his old room at the back of the house overlooking the backyard. The last time he'd slept there was Christmas Eve more than a year ago. Last Christmas Eve he'd spent at Edie's place. They'd put up a tree together and exchanged presents, and Edie'd cried a little because it was the first Christmas she hadn't gone to Texas to be with her folks.

Halfway up the stairs, he heard his father speak.

"Paulie?"

He said, "Pop? What's the matter?"

"No! No!" his father said.

Alex went back and stood over the chair. "I'm here, Pop. You want to talk about it?"

"It's Alex, isn't it? For a minute, I thought I heard Paulie trying to sneak in. Get me a beer, will you? Get one for yourself."

"There's one right next to you." Alex sat down on the couch again, facing his father. With the television off, the only light came from a floor lamp that shone down on his father's balding head. A few grayish wisps were standing straight up at the back of his head, quivering as he leaned forward to pour his beer.

"It always tastes better in a regular mug," Theo said.

"It stays colder in a can," said Alex, instantly regretting the remark. They never could agree on even the most insignificant thing, but this was no time to be nit-picking.

"I don't know," said Theo. "You work hard all your life just to give your kids a chance, and then something like this happens. Maybe if we'd moved out to New Jersey . . ."

"Pop," said Alex, "do you believe it was an accident?"

"What else?" said his father, watching the foam rise in his stein. "It was his own dumb fault."

"But what if somebody pushed him?" Alex said. "Or did something to him?"

72

"What are you talking about? I never heard anything so stupid. Did what to him?"

"I don't know," said Alex. "It's just a thought, just an idea."

"Well, don't think. You were never very good at it." Theo drank deeply from his beer stein. "Can't we just sit here and have a beer together? Father and son? You're all I've got left now, Paulie."

"I'm Alex."

"That's what I meant. Alex. Did you know you were named for Alexander the Great? Your mother's idea. She got everybody in the family upset about it. It wasn't a family name. On her side or mine. Nobody'd ever been named Alexander before. Nobody'd even heard of Alexander the Great. If we'd named you after my uncle, he might have left me the shop. I'd be the boss now. You and Paulie could have come into the business with me. Father and sons. Carlson's Prime Meat."

"I know all that," said Alex. "I thought you named Paulie after your uncle."

His father nodded morosely. "It was too late by then. The damage was done. Ah, what the hell! Maybe he wouldn't have left it to me anyway. He was a stingy old bastard and a slave driver. Thought he could pay me nigger wages because I was a relative. All those years, ten hours a day, kissing his ass all the way, and then out on the street with nothing when he died. Don't you think I wanted to do something else? Don't you think I had dreams? Do you think I *wanted* to be a butcher?"

Alex sighed. He'd heard it all before. His father had never had anything good to say about the old uncle whom Alex could barely remember. The butcher shop had been in Bay Ridge and he could only remember going there a few times when he was very little. A stout white-haired man had teased him and then given him a slice of bologna which

73

Alex had dropped on the sawdust covered floor. His mother had quickly picked it up and stuck it in her pocket so the uncle wouldn't see it was wasted. But what his father had said about his dreams was new. He'd never spoken about that before.

"What did you want to be, Pop?"

His father stared at the blank television screen as if he could see his youthful dreams and ambitions flickering there.

"I used to draw pictures," he muttered. "Kid stuff. Dogs. And horses. I used to draw the horse that pulled the vegetable wagon. And buildings. I got real good at drawing buildings. First, I drew the houses in the neighborhood. And then one day, I found a magazine with drawings in it. Houses that hadn't been built yet. I copied those, and then I started drawing my own houses, floor plans, everything. I guess I thought I wanted to be an architect. But times were tough, so I went into the Navy before I even finished high school and by the time I got out, I was married and you were on the way and that was that. Into the butcher shop."

"I never knew that," said Alex. His father's stunted dream saddened him, and he cast about for something to say to show that he cared. "I remember the monkeys you used to draw for me years ago. They lived in a castle in the jungle and they were always jumping out the windows."

His father smiled. It wasn't much of a smile, but it was there on his face, almost erasing the lines of bitterness and disappointment. "Ah, that was nothing," he said. "I just did that to make you stop being such a pest. You should see some of my old drawings. I think your mother still has them up in the attic. You know her. She never throws anything away. Maybe I'll show them to you some day."

"I'd like that," said Alex, congratulating himself on how well this conversation was going. It was turning into the

74

first real talk they'd ever had. Maybe there was hope for the old man yet. "I guess that's where Paulie got his talent."

"Talent!" his father roared. "You call that talent!"

Suddenly, Theo was out of his chair and looming over Alex. Beer sloshed out of his stein and drenched the front of Alex's shirt. He dropped the stein on the floor and the remainder of the beer soaked into the carpet.

"You don't know anything about it," his father raged. "Why did you come here? Just to torture me? I ought to knock you cock-eyed."

Alex slithered off the couch, evading Theo's wildly flailing fists. "Take it easy, Pop. I didn't mean anything."

"The hell you didn't! I know you. You're nothing but a sneak and a liar. You've always been against me and then you wonder why I try to straighten you out. I ought to beat the shit out of you right now for saying such a thing."

"If you hit me, Pop, I'll have to hit you back. And I don't want to do that." Alex put his beer can down and stood with his arms at his sides, not threatening but ready for anything that might happen.

"Think you can?" Theo sneered. "You're such a big tough guy now, huh? I could deck you with my little finger." He grabbed the front of Alex's shirt in one fist and waggled the fingers of his free hand under Alex's nose. "See my pinkie, see my thumb, see my fist, you better run."

Alex caught hold of the waggling fingers and twisted his father's arm behind his back, spinning him around. "Calm down, Pop," he said in a level voice. "There's nothing to get so upset about. You don't want to fight with me any more than I want to fight with you. How many beers did you have?"

"Enough. None of your business," Theo muttered. "Let go my arm."

"I will when you promise to go to bed and sleep it off.

We've got some tough times ahead. You don't want to make them tougher."

"Stop telling me what I want. I know what I want." He struggled against Alex's grip, but couldn't free himself. "You're hurting my arm, you bastard."

"You're doing it to yourself. Just relax and it won't hurt. Does it make you feel good to call me names?"

"The truth hurts, doesn't it?" Theo snarled.

"What does that mean?"

"For me to know, and you to find out." Theo went limp and Alex had to support him with an arm around his middle. "Okay," he muttered, "I give up. You win. This time. Only because you're younger and I'm out of shape. But I'll remember this. Don't think you're gonna get away with it."

Cautiously, Alex released his hold on his father. Theo, still with his back to Alex, worked his arm and rotated his shoulders, as if trying to relieve the stiffness. Then he bent into a crouch, reaching for the floor. Alex watched him, wondering if he'd really hurt him. When Theo came out of the crouch, Alex wasn't ready for him. He backhanded Alex across the face and knocked him through the open double doors and into the hall, where he sprawled against the bottom step of the stairway. Then Theo laughed, loud and ugly. He stood victorious, hands on hips, his jiggling paunch overhanging his belt, and shouted his triumph to the four walls.

"Guess the old man can still teach you a few tricks!"

Alex scrambled to his feet. Blood dripped from his nose and spotted the front of his blue shirt. "You asshole," he grated as he stalked back into the living room. "Is that all you ever learned from life? I know what you're thinking. 'An honest man's answer is a punch in the nose.' Well, now you've done it, and let me tell you, it's no answer at all.

76

You're still going to have to deal with tomorrow and all the days after that. I could have helped you. I could still help you, but now you're going to have to ask for it. Someday, you're going to learn that bulldozing your way through doesn't mean shit. You're going to come up against some hard guys who won't stand for it, and I want to be there to see it."

"Blabber, blabber, blabber," Theo taunted. "All you know how to do is talk. Come on. Hit me. I'd love to knock you on your ass again."

"Much as I'd love to, it's not worth it. I'd be too ashamed of myself."

"You ought to be. Let that be a lesson to you. Don't you ever again even so much as hint that I'm to blame for what happened to Paulie. You had as much to do with it as I did. Maybe even more."

"Pop," Alex protested. "I never said that."

"Not much, you didn't. You said he got his talent from me."

"I only meant that he was artistic. And you used to be. I'm sorry if you misunderstood me."

"Apology accepted."

"Well, how about you apologizing to me? This is my nose that's bleeding."

"I've got nothing to apologize for. Look out, you're getting it all over the rug. Can't you go get a towel or something?"

"Here's one. Is it all over?" Dorothy Carlson stood in the doorway, looking faintly disgusted. She handed the towel to Alex and took her husband's arm. "Come on, Theo. Time to go to bed. It's almost one in the morning."

"Don't say anything, Dottie. Don't say a word. Not now, not tomorrow, not ever. He was asking for it."

"Yeah. Sure. And you were giving it. And now it's all

over. Go to bed." She pushed him toward the stairs and he went, mumbling to himself all the way.

After he was gone, Dorothy slumped onto the couch and stared at her son. "What happened, Alex?" she asked.

"Just the usual, only worse. I guess he's feeling lousy about Paulie and had to take it out on somebody."

"Ohmigod!" Dorothy exclaimed. "A saint and martyr! Why didn't you hit him back?"

"How do you know I didn't?"

"I know you, Alex. You're always trying to get on the good side of him. How long is it going to take you to learn that as far as you're concerned, he doesn't have a good side? Has it stopped bleeding yet?"

Alex removed the towel from his face. The white terrycloth was stained deeply red with blood. "I guess not. Maybe I should put some ice on it."

"Good idea. Come with me. There's something you ought to know. I guess now's as good a time as any to tell you."

Dorothy led the way into the kitchen. Alex followed along, wondering what his mother was getting at. She didn't seem at all surprised about the fight. He watched her open the refrigerator, get out an ice cube tray, and dump the cubes into a plastic bag. She wrapped the bag in a dishtowel. Finally, she was ready.

"Here," she said. "I don't know whether it's better to put it right on your nose or hold it against the back of your neck. I've heard it both ways." She handed him the ice pack.

"What did you want to tell me?" he asked. He sat down on a kitchen chair, put the ice pack on his nose and peered at her over it.

"I don't know how to start," she said. She leaned against the kitchen counter, hugging herself and staring down at the floor. "I've never told anybody, not even my own mother."

78

"If you don't want to tell me, it's okay. This is really cold." He shifted the ice pack to the other side of his face.

"Do you think your nose is broken?"

He took the ice pack away and felt his nose. "No. It feels okay. Why don't you go back to bed?"

"No. I've made up my mind. I should have told you before now. It might have saved you a lot of grief."

"Tell me, then. After what we've all been through today, what could be worse?"

"That's right. That's what I thought. I've been lying up there in bed, thinking about it. And then, when I heard you two fighting, I decided enough was enough. You don't deserve the way he's treated you all these years. Of course, he wasn't that much nicer to Paulie, but he did try. Alex, please don't hate me for this."

Alex waited. He hadn't the foggiest idea what was coming, and anything he said could make it that much harder for her.

Dorothy threw her head back and gazed at the ceiling. "The thing is, oh, God, this is hard for me to say."

"Just say it, Ma. Plain and simple."

"Okay. Here goes." She lowered her gaze and looked Alex straight in the eyes. "Theo isn't your father."

Alex put the ice pack over his eyes and let the cold penetrate his brain. How many times, when he was little, had he dreamed that he wasn't their kid at all, that he was a foundling, separated from his real parents, and that someday his real father would drive up in a big, fancy car and take him away. Now the childish fantasy was half-true. If he could believe her. But why would she lie?

"Did you hear me, Alex?"

"I heard you. I just don't know what to say."

"Say anything you like. Ask any questions you want to. I'll try to give you straight answers."

"Does he know?"

79

"Yes. Of course. I was pregnant with you when he married me. I wouldn't play that kind of dirty trick on anybody. I told him what he was getting. But he's never talked about it since the day I told him. He's never thrown it up to me or used it against me. You have to give him credit for that."

"What about Paulie?"

"Paulie's his kid. And believe me, we waited long enough for him to come along. We'd almost given up hope. Can you understand a little better now why this is so rough on him?"

"Yeah. I guess so. I guess I understand a lot that's been going on here."

"Don't hold it against me, Alex. In those days, it wasn't easy to have a kid on your own. Your father came along like the answer to a prayer. He was different then. He said it didn't matter and he would raise you like his own son. And he did. You can't say he didn't."

"What about my real father? Who is he?"

"I can't tell you that."

"Don't you know?"

She took a deep breath and her voice trembled when she spoke. "I guess I deserve that."

"I'm sorry, Ma. That was a rotten thing to say. It's just so hard to make sense out of this."

"No. It's okay. I said you could ask anything you wanted. It's just, I don't know what happened to him. He could be married and have a family of his own by now. I don't want to make any trouble for him."

"You still love him?"

"Love? I don't know anymore what that means. I love you, and God knows, I loved Paulie. But that's different. I haven't thought about that other kind of love for years. Why should I? I've been a married woman for most of my life."

"Why didn't you marry him instead of Pop?"

"You know, I don't really know the answer to that. It seemed like there were good reasons at the time. He was Catholic and I wasn't. His family was against it. So was mine. I never told him about you. When we broke up, I didn't know you were on the way. By the time I found out, he'd left town and I just couldn't face asking his mother where he was. Maybe we could have made a go of it. Maybe not."

"Did you ever have any regrets?"

"About what? About having two wonderful sons and a marriage that's lasted twenty-five years?"

"It hasn't been easy for you."

"Who said it was supposed to be? I don't see you looking for an easy life. Being a cop has to be just about the toughest job there is. Did I ever say I'm proud of you? I am, you know."

"Thanks, Ma. I wish he'd tell me that sometime instead of always trying to put me down. But I guess he never will. And thanks for telling me. Now it won't hurt so much when he hassles me."

"Just do me one favor. Don't ever let him know I told you. He made me promise years ago that you'd never know."

"Okay. But I can't help wondering . . ."

"What?"

"If he's not my father, I don't have to worry anymore about inheriting his rotten temper. But what did I inherit?"

A smile lit Dorothy's face. "Your dark hair," she said. "Your big brown eyes. And the way you won't take no for an answer. Now, let's drop this for a while. If you want to talk about it some other time, I'll tell you everything I remember about him. Everything but his name. How's your nose?"

Alex had forgotten all about his nose. The ice pack lay

81

melting on the bloody towel, both resting on his lap. His nose had stopped bleeding.

"It looks okay to me," said Dorothy, picking up the towel and emptying the icepack in the sink. "Take off your shirt. I'll stick all this in the washing machine and it'll be nice and clean for you in the morning."

"Ma," Alex protested, "I've been doing my own laundry for two years now. I can do it."

"You're not so big that I can't mother you once in a while. Take it off before I take it off you."

"Okay. Okay. But while you're doing that, I'll clean up these dishes in the sink. Fair exchange."

"It's a deal," said Dorothy.

9

In the morning, there was snow. Not the clean sugar-frosting kind that iced the city with whiteness and covered over its ulcers with a fragile wedding cake beauty. This was wet, sleety snow that turned to slush underfoot and multiplied the ugliness with its penetrating gray chill.

Alex was up and out of the house before his parents were awake. He'd slept off and on, but by five-thirty saw little point in trying to force his churning thoughts to quiet down for another half-hour or so of restless dozing. At six o'clock the streetlights shone sickly yellow, feebly attempting to cheer the dreary morning. Alex left by the front door, easing it closed behind him with only the soft click of the lock to mark his passing. It was too early to head for the Academy, too nasty to walk through the park to pick up Edie and ride the subway in together. Alex stood on the front porch and scowled at the weather.

"Hey, man!" The voice came from a shadowy corner of the porch.

Alex saw a dark bundle unfold itself and stand up. A bum, he thought, about to panhandle me. "Who's that?" he asked, ready to run the sucker off.

"Yo, man. It's me. I been waiting for you."

Enveloped in a dark poncho, face hidden by a hood, the figure came out of the shadows and extended a gloved hand.

Alex whipped into a crouch. This was no bum. The neighborhood was really going downhill if muggers attacked you on your own front porch. He was prepared to defend himself and haul the dirtbag into the nearest precinct house.

"Hey! Cool out! I'm here to tell you something. Don't you know who I am? I'm Juice."

Alex looked closer. Inside the hood, he caught a glimpse of wispy black moustache against olive skin, a flash of a smile.

"The guy on the phone? Paulie's friend?"

"Right on."

"How'd you find this place?"

"I been here before. Dreemz brought me here once to work on his piecing books. You wasn't around. He said you didn't live here anymore. But you was here last night, so I figured you'd be here this morning. Someplace we can talk? I don't want to mess around with no mothers and no fathers."

Alex glanced back at the front door. His parents' bedroom was right above the porch. "Not here," he whispered. "You hungry? Want some breakfast?"

"Bacon and eggs! Dig it. You buying?"

"Let's go."

They slogged through the slush to the corner and turned toward the subway station. As early as it was, there were people hurrying along the sidewalk, huddled under umbrellas, intent on avoiding puddles and slippery patches of sidewalk. The diner on the corner opened early. Alex stopped at the newsstand to pick up a copy of the *Daily News*. At least Paulie wasn't on the front page this morning.

There'd been a fire in Brownsville during the night. An illegal oil heater had exploded. Two babies had died. Their mother, photographed in the restraining arms of a fireman, screamed her anguish off the page. Alex led the way into the warm, grease-smelling fug of the diner and chose a table near the rear.

"What did you want to tell me?" he asked.

Juice slipped his wet poncho over his head and draped it over the back of his chair. Underneath it, he wore an old army field jacket, worn and stained with grimy smears of paint that had once been bright. He looked about Paulie's age, maybe a little older.

"Feels good in here," he said. "Nearly froze my *cojones* waiting for you."

The waitress stood over them, sleepy-eyed and gray-faced except for the red lipstick smeared across her thin lips. Alex remembered seeing her around the neighborhood, walking a toy poodle, carrying shopping bags, just another of the middle-aged ladies who walked in fear of muggers and triple-locked their doors against burglars and rapists.

She recognized him too, and her face rearranged itself into appropriate lines of mournfulness. "God!" she said, "I heard about your brother. What a shame! What can I get you? Coffee?"

"Thanks," said Alex. "Bacon and eggs, I guess. Scrambled." He glanced across at Juice, who nodded. "Two of them."

The waitress looked at Juice and just as quickly looked away, frowning. Juice gave a small shrug and twisted his mouth into a rueful smile, as if to say, "It happens all the time. They don't like to wait on us spics."

"Let's have some orange juice, too," said Alex.

The woman wrote the order down and went away. Alex watched her whispering to the fry-cook and both of them sneaking curious glances at their table when they thought he might not see them. Juice sat fiddling with the salt and pepper shakers, staring down at the formica table top.

"What does it mean? Juice?" Alex asked.

The boy shrugged again. "Ah, it don't mean nothing. It just makes a good tag. My name is Jesús, but that wouldn't look too swift on the trains. So I write Juice instead. Paulie, man, he had a really chill tag. Dreemz. I don't know where he got it from, but it really puts your eyes out. Makes you think. And those scenes he did. Real weird shit. Man, I wish he wasn't dead."

"Me, too," said Alex. "You wanted to tell me something?"

"Oh, yeah. Well, it's this. We all got together last night, you know? And we wanted to do something for Dreemz. So we did." Juice fished a crumpled pack of Kools out of one of his pockets and made a prolonged ceremony out of lighting up.

"What did you do?" Alex prompted.

"I don't know if I should tell you this, you being a cop and all."

"I'm not a cop yet."

"Yeah. But almost. And you hang out with cops."

"I don't tell everything I know."

"So you say." Juice dragged on his cigarette and flicked ash into the battered metal ashtray. There was challenge in his taut, controlled movements.

"Well, let's just eat our breakfast then." Alex had seen the waitress coming toward them. He opened up his newspaper and pretended to read while she laid plates of food in front of them. She went away and came back with mugs of coffee. All the while she was serving them, Alex kept his eyes fastened on the page, scanning the print but not comprehending a word, waiting. After she went away for good, he turned the page and picked up his fork.

86

"Don't you want to know?" Juice asked.

It was Alex's turn to shrug. "If you want to tell me, go ahead. Otherwise, eat your breakfast. I owe you that much for waiting out in the cold."

"Oh, shit, man. That's nothing. I was out all night. We all were. That's what I wanted to tell you. All us writers, we got together last night, even some guys from the Bronx, and we went bombing. It was kind of like a memorial for Dreemz. Oh, man! Wait'll you see those trains this morning! There must have been about a hundred of us. We had a meeting, and then we split up and went to every yard and every lay-up in the city. We all wrote Dreemz on everything we could find. He always wanted to be a king of the line. Well, now he's king of the whole fucking city." Juice choked up and stopped talking. Tears spurted uncontrollably from his eyes and ran down his agonized face. He scrabbled in the steel napkin holder and pressed a fistful of paper napkins to his cheeks.

"Sorry, man," he mumbled. "I don't know why I'm pissing off like this. He was *your* brother. But we was tight, Dreemz and me. Real tight."

"It's okay," Alex soothed him. "It's okay. I did some crying myself yesterday. Thanks for telling me. Paulie would have liked what you did. I wish he could see it."

"You think he can see it?" Juice asked hopefully. "From wherever he is? The priest is always going on about heaven. You think there's a graffiti heaven? I can just see him tagging up on the pearly gates."

Alex shook his head. Religion was one thing he tried not to think too much about. He knew there'd have to be a funeral for Paulie, probably in the Lutheran church where the two of them had gone to Sunday School a long time ago, and his mother still went. She'd probably have to take care of that. He had other things to think about. He shoveled eggs into his mouth and bit off the end of a strip of bacon.

"But something else," Juice was saying. "And this is really weird."

Alex nodded his interest.

"While we were meeting and trying to decide what to do, one of the guys got up and said, 'Somebody tried to waste *me* last week.' Everybody shouted him down, 'cause we thought he was trying to steal some fame away from Dreemz. But then another guy gets up and goes, 'Hey! Me, too! Some turkey took a shot at me a few weeks ago. He couldn't shoot for shit.' So then we heard from a couple more and they all said the same. About a month now, and four graffiti writers been shot at. That's just the ones we know about, 'cause not everybody was there. So, what I wanted to ask you was, is that what happened to Dreemz?"

Alex sat up straight and swallowed the food in his mouth. Was this what he'd been hoping for? Something that would *prove* what he'd only been feeling instinctively? "Do they know who did it?" he asked.

"Nah. They weren't about to stick around and find out. They all thought it was the cops out hunting them."

"Cops wouldn't do that."

"Hah!" Juice's scorn was almost tangible.

"Would they talk to the cops about it?"

"No way. You think they want to get beat up on and maybe killed?"

"Would they talk to me?"

"I don't know. Maybe. But only because you're Dreemz's brother. They can respect that."

"Would you set up a meeting?"

"Oh, man! You know what you're asking? Suppose I do it and you show up with an army? My ass is grass. I'd be the next subway accident."

"I'd be alone. I'd go wherever they say." As he said the words, Alex felt foolish. He'd heard them so many times on TV cop shows and in the movies. Real life shouldn't sound like a movie.

"Oh, shit! Why did I ever come to see you?"

"Don't they want to find out who's been shooting at them?"

"They know. They think they know. It's the cops. Some of them want to get guns and declare war."

"Don't *you* want to find out who killed Paulie?"

"Yeah. I'd like to know that. I'd like to cut my tag into his guts. Slow, so it hurts. So he'd never forget he killed my friend."

"And my brother. I can't do it without your help, Juice. I'm just a recruit. A nobody. The big guys won't listen to me. And if it officially turns out to be murder, they won't let me work on the investigation. It's against the rules. I've got to have something to make them listen. If I can tell them, with witnesses, that somebody's been trying to kill off graffiti writers and finally got one, they'd have to listen. Even if it's a cop, they'll have to listen."

Juice pushed his remaining eggs around on his plate. He sipped at his coffee. Lit another Kool. Frowned and stroked his embryonic moustache. Finally, he said, "Okay. I'll try. But that's all I'm going to do. I'll talk to them and see if they'll meet with you. But I ain't talking to no cops. My mother'd kill me, they been giving her such a hard time over me and my brothers. Later, man. I'll be in touch."

Juice was up and out of the diner, whirling his poncho over his head, before Alex could ask him anything else. Like what his phone number was, or how he could find some of Paulie's other friends. Alex thought about following him, but decided that if Juice spotted him, that would only make him more nervous and reluctant to set up the meeting.

The waitress was standing over him with a glass coffee pot in her hand. Her eyes were greedy for news. "How's your poor mother taking it?" she asked. "I saw her on TV last night. She looked terrible."

"She's dancing in the street. What do you think?" Alex laid a ten dollar bill on the table and pushed back his chair.

"Well. I was only asking. You don't have to get so snotty."

"Can I have the check, please?"

The waitress put the coffee pot down and added up the check with quick little stabs of her pencil stub. "Pay the cashier," she snarled at him, slapping the check down on the table and stomping away with the coffee pot.

Alex left her a dollar tip, more than she deserved, and took the ten dollar bill to the cashier, who was also the fry-cook this early in the morning. As the man gave him his change, he muttered, "She's nosy, but she don't mean no harm." There were questions in his eyes, too.

Alex left without answering. Everybody wanted to know about death. How it felt to those who were left behind. Relatives. That woman in the paper whose babies had burned. There'd be people wanting to know how she felt, too. It was gruesome, morbid, and tantalizing. And it sold newspapers. Everybody wanted some kind of clue. How will it be when it comes to me? Or to my husband, wife, father, mother, kid. Brother. Well, now he knew how it was. And it wasn't anything you could make anybody else understand. It was anger so deep, he could hardly recognize it as springing from his own heart. If he ever came face-to-face with whoever had murdered Paulie, he'd probably try to kill him with his own hands. And then there was the thing his father . . . no, not his father, but it was hard to stop thinking of him that way . . . Paulie's father had said last night. "Why couldn't you have made him stop? You should have done something." Sure he should have. He'd tried, but not hard enough. If he'd tried harder, maybe Paulie'd be home this minute, getting up and getting ready to go to school. He shook the thought away. Nobody could have stopped Paulie from doing what he wanted to do.

It was still too early for the subway platform to be very crowded, too early to be heading for the Academy, but he didn't know where else to go. Waiting on the outdoor platform, under the shelter of the overhanging roof, he watched the wet, gray snow splatter down onto the tracks and turn into streams of filthy water. Far up the track, he saw the lights of an oncoming train. Sweet Jesus! Would he ever be able to ride the subway without thinking of Paulie?

The train, a QB, slid into the station, and the gray morning burst into color. Every car had been spray-painted, top-to-bottom and end-to-end, in colors so bright, in combinations so garish, it almost hurt your eyes to look. Flaming red and sky blue, hell and heaven in one piece. Pale pink shading to fierce purple. Loud orange splotched with muted olive drab. Every color in the spray paint spectrum was there, in letters that marched or strolled or strutted along the sides of the cars. And every letter spelled his brother's graffiti name. DREEMZ. DREEMZ. DREEMZ. DREEMZ. DREEMZ. As far as the eye could see. The name. On some cars, it curved gently as if it were made of marshmallows. On others, it was knife sharp and angular, a cutting edge. On all, it was surrounded by messages, tags, signatures, initials. A grinning Felix the Cat filled the center of one D. Howard the Duck pointed, trembling, toward a Z. Beneath one DREEMZ, Alex read, "This writer died for your sins."

He got onto the train, listening to the excited chatter of the other passengers. No one read newspapers this morning. People who would ordinarily be afraid to talk to the strangers standing next to them sounded off in wonder or dismay.

"What does it mean?"

"Have they painted all the trains?"

"You have to admit, it sure brightens up the crummy day."

"Ah, it's crap. They ought to throw them all in jail."

"For this, I pay a buck a ride?"

"It's about that kid who died, isn't it?"

"They ought to make them lick it off."

Alex listened and said nothing. Although Juice had told him what the writers had done, he hadn't been prepared for its effect on him and on the rest of the city. While around him, the passengers laughed and argued about the painted trains, Alex felt that Paulie's death had been turned into a sideshow. The graffiti writers had taken over and made an event out of it. No doubt the newspapers and television would pick up on it. There'd be pictures of the trains and some of the writers would be on TV again. They'd talk about Paulie. They might even go out to the house again to talk to his mother. He ought to warn her. As soon as he got to Fourteenth Street, he'd give her a call.

At each stop along the way, as more people got on the train, the conversations grew louder and more heated, with some people, usually the younger ones, defending what had been done, while others, the majority, condemned graffiti and all who did it to extreme and inventive punishments. One man recommended shipping them all to the middle east in exchange for hostages.

A woman standing near Alex said to a young girl, "It's too bad about that kid, but if he was mine, I'd have chained him to his bed."

The girl smiled sweetly and said, "Get fucked and die, lady. Somebody ought to keep you chained up. In a sewer."

And a dignified gray-haired man next to her whispered conspiratorially, "I used to write 'Kilroy was here' all over the barracks when I was in the Army. You wouldn't remember Kilroy."

As the train crossed the Manhattan Bridge, everyone craned to watch a D train going in the opposite direction. It, too, had been painted top-to-bottom and end-to-end. Alex watched the DREEMZ flash by, wishing the world could turn back two nights. He wished he *could* chain Paulie to his bed, or sit on him, or break his arm just enough to put him in the hospital for a week.

At Fourteenth Street, a television crew was already on the job, setting up their lights, testing their microphones. A blonde woman, her face glowing with make-up, was stopping passengers as they got off the train.

"Can I ask you a few questions? What do you think of the graffiti on the trains this morning?"

But the camera wasn't recording yet. Alex guessed that she was just warming up, testing the answers she would get, trying out faces for the evening news. He skirted the small crowd that had gathered around the crew and ran up the stairs.

Outside, Union Square Park cowered under the onslaught of the weather. It was looking good these days, after a complete renovation. New grass, new trees, and brand-new subway entrances that looked like old-fashioned gazebos. The winos and junkies who used to live in the park had gone someplace else. It was one of the good things the city had done lately, but the weather was too crummy to stay in the park.

Nowhere to go but to the Academy. At least, he wouldn't be late this morning. As he hurried along the dreary streets, Alex wondered if the autopsy had been done yet. Was it too much to hope they'd find a bullet inside

Paulie? What a thing to hope for! But it would mean they'd have to investigate. He shook his head to clear away the image of Paulie in that place, a piece of dead meat, cut open from neck to groin, his heart taken out and dumped into that scale. But how else could they find the bullet? If there was one.

He'd almost reached the Academy when he realized he'd forgotten to call his mother. Should he do it now or wait until he got there? He spotted a phone on the corner of Third Avenue and groped in his pocket for a quarter. Damn! Nothing but a dime and some pennies. He'd have to buy something, a cup of coffee or another newspaper, to get change for the phone. He walked on, past the steel-shuttered shops of Third Avenue. The snow was beginning to let up and the morning traffic had started its rumble. Soon there'd be as much light in the sky as they were likely to get on a gloomy February day, not enough to prove that the sun ever shone on these streets. He walked past a heap of old clothes in a doorway, only the smell betraying the presence of a human being underneath the wet, filthy layers, and found a coffee shop a few paces beyond.

He went in, red plastic and fake Tiffany lamps a contrast to the gloom outside, and ordered a regular coffee to go. There was a pay phone on the wall near the entrance where he could be warm and dry, but there were people sitting at the long counter and at some of the tables. He didn't need an audience. When his coffee came, a cardboard container in a brown paper bag, he paid for it and helped himself to a handful of sugar packs. With the change in one hand, the coffee in the other, he went back out onto the street and retraced his steps to the phone, stopping to put the coffee down next to what he judged must be the head end of the bundle of clothes.

"Hey, pal," he said loudly. "Wake up and smell the coffee." He nudged the bundle with the tip of his shoe. A cup of coffee wouldn't do much good. This one already smelled like the morgue would be his next stop. The bundle groaned and moved. The face that peered up at him, crusted with dirt, was unmistakably a woman's. When the bleary eyes focused, the face leered and the mouth said, "Fifty cents, sonny. You got a room?"

Disgusted, Alex backed away. The bundle heaved itself upright. Alex saw a pendulous gray breast flop out of the layers of clothes. The woman held it up and offered it to him. What was once a nipple was an open, oozing sore. Alex turned and ran, trying not to hear the stream of obscenities she howled after him.

At the telephone, he shoved a quarter into the slot, then changed his mind and punched the coin return. That woman. She'd been old enough to be his mother, maybe even his grandmother. Didn't she have anyone who cared about her? How had she got like that? Did she have a son once, and had he been killed? His mother had been acting strange last night. And the things she'd told him. They must have been preying on her mind for years. It was all enough to make her lose her marbles. What would happen to her if she did? Would she go out wandering in the streets? Would she end up like that? What was she doing right now?

He retrieved the quarter and tried again. The phone rang three times before it was picked up. Alex shouted, "Hello, Ma?" without waiting for a voice on the line.

"Alex. Where are you?"

She sounded normal, thank God. A little sleepy. Groggy. But that was normal, wasn't it? She'd still been up when he went to bed last night.

"I'm here, Ma. On my way to the Academy. I just wanted to be sure you're all right."

"I'm all right. How about you? You left so early. You couldn't take a day off?"

"I'm fine, Ma. I couldn't sleep anymore, and I didn't want to be just hanging around the house. So I came here."

"I would have made breakfast for you."

"That's okay, Ma. I ate at the diner. Listen. I have to tell you something. All the subway cars? They're all painted with Paulie's graffiti tag."

"That can't be. Paulie's dead. Don't tease me, Alex."

"I'm not teasing, Ma. His friends did it. Last night. I saw one of them this morning and he told me about it. You should see it."

"Some friends," she remarked. "Will you be coming back here tonight?"

"I'd like to. You want me to?"

"You don't even have to ask. Maybe you can help me go through Paulie's things, clear out his room."

"Do you have to do that right away? Can't it wait a few days?"

"I want to do it now. I need the room."

"What for?"

"I just need it."

"How's Pop?"

"Still sleeping. I don't think he's going to work today. He'll have some hangover when he wakes up."

"Maybe I ought to go to my place tonight. He might not be crazy about seeing me there."

"He'll be okay. How will you be? Are you upset about what I told you last night?"

"Upset? No, I don't think so. I think it's gonna take a while for it to sink in. Anyway, I've got other things to worry about."

"Like what?"

"Like not letting any of this interfere with my work at

96

the Academy. Well, listen, I just wanted to let you know about the trains. Don't be surprised if those TV people come back."

"I'm not talking to anybody. If your father wants to, that's his business."

Alex laughed. "Good idea. He'll give them a lecture on how to run the city. Got to go, Ma. I'm on a street corner, and it's cold."

"Come straight home, Alex. Don't make me worry about you."

"Bye, Ma." Alex hung up. Straight home? Maybe. If there wasn't something else he had to do. Juice knew where to find him. The sooner he set up the meeting, the better. Tonight would be just fine.

He crossed the avenue to avoid passing by the woman in the doorway and walked on toward the Academy.

10

"I'm going with you."

"No, you're not. I promised I'd go alone."

"You can't go alone. You know that. It's one of the first things they taught us. Never get into a situation where you don't have a back-up."

"Edie, this is different. It's not police business. It's my business. I don't even know yet if they'll meet with me. But I promised Juice I'd be alone. If I turn up with you, it could ruin the whole thing."

Alex and Edie sat in the middle of the back row of the auditorium, staying on for a few minutes after a lecture class had ended. Everyone else had hurried off for lunch. The knowing looks they'd got from the rest of the class meant that they'd soon be a hot topic for gossip all over the Academy. After they'd been so careful never to be seen alone together, always making sure that either Beatty or Maldonado or both were around to form a group.

"I wish Maldonado were here today," Edie said. "He'd back me up. He'd want to go, too. What if they want you to go to the Bronx? That could be dangerous."

"Edie, the Bronx isn't a war zone. People live there. Maldonado lives there."

98

"Yeah. And you've heard his stories. It's not safe. You don't look like you belong there. Face it, Alex, you look like a cop. People who don't like cops'll be able to make you a mile away. It's not the graffiti writers I'm worried about. If they agree to meet with you, it means they think they need you. But there are others. There's a world full of creeps out there."

Alex was flattered by the notion that he looked official, but refused to give in to her objections. "I only look that way in my uniform," he said. "I'll wear jeans and sneakers, just like everybody else. Nobody'll notice me."

"It's the haircut," she persisted. "It's a dead giveaway."

"So, I'll wear a hat. I think I've got an old Yankees cap in my locker. Edie, give up on it. If I go, I go alone. Let's get some lunch. I'm starving."

He got up and started edging his way along the row of seats toward the aisle. Edie followed him. They both carried their bulky black recruit's satchels. Alex was almost sorry he'd told her about the meeting he'd asked Juice to arrange. He hadn't really expected that she'd want to go along, but he should have known. Edie was like that. It wasn't just his promise to Juice that made him adamant about refusing her. She was right. It could be dangerous. No way would he ever put her in a situation where she could get hurt. And he hoped, although he'd never admit it to her, that when they graduated, she'd be assigned to a nice, safe precinct where she'd never have to deal with anything more threatening than shoplifters or traffic accidents. He knew he was being unreasonable, but he couldn't help it. She was beginning to mean too much to him.

Together, they ran down the stairs and out into the parking area in front that was always dark and gloomy, even on the brightest of days. If there was one thing about the Academy that Alex disliked it was the creepiness of the entrance to the building. A street-level set-back, with parking spaces for patrol cars and VIPs, it was shrouded by the building's overhang. And despite the guard stationed at the entrance, it had plenty of dark corners for lurking surprises. He examined the area carefully to see if Juice might be waiting for him with a message.

Edie said, "Will you at least tell me where you're going to meet them? In case something happens, I'll know where to start looking."

Alex shook his head and walked faster. She hurried along beside him.

"Alex, talk to me," she pleaded. "This isn't fair. I thought we weren't ever going to have any secrets from each other."

"It's not my secret, Edie. Can't you understand that?" For the first time since they'd been seeing each other, he wished she'd go away and leave him alone. If she knew that he was harboring another secret, the one his mother had confided in him last night, she'd really freak out. But he wasn't ready to talk about that with anybody yet. He wasn't sure he was ready to admit it to himself. Even his mother, on the phone that morning, was still talking in the old way about his father. Well, hell, what else was he supposed to call him? The guy'd been there all his life. He'd never known any other father, and while he was glad to know the truth, he didn't know what he was supposed to do with it. As far as he could see, it wouldn't really change anything.

They were headed toward Second Avenue and the pizza parlor two blocks uptown, a favorite hangout of theirs. Usually, there were four of them, Edie, Alex, Richie Maldonado, and Jim Beatty. Beatty was on a different schedule, so they hadn't seen him since roll call that morning. And Maldonado was sick. Alex hoped Beatty would be waiting for them so Edie couldn't continue the argument over lunch.

Alex heard the running footsteps coming up behind them, but didn't turn to see who it was. Runners were common on the city streets. The really dedicated ones ran even in snowstorms. He was unprepared for the thump on the back as the runner passed by. He recognized Juice's poncho flapping toward the corner.

He handed Edie his black bag and said, "Hold this. And don't follow me." He didn't wait for her reply.

Juice was running in place at the corner, ostensibly waiting for a traffic light to change. Alex followed him, walking at a normal pace. No point in looking as if he were pursuing a suspect. There were so many cops and recruits in the neighborhood, somebody was bound to see him and wonder what he was doing. He hoped Edie had the good sense not to try to horn in.

On the corner, he stood beside Juice but didn't speak to him. Juice eyed him and nodded toward a playground on the other side of the avenue. Juice didn't wait for the light to change, but darted out into the street, dodging traffic. Alex waited for the light and followed, walking. He looked back once and saw Edie still standing where he'd left her. She looked angry, but she wasn't following. So far, so good.

In the playground, Juice sat wheezing on a bench. "Oh, shit, man. I don't know how them runners do it," he said. "I just run one fucking block and I can't breathe. I think I got asthma."

Alex sat down beside him. The playground was deserted. On sunny days, it was usually full of screaming children from the school across the street. "What did they say?" he asked.

"Who's the chick? Your old lady?"

"Just a friend."

"She a cop, too?"

"A recruit. She's in my class."

"She know about this?"

"She knows what happened to Paulie. They all do. I told her what I think, that somebody killed him."

Juice lit up a Kool. "You said you was in this alone. Nobody else. No cops. Now you got a chick who's a cop. I'm gonna call it off."

"Then it's on? When?"

"It's not on. Not if you're dragging her into it. Or anybody else. My mother told me never to trust a cop."

"She's not in it. We eat lunch together practically every day. She'd think it was strange if I didn't eat lunch with her today. That's where we were going."

"Yeah? Well, what does she think about you coming over here and talking with me? Look at her, just standing there eyeballing us. Can't you make her go away?"

Alex turned and looked over his shoulder. Edie was, indeed, standing on the corner, glaring in their direction. He waved to her and pointed up the street toward the pizza parlor. She shrugged, picked up the two satchels, and stalked stiffly away. Alex watched her go until she was out of sight. Then he turned back to Juice. "Is that better?"

"What are you gonna tell her about this?"

"I don't have to tell her anything."

"A chick?" Juice laughed. "She won't let you pull that. Chicks ask questions. They're worse than cops. They never let up."

"Why don't I just tell her the truth? That you're a friend of my brother's."

"Uh-uh. Never tell them the truth. About anything. They'll always get you with it."

"I'll tell her I was buying some weed."

"You want some?" Juice started groping inside his poncho. "I got some good Jamaican ganja. Just got in this morning. Some of my best customers are cops. I could put you on my list."

"No. Forget it." Alex looked around nervously. If anyone from the Academy saw him, they'd think that's exactly what he was doing, making a buy. "I'll think of something to tell her. I don't want her in on this either."

"And nobody else."

"Nobody."

"If you fuck this up, I'm coming after you."

Alex looked down and saw a knife lying in Juice's lap. He'd seen knives before. His father's butcher knives, the switchblades that some of the kids in high school had carried, the knives they'd exhibited in the Academy's self-defense class. But he'd never before seen one pointed at his gut.

Without a second thought, he gripped Juice's wrist in one hand and twisted until the knife dropped onto the pavement. "Now pick it up and put it away," he said, his voice as hard as the steel blade.

"You didn't have to do that," Juice complained. "I was just trying to make things clear to you."

"They're clear enough," said Alex. "If you've got something to say to me, say it and let's quit trying to fake each other out."

"Okay, okay. Here's what's happening. Tonight at six o'clock you be at the Ninety-sixth Street station, Seventh Avenue line, uptown platform. That's all."

"And then what?"

"Just be there. Somebody'll pick you up."

"How'll I recognize him?"

"Don't worry. You'll be contacted. I gotta go now." Juice dropped the stub of his cigarette into a puddle. "You do much running?" he asked.

"Some," said Alex.

"Funny, I can run like crazy if somebody's chasing me

103

through the yards, but just running along like these joggers do, it makes me tired. Dumb boring shit, right?"

Alex smiled. "Will you be there tonight?"

"Not me, man." He grinned. "I got a date with a lady who don't like to be disappointed."

Juice strutted away, his poncho flapping in the wind that cut through the playground and set the swings jangling on their chains.

Alex found Edie waiting for him in the pizza parlor, scowling over a half-eaten slice and a can of Sprite. He got himself two mushroom and pepperoni slices with extra cheese and a Cherry Coke.

When he sat down, Edie got up.

"Don't leave," he said.

"Nothing for me to stay for," she answered. "I only waited because you left me holding your bag. There it is. Good-bye."

"Edie, wait. Don't go. You're acting like a spoiled child."

"*I'm* acting like a child! You should take a good look at yourself. You think this is some kind of game. You think you can tell me what you like and keep the rest to yourself. It doesn't work that way, kiddo. I'm the all or nothing type, and right now it looks to me like a big, fat nothing."

"Sit down, Edie. Don't make a scene."

The pizza parlor was crowded. About half of the crowd was made up of police recruits, all of them paying close attention to the pizza slices they were gorging on, but not a single one of them was talking. Edie sat down.

"I wouldn't be making a scene," she hissed, "if you had any sense. Beatty was in here a while ago. He asked me if there's anything he can do for you. I told him no. I told him you had everything under control. Funny thing. He didn't believe me."

"Thanks a lot," said Alex.

"Beatty's a nice guy in spite of being a hypochondriac. He skipped two classes this morning to go up to the Bronx and see how Maldonado's doing. That took courage."

"How is Maldonado?"

"He's got strep throat and his wife's gone back to her mother."

"That's good."

"Her mother's the one who put her on the street in the first place."

"Oh. Then that's not so good."

"No. Especially since she's pregnant."

"Poor Richie. Is it his?"

"He doesn't care. He just wants her back. Beatty said there was a terrible scene while he was there. She won't come back unless Maldonado drops out of the Academy. But her mother's behind it all. She's got a finger in all kinds of trade, and she doesn't want a cop in the family. Not unless she can control him, and Maldonado won't play along. But he's so upset, he's talking about doing anything to get Idalinda back. So you're not the only one who's got troubles."

"We ought to do something," said Alex. "I'd hate to see him give it up. It means a lot to him."

"How much does it mean to you?"

"Edie, you know how I feel about it. It's the only thing I've ever really wanted to do. For two years after college, I just went from job to job. Nothing was ever right. Until one day, I saw the NYPD ad in the subway. So I took the exam and here I am. It's the best thing that's ever happened to me."

"And you're willing to risk it all, just to go chasing after some harebrained idea that can only mean trouble for you."

"Paulie was my brother. I have to do it, Edie."

"And you won't let anybody help you or do anything for you."

"Why should you risk getting kicked out? I know I'm taking a chance on that. I'll just have to hope it won't happen. But it's not your problem."

"Alex, Alex. Either you're dumber than I thought, or you're so pigheaded you won't let yourself see what's right in front of your face."

Alex stopped chewing on his pizza and stared at her. "What do you mean?"

"I mean, how much do you think all this would mean to me if you weren't around to make my life miserable?"

"Do I, Edie? Make your life miserable?"

She took one of his hands, the one that wasn't clutching the remains of his second slice of pizza. "Oh, you know what I mean. Now, finish your lunch and let's get back. I wish we didn't have gym right after lunch. It makes me feel like a tub of lard."

Alex wolfed down the rest of his lunch, and was still hungry. On the way out of the restaurant, he bought a candy bar to eat later.

Walking back to the Academy, Edie said, "Will you call me later tonight and let me know how it goes?"

Alex looked straight ahead and said, "How what goes?"

"Okay, okay," said Edie. "But if I don't hear from you, I'm going straight to the commissioner."

Alex laughed. "I'll call you, Edie. Just to keep *you* out of trouble."

11

They came for him before he had a chance to change for gym. They were waiting for him in the locker room when he got back from lunch, two of them, standing one on either side of his locker. Beatty, in his underwear, eyed him from across the room but didn't say anything. The rest of the guys were keeping quiet, too. A whole locker room full of recruits, normally boisterous and horsing around, was suddenly behaving like a squad of Sunday School teachers, all of them looking at the ceiling or into their lockers, anywhere but at him. The silence was eerie. Alex knew all ears were on the alert.

The two men were dressed as civilians, the tall, dark one in a fedora and dark gray cashmere overcoat that shouted big bucks, the shorter one in a trenchcoat, no hat, but Alex could tell they were cops. They had the aura. And who else could get this far inside the Academy?

"You Carlson?" the shorter one said. Nothing in his voice revealed his purpose. He sounded indifferent, almost bored.

Alex nodded. He noticed a faint scar on the man's cheek, arrowing up toward his right eye.

"I'm Detective Sergeant Lawrence Farley. This is Detective Sergeant Frank Bruno."

They both offered hands to shake. Alex gripped each in turn, trying to conceal his nervousness. Sweaty palms, shaky knees, dry mouth. He had them all. These guys must be hell on felons if they had him sweating already, and he hadn't even done anything. He murmured something; he didn't know what he said.

"We'd like to talk with you," said Farley. "It's okay. We've cleared it with your instructor."

Alex nodded again. He couldn't figure out why he felt so guilty. So far, he'd done nothing except sit in the playground and talk to Juice. Yet he was sure they knew he was up to something. This had to be about Paulie. The investigation had started. They'd be looking into every nook and cranny of Paulie's life, and probably his own. He started thinking about all the things he'd done in his life that could be held against him and make him look bad. He'd once stolen a Hot Wheels car from a neighborhood toy store. His mother had hauled him back and made him return it to the manager. The first time he'd smoked grass way back in junior high, he'd gotten violently ill, thought he was going to die, and sworn he'd never do it again. He had, of course, but only now and then, not a regular thing. And once, he and some of his high school buddies had "borrowed" a neighbor's junk heap of a car, driven it out to Jones Beach on a hot summer night, and returned it at four in the morning, with no one the wiser.

But that was all kid stuff. They wouldn't be interested in any of that. Or would they? What Paulie'd been doing was kid stuff, too. Until suddenly it wasn't, and Paulie was dead.

"Let's go someplace and sit down," Farley was saying.

So far, Bruno hadn't said a word, but now he took Alex's arm and led him toward the door. The man smelled of some kind of cologne or aftershave, sharp and pungent, but

108

not offensive. Alex noticed that his fingernails gleamed from buffing, and his expensive-looking black shoes sported the kind of shine Alex had never been able to achieve on his own thirty dollar cop clodhoppers. A real dude.

As they moved in a tight little phalanx toward the door, Bruno said, "They still teach you guys judo?" His voice was deep and tinged with the familiar accents of Brooklyn.

Alex found his own voice and felt himself warming to the tall, sharp-featured detective. "Some of that," he said. "Karate, all kinds of hand-to-hand, even the dirty stuff."

"Yeah," said Bruno with a slight smile, "comes in handy."

As the door closed behind them, Alex heard the locker room resound with a babble of excited conversation. Farley led the way to the stairwell and up to another floor where they found an empty classroom. They sat in student chairs at the back of the room, and both men produced leather-bound notebooks which they opened to blank pages on the formica desk arms. Both unbuttoned their coats but kept them on despite the warmth of the room. Alex noticed that while Bruno was wearing a dark suit of fine wool, Farley wore a rumpled tweed jacket and wrinkled twill slacks with street slush stains around the bottoms. Alex set his satchel down on the floor between his feet and gazed out the window at the back of Cabrini Hospital across the street, waiting for the questioning to begin.

He didn't have to wait long. "We have to ask you about your brother," said Farley.

"I figured," said Alex. "Does this mean he was murdered?"

"Oh, yeah," said Bruno. "It's a homicide all right."

"Got any ideas about that?" Farley asked.

"Me?" said Alex. "No. Only that I didn't think it was an accident."

"Why not?" Farley asked.

Alex shrugged. He couldn't tell them about Juice and the four graffiti writers who'd been shot at. Not now. And probably not even after he'd had a chance to sound the writers out about going to the police. He was sure they'd never agree to do that. "Paulie never had accidents," he said. "Even when he was little, he was always so careful."

"First time for everything," Bruno suggested.

"Maybe," Alex agreed, "but you just said it was homicide."

Bruno laughed. "Hey, Larry," he said. "This guy should be a lawyer. Watch out what you say to him. He doesn't miss a trick." He turned on Alex and his face was suddenly fierce. "Listen, shmuck. Let's just stop all this farting around. Answer the questions and don't get fancy with us. Go ahead, Larry."

Farley slammed his notebook closed. "Ah, shit, Frank. I couldn't care less who offed the little animal. I didn't want this assignment. You're the one who asked for it. You ask the questions."

"My brother wasn't an animal!" Alex flared.

"Don't pay any attention to him," said Bruno. "He's got a bug up his ass about graffiti. He thinks it's not worth his esteemed attention. He's just off of vice and he'd rather be consorting with pimps and whores. I guess he's more comfortable with his own kind and doesn't know how to act around human beings."

"Lay off, Frank," said Farley. "Let's get this over with. I don't know what I did wrong to get teamed up with you." He shifted his chair a few feet away from Alex and pulled a paperback novel out of his trenchcoat pocket. He was reading a Louis L'Amour western.

Meanwhile, Bruno edged his chair a little closer to Alex's until their knees were almost touching. He looked into

110

Alex's face and said softly, "Tell me about your brother's friends."

"I didn't know his friends. I haven't been living at home for two years."

"Before that. Didn't he ever bring his friends home?"

"No."

"Not even his school friends?"

"Oh, them. Sometimes. Not too often. I didn't pay much attention. They were just kids."

"Who did you think I meant?"

Alex looked away from Bruno's hard, dark, probing eyes. No way could he ever get away with lies or evasions with this guy. He could only hope Bruno wouldn't pop the right questions. On his other side, Farley was engrossed in his book, but Alex had the impression he wasn't missing a word.

"Well, you know," he said, "he mostly hung out with graffiti artists. He never brought them to the house, at least when I was around. I never saw any of them." That was the truth. Until he'd met Juice, Alex had never laid eyes on any of Paulie's graffiti friends.

"Somebody sure did a job on the trains last night," Bruno remarked.

"Yeah, I know," Alex said. "I saw it this morning."

"They must have thought a lot of your brother, to go out and do a thing like that."

"I guess so."

"They all loved him, huh?"

"How should I know?"

"Do you suppose one of them could have been jealous of him?"

Alex shrugged.

"Or mad at him?"

"I don't know. I just don't know."

111

"How about you? Were you jealous of him? Did you get mad at him?"

Alex leaped out of his chair. "What the hell kind of question is that?" he shouted. "He was my brother."

"Sit down," Bruno said wearily. "Brothers get mad at each other. They fight. Brothers kill each other. If you believe the Bible, the first murder was brother killing brother. It happens all the time."

"Well, not this time! Jesus!" Alex dropped back into his chair and covered his face with his hands. How could the guy be so hard? If that's what being a cop did to you, maybe Pop was right. It was time for him to quit.

He felt a hand on his shoulder and jerked his head up, ready to brush it away. It was Bruno's hand, and Bruno was smiling at him. The smile didn't do much to soften the man's features, but at least his eyes had lost some of their ferocity.

"Take it easy, Alex," he said. "I have to ask you these questions. Most homicides are family matters. They taught you that, didn't they?"

"Yeah. But not this one."

"You got any ideas who would have wanted your brother dead?"

Alex shook his head.

"What did it mean? That name he used? Dreemz?"

Alex thought the question over. He'd asked Juice what *his* name meant. Juice had said it didn't mean anything. But Paulie was different. He would have chosen a name that meant something to him. Alex could only guess.

"He never told me what it meant. But Paulie was a dreamer. He wanted the world to be beautiful. Peaceful. He thought he was doing something important, writing his messages on the trains. I guess that's what it meant. He wanted people to dream like he did."

"A dreamer," Bruno echoed. "Dreamers have a hard time of it. They never know what it's really all about. Are you a dreamer, Alex?"

"Me? No. Would I be in the Academy if I was?"

"Don't you dream about being a detective, getting a gold shield?"

"Well, maybe that. But I don't dream about changing the world."

"Don't you? Funny. I thought all young cops believed they were gonna make a difference. Maybe times have changed." He called across to Farley, "You want to take over for a while?"

Without looking up from his book, Farley said, "You're doing wonderful. Lemme know when it's over."

Bruno looked over the notes he'd been jotting down throughout the questioning. Then he began again.

"Was your brother on dope?"

No point in lying about that. Alex didn't think Paulie's death was drug-related. "A little weed sometimes. Not so much lately. I think he quit it altogether. He was into yoga."

"Was he dealing?"

"No. At least, I don't think he was." But he remembered Juice's offer in the playground. There might be some connection. He'd have to remember to ask Juice about that.

"Did he have any girlfriends?"

"Not that I know of."

"Was he a faggot?"

"Hey! Wait a minute! I don't have to listen to this shit!"

"Just answer the question."

"No! He wasn't!"

"How do you know?"

"I'd know it if my own brother was gay."

"You don't seem to know much else about him. You

don't know his friends. You don't know if he had any girlfriends. What if he got some girl knocked up and her brother went after him?"

"Paulie was only sixteen."

"And when did you lose your cherry?"

Alex was silent. He felt the red flush rising up his neck and flooding into his face as he remembered. His girlfriend of the moment had been babysitting. She'd heard a noise in the backyard and called him up, panicky. He'd rushed over and calmed her down. Like a hero, he'd gone out into the yard with a flashlight in one hand and a baseball bat in the other. There was nobody there, but when he came back in, she'd been so grateful. He almost couldn't do it for fear that the kids would wake up or the parents would walk in on them. It was all over in five minutes. He'd been fifteen.

"I don't think anybody gets murdered for that," he muttered.

"No, you're probably right," said Bruno. "In the old days, maybe, but not anymore. Kids, these days, they're playing doctor before they're out of diapers."

Bruno was on his feet, groping in his inside jacket pocket. Alex caught a glimpse of a shoulder holster. His clothes were so well-tailored, you couldn't tell it was there unless you actually saw it. Bruno handed him a business card, white with the blue police department shield in one corner. There were two phone numbers.

"I guess that's it," he said. "For today anyway."

"About time," said Farley, turning down the page of his book and stuffing it back into his pocket. "Think I could get a transfer to some police department out west? I'd like to see some of those mesas and prairies and things."

"You'd hate it," said Bruno. "The cowboys all ride around in jeeps and the traffic's as bad as the Fifty-ninth Street Bridge at rush hour." He turned to Alex. "Call me if

114

you think of anything else. Call anytime. I'm out a lot, but just leave a message and I'll call you back."

"Wait a minute," said Alex. Now that it was over, he had a few questions of his own. "Tell me one thing. I know how he died . . . the train and all that . . . but was he shot, too? Were there any bullet wounds?"

"Yeah," said Bruno, "somebody shot him. In the leg."

"What about his head?"

"How did you know about that?" Bruno was giving him the hard look again.

"I saw it," said Alex. "At the morgue. It looked like a bullet had grazed his head."

"Well, aren't you the smart one," said Bruno. "Maybe we should have you working this investigation."

"Do you mean it?" Alex blurted, not believing he'd heard Bruno correctly. "I want to help out. Is there something I could do?"

"No, I don't mean it." Bruno sat down again and motioned Alex back into his chair. "And I'll tell you exactly why. It's got nothing to do with the rules. As far as I'm concerned, the rules can go take a flying fuck at themselves. I'm not saying don't learn them. I'm saying learn them and then learn how to get around them."

"Don't listen to him, kid," Farley interrupted. "Old Bruno could've made captain by now if he'd played it by the rules."

"Shut up, Larry," said Bruno. "I'm telling this. And it's about how sometimes the rules are right, but mostly it's by accident. Listen to me, Alex. I'm gonna tell you a true story. Once, years ago, when I was still a patrolman, my mother was mugged. She was really hurt bad. The guy broke her arm and slashed her face. She almost lost an eye and she still has the scar. All for twelve dollars and change. Well, you can imagine how I felt. Me, a cop, and I can't

115

protect my own mother. I wanted to get the bastard and crucify him. I wanted to cut him into little pieces and flush him down the toilet. I begged them to let me work on the case. But you know what they said? They said no. The rules said no. And you know what else? They were right. Not because of the rules, but because they caught the guy without my help. My mother identified him. But if I'd been there, I'd have found some excuse to blow the guy away. That would have made me feel pretty good for the moment, but pretty lousy later on. And it probably would have got me discharged if not a jail term. I resented it like hell at the time, but I got over it. And so will you. You understand what I'm saying?"

Mute, Alex nodded. He understood it all right, but he wasn't sure he could buy it. Paulie wasn't just hurt. He was dead. And Alex had already set something in motion that he didn't want to stop. If he didn't do something, he wouldn't be able to live with himself. But he nodded again and said, "Okay. I hear you."

"Good," said Bruno, rising and buttoning his overcoat. "I'll be in touch. I understand you'll be staying with your folks for a while."

"What?" said Alex. "Who told you that?"

"Your mother," said Bruno. "She also gave me your address and phone number, just in case."

"You've been to see my mother?"

"And your father. They're both holding up pretty well."

"Let's go," said Farley, heading for the door. "I don't know about you, but my stomach's beginning to think my throat's been cut. I wish Luchow's was still in business. I could sure go for some wiener schnitzel right about now."

"What did they tell you?" Alex asked.

"About as much as you did," said Bruno. "This time. You'll all be seeing a whole lot of us until we get this thing squared away."

116

"Filed away, you mean," said Farley. "This one's got un-solved written all over it. And who cares? As far as I'm concerned, if all the graffiti dirtbags in the city start picking each other off, they'll be doing us all a big favor."

Alex decided to ignore Farley. There were too many peo-ple in the city who felt exactly the same way. It wouldn't do him any good to do battle with all of them, or any of them, or even with this one who was obviously just putting in his time until the big twenty when he could collect his pension and go live out his fantasy in some jerkwater town out west.

"This one isn't gonna get filed away," said Frank Bruno. "I don't like kid killers even worse than I don't like mafia hit men."

"Oh, boy," said Farley. "You and Giuliani, a couple of wop saints. He's gonna bust organized crime wide open and you're gonna bring in the Graffiti Gonzo. Hey, Frank, sup-pose Giuliani finds out who did your old man? What'll you do with the rest of your life?"

"Shut up, Larry. Your mouth is only bigger than the empty space between your ears."

And then they were gone. Alex listened to their uneven footsteps echoing away down the corridor. He sat with Frank Bruno's business card in his hand until long after the sound had died away.

12

The subway platform was narrow and crowded, with tracks on either side. Ninety-sixth Street was an express stop, the last one before the local took over on its slow crawl through the Upper West Side and on into the Bronx. The express trains branched off here to shoot through Harlem along Lenox Avenue where the No. 3 train ended its run and the No. 2 continued on into another part of the Bronx.

Alex had been standing on the platform for almost half an hour. He'd got there early, leaving the Academy before his usual time, skipping out on Edie so he wouldn't have to answer any of her questions or argue with her anymore about whether she could come along. Alone meant alone, solo, nobody hiding in the wings to play back-up. And just in case Bruno had put a tail on him, he'd taken the precaution of going all the way out to Brooklyn on the Lexington Avenue train, as if he were heading home, and then doubling back on the Seventh Avenue line from Atlantic Avenue. In the midst of rush hour, the trains were crowded. Twice, he'd spotted men who had the look of cop about them, but they were probably plainclothes transit cops on the lookout for ass-grabbers and purse-snatchers. If he was

118

being followed, the follower was doing a good job of staying unseen.

At Ninety-sixth Street he'd taken up a position in the middle of the platform so it would be easy for the graffiti writers to spot him from either end. Despite the hordes of people who poured off the trains and swirled around him to hurry up the stairs or onto another train, he felt out of place and exposed just standing there. A sitting duck for anybody who wanted to sneak up behind him and shove him onto the tracks.

The station was dirty and dank, and despite its fitful fluorescent lighting, dark. Most of the trains that swept through carried big DREEMZ pieces, in as many different styles and colors as there were graffiti writers, but the people who rode the trains, weary after their day's work and struggling for space on the teeming platform, scarcely noticed. It had been the sensation of the morning; by evening it was just another part of the underground scene.

The two men Alex had made as transit cops passed him twice, the second time giving him the once-over. He'd changed out of his uniform and into a pair of jeans and a sweatshirt that he kept in his locker. Remembering Edie's comment about his haircut, he'd put on his old Yankees cap. His down jacket was ordinary enough. Everybody wore down jackets in the winter. And he'd left his black bag in the locker, so there was nothing to identify him as a recruit. The next time the transit cops came by, they might stop and question why he was standing there so long. Waiting for a friend. What else could he say? But he hoped they wouldn't. If the contact spotted him talking to cops, to anybody, he'd split, sure as hell.

For about the hundredth time, he scanned the platform looking for a face he'd seen before, someone who was watching and waiting to be sure he was alone. He dismissed

119

all women and girls, all guys who looked older than twenty or twenty-one. Graffiti was a male preserve, mostly teen-aged boys, although there were a few girls and some old writers who kept on doing it even after they were married and had jobs. They couldn't get it out of their blood. Paulie'd told him that once, in one of the rare confiding talks they'd had. He wished he'd talked to Paulie more. Listened to what he had to say.

He was watching a tall thin black kid plugged into a Sony Walkman who'd let two trains go by, when he felt a tug at his sleeve.

"You're Alex, right?"

He didn't hear what she said. A train had just rumbled in. He thought she was trying to pick him up and shook his head.

"You're not Alex?" She was tiny, barely reaching his bicep even in high-heeled boots, and she was beginning to look exasperated.

"Yes. I'm Alex."

"Well. Come on, then." She took his hand and tugged him toward the train.

He held back. "Wait a minute. Where are we going? Where are the rest of them?"

She dug her long fingernails into his hand. "Come on, turkey. They're waiting for you."

The train doors started to close. She wedged her small body between them and held them open. "Come on!" she shrieked at him.

The doors sprang apart and she leaped into the train, still holding onto his hand. The doors slammed shut again before he could follow. She was on the train and he was on the platform with his arm stuck between the two doors. He had a vision of the train starting to move, dragging him along the platform and into the tunnel. Even worse, the girl could lose her grip on his hand and the train could roll off with her on it, leaving him behind on the platform.

He tried to get his other hand into the opening between the doors to force them open. The doors wouldn't budge. The passengers inside the train were beginning to look impatient and one of them shouted, "Pull your arm out, jerk! I wanna get home tonight."

The girl clung to his hand and pulled on it until he thought his arm would break. Shit! Did she think she could pull him *through* the doors?

The conductor's head popped out of a window at the end of the car. "Let go the doors!" he bawled. "There's another train right behind this one."

"I can't!" Alex shouted back. "My arm's stuck. Open the fucking doors."

The conductor muttered to himself angrily and withdrew his head. The doors sprang open again and Alex stumbled onto the train, lurching into the knot of passengers standing near the door. They gave him resentful looks as they tried to make room for him. The girl burrowed through the standing crowd, deeper and deeper into the car, dragging him along behind her. At last, she reached a spot that seemed to suit her. She gripped a pole and stood still, not saying a word to Alex, not even looking at him, although her hand still clung to his with a numbing strength.

Alex rubbed his arm. It felt like it had been run through one of his father's meat grinders. And for the first time, he got a good look at the girl. Although she was small and at first he'd thought she was about twelve or thirteen, her face was older, pretty enough but pinched. Impossible to tell whether she was black or Hispanic or even some kind of Oriental. Maybe a little of each. She wore a ratty fur jacket, and her slanted eyelids were smeared with green shadow. Her high-bridged nose hinted at Indian blood, but it arched over wide full lips thickly coated with purple lipstick. She stared straight ahead, swaying with the motion of the train. When Alex tried to free his hand, she tightened her grip.

"I won't run away," he whispered to her.

No answer.

"Where are we going?"

Nothing.

"What's your name?"

She ignored him. Alex gave up and rode in silence. The train stopped at 103rd Street and a few people got off, not enough to relieve the pressure of the crowd. The car was overheated and Alex felt the sweat soaking his clothes and trickling down his face. Little by little, at successive stops along the way, the train began to empty out. At 125th Street, a pair of seats became vacant and the girl plopped herself into one of them, forcing him to take the other. Their joined hands rested on his knee.

Alex looked down at her and said, "Isn't this romantic?"

She refused to answer or even meet his eyes. Instead, with her free hand, she took a stick of gum from her pocket, unwrapped it, and folded it into her mouth.

"Got any more?" he asked.

She chewed the gum noisily, but made no other sound.

At 157th Street, just as the doors were about to close, she got up suddenly and dragged him off the train. She ran and he ran with her, up the stairs and out into the street. He knew he was on Broadway in Spanish Harlem and the storefronts confirmed that knowledge. Their signs proclaimed: *Bodega, Comidas, Cerveza Fria, Viajes, Botanica.* You could buy groceries, eat a meal, drink cold beer, take a trip back to Puerto Rico, and get a potion or an amulet to help out your love life. You could also hang out in the littered doorways of abandoned shops and kill time in whatever way suited you. The girl steered him into one of these and pulled a pair of dark glasses from her pocket.

"Put 'em on," she ordered.

"I don't need them," Alex said. "It's not sunny."

She glared at him. Alex took the glasses and put them on. Might as well humor her, he thought. She's only the messenger, but she's the only way to get where I want to go. At first, they seemed like ordinary sunglasses, but once he got them in place, he realized that the lenses were completely opaque, black. He could see only by swiveling his eyes to one side or the other, but not enough to give him any sense of direction.

"You take 'em off, I leave you right here," she said.

Alex nodded, and off they went. She led him by the hand across streets and around corners until he was completely disoriented. She gave no warning when they were approaching a curb and several times he stumbled. Her hard heels clacked along beside him, keeping up a rapid pace. He lost track of time and distance. A dog barked and cars honked at them. He caught a whiff of rotting fruit. And all the while, she pulled him along by the hand. She never let go for an instant. His fingers were completely numb.

Suddenly, they were going up some stairs. She opened a door and pulled him through it. Then another. He smelled pungent cooking and the presence of cats. More stairs. A long flight and then a landing. Her heels rang out as if on concrete or tile. Stairs again. He counted four flights of stairs. And there were sounds along the way, television, a baby crying, voices laughing and talking, sometimes in Spanish, sometimes in English. He guess that he was inside one of the many old tenements that still dotted the neighborhood; condominium gentrification hadn't yet crept this far north. But which one? On what street? Obviously, he wasn't supposed to know.

She stopped at last and he heard her knocking on a door. A voice murmured a question from the other side.

"It's me," she answered. "I got him."

123

The door opened. She let go of his hand and pushed him through it. Before the door closed, he heard her heels clacking away down the stairs.

Behind him, a voice said, "Fun, huh? Cops and robbers. Just like in the movies."

Hands landed on his shoulders and propelled him forward. There was little light in the apartment, but he got the sense of moving through one room and into another. A railroad flat. He reached up to take the glasses off, but the hands on his shoulders tightened warningly. "The shades stays," said the voice.

In the third room, he was led to a chair and told to sit. Another voice said, "He don't look like Dreemz. You sure it's his brother?"

"Do you look like your brother? Juice said he was okay."

"I still don't like it. A cop is a cop."

"You didn't have to come."

"Yeah, man. But I'm the one got my ass shot at. I want to find out who the fuck's been doing that."

"You wasn't the only one. Don't try to make yourself out some kind of hero."

"I can get a gun, too. Next time, it's gonna be war."

"That's dumb shit, man. Who you gonna shoot? You can't even see the sucker. He hides out somewhere and all of a sudden, blam! He shot out the window of the car I was working on. Glass all over everything. I thought it was the cops."

A silence fell. Alex had been listening to the voices, trying to figure out how many people were in the room. So far, he'd counted four, but there might be others who hadn't spoken yet.

Another voice spoke up now, deep, authoritative and slow. "What say, brother of Dreemz? You asked for this meeting. We came. What you want from us?"

124

Alex searched for the right words. It was hard to talk when he couldn't see who he was talking to. He sensed that the group, however many there were of them, was divided. Some wanted to hear him out and maybe work with him; others wanted to strike back on their own, with guns. All of them distrusted cops. To them, he was a cop. But he needed them, and he hoped Edie was right in her judgment that they needed him, too.

"My brother was killed," he said. "Murdered."

The room murmured approval and settled down to hear his story.

Alex took a deep breath and went on. "I don't know who did it. But I do know he was shot, wounded and left on the tracks. A train finished him off. I saw his body. His head was cut off and his right hand. It was a hard thing to look at. My brother." He stopped to let them absorb what he'd said and to listen for any reaction. He hoped he wasn't overdoing it.

There was only the sound of steady breathing.

"You guys can take the easy way out," he went on. "Say it was the cops and feed on that. Me, I can't do that, because I don't *know*. And I won't rest until I *do* know. It would be easy to say I'm making a big thing out of it because he was my brother. Yeah, I guess I am. Wouldn't you? I came here tonight because I was hoping you guys could tell me something. You were my brother's friends. You probably know more about him than I do, who his enemies were if he had any, who would want to do this to him. Between us, maybe we can figure out who this sniper is. I don't want it to happen to anybody else."

The voices started up again.

"He say right. I don't want no more shooting. Next time, that motherfucker might get me between the eyes."

125

"Dreemz, he didn't have no enemies. He was one righteous child. Too good to be for real."

The deep voice overrode all the others. "How come you don't go to the cops? You supposed to be one of them."

"I didn't have to go to them. They came to me. This afternoon."

The room exploded with noise. Shouts and curses filled the air. Chairs scraped against the floor. Footsteps pounded through the apartment. Alex sat tight and listened to the turmoil, waiting for a lull and hoping no one would take a notion to pitch him out the window or slip a knife between his ribs.

"Listen!" he shouted above the din. "Would you believe me if I said they hadn't talked to me?"

"Who the fuck cares?" someone yelled. "If they did it, they not gonna tell you, asshole."

Alex stood up. Although he couldn't see any of the graffiti writers, he moved his head to wherever he heard a voice or a footstep. "They came this afternoon," he said. "They asked me a lot of questions about my brother. That's normal. But do you think it was fun?"

The noise diminished rapidly, and he heard the creak of chairs. They were settling down again. Alex remained standing. "They always talk to the family. That's the first thing they do."

"He got it," someone whispered. "I get busted, they all the time hassling my mother." A giggle. "She burn their ears all right. She throw their ass down the stairs."

Alex nodded. "That's right," he said. "They went to see my mother, too." He decided not to mention his father. A lot of these kids probably didn't have fathers in residence. Although Bruno had said they were holding up pretty well, he wondered. His mother would have been okay, but Pop was likely to have flown off the handle and talked a lot of garbage. Against Paulie, against him, against the police. Alex tried to imagine his father standing where he was now. Not in a million years! Because . . . a faint glimpse of the reason shimmered in his mind. Because he'd be scared? He pushed the thought away, but it came back with certainty. His father was always shouting things down because they scared him. The insight roused a rush of pity for the old man, but now wasn't the time to think about it. Now he had to deal with a roomful of graffiti writers who were suspicious at best and hostile to the idea of having anything to do with the police. Come to think of it, they were scared, too. That was the reason they'd agreed to see him, not because of Paulie. They could spill their fears to him and still preserve their illusion of not talking to the cops.

"I didn't tell them anything," he said, "because I don't know anything. I didn't tell them about this meeting because I gave Juice my word. But I'd like to be able to tell them about the four of you who were shot at before my brother was killed. I'd like it better if you'd tell them yourselves, but that's up to you. Whatever we do, we've got to let them know there's a sniper out there. You can't stop him, but they can. Before he kills another one of you."

Murmurs of protest and tentative agreement rumbled around the room.

"Shit, man. They don't do nothing they don't want to do. Why should they do something for us?"

"They got killer dogs. Who's to say they don't got killer cops out hunting us down?"

"I say we all get guns and waste the motherfucker."

"Yeah? And I say we cool out for a while. No more writing until this is over."

"How you gonna enforce that, man? When the urge to write, we out in the night, spreadin' our fame on the

Number Two train. It's like the full moon, man." The voice gave a high-pitched howl and everybody laughed.

Alex spoke again when the laughter died down. "I saw my brother's last piece. He didn't finish it. Somebody stopped him from finishing it."

"I seen it, too," said the voice that had howled. "Old Dreemz, he had some bug ideas. He was a chill artist. He had good style. I'm sorry he got offed."

"Thanks," said Alex. "And thanks for remembering him the way you guys did. I saw a lot of trains today."

"Did you see mine? I did a whole car, window-down, wild-style Dreemz with angel wings. I write Mello."

The deep voice sounded warningly. "We said no names. Listen up, brother of Dreemz. We got to think this over some more. It's not just us. It's every graffiti writer in the city. Meantime, suppose you find out what the cops plan to do about this situation. You let us know what's going down."

"Will you talk to them?" Alex asked.

"Not to them. To you. Nobody else. That way, if something gets screwed up, we know who to blame. We gonna be watching you, brother of Dreemz. They talk to you again, you find out what they doing. Then we decide what to do. But you say nothing to them about us, you understand? Some of us could get busted for just breathing on the trains."

"They'll find you without my help," Alex warned. "They'll be looking for Paulie's friends."

"I hear you," said the deep voice. "We'll deal with that. You do your part and we'll do ours."

"What are you going to do?" Alex asked.

No one spoke. They weren't going to tell him anything else. Maybe they didn't know what they were going to do. He hoped they wouldn't do as some of them wanted, get

128

guns and start popping off at every noise they thought might be the sniper. They'd wind up shooting each other, or some poor yard bum. But at least the one with the deep voice seemed to have some sense. He sounded older than the others. Alex wanted to rip the dark glasses off and see their faces. But he didn't dare destroy the fragile commitment he'd got from them. There'd be other times, he was sure. "Okay," he said. "I'll see what I can do. How do I get in touch with you?"

"Juice. He'll be around," said the deep voice. "Get the girl up here."

Alex heard footsteps going into another room and then the sound of a window being raised and a piercing whistle.

While they waited for the girl, a hush settled over the room. Alex sat down again, in darkness behind the dark glasses, and wondered if there was anything else he could have done. He was startled when he felt his hand being gripped in a soul brother handshake.

"I'm sorry about your brother, man," a voice he hadn't heard before whispered.

One by one, the people in the room came up and gripped his hand, murmuring rough condolences. He counted eight or nine of them, more than had taken part in the discussion. Then he was led back to the door where once again he was taken in tow by the girl who had brought him there. She was still chewing her gum, cracking it loudly between her teeth. Her small hand took charge of his just as firmly as before and her heels rang out on the stairs as she hurried him down and out onto the street.

When she finally snatched the glasses off his face, he blinked and found himself back at the subway station on Broadway. He saw her ratty fur jacket disappearing around the corner. To his surprise, Juice was standing next to him.

"So how'd it go?" he asked.

"All right," said Alex. "I thought you had a date."

"I did. I was right there in the room, keeping quiet. I was kind of like an insurance policy. If you fucked up, I wouldn't be standing here. So you did okay."

"You think they'll help me?"

Juice nodded. "If you help them. You just got to prove yourself. You do what they want and they'll be on your side. Hey, how'd you like that bit with the dark glasses? That was my idea. I seen it a long time ago on 'The Rockford Files.'"

"I still can't see too good."

"Want to go for a beer?"

Alex hesitated. He might get something more from Juice with a few beers in him, but he doubted it. He'd had enough of graffiti writers for one night. More important was finding out what Bruno and Farley had asked his mother and father. And whether Edie was still speaking to him. "Thanks," he said. "I think I'll be heading out to Brooklyn."

"Well. See you around." Juice gave him a mock punch on the arm and took off down Broadway, his poncho flapping around him like the wings of a giant bird.

Alex went down into the subway where he hoped to find a phone that worked.

13

Edie wasn't answering the phone. Didn't mean anything. She could be out. On the other hand, she could be so mad at him, she wouldn't answer the phone no matter who called. He retrieved his quarter and was about to call his mother when he heard the train pulling in down below.

He ran down the stairs to the downtown platform. It wasn't yet eight o'clock, but the platform was nearly deserted. There were just a few people scattered up and down its length. He got on the train and slumped into a seat. It was a long way home, and he was hungry and tired. But despite his fatigue, he felt there ought to be something else he could do tonight. Just going home, after the tension of meeting with the graffiti writers, seemed stupidly anticlimactic. He wondered if Bruno and Farley just went home after a hard day among murderers and suspects. He wondered what kind of homes they had, and what they told their wives, if they had them, about their work. But their wives couldn't be anything like Edie. He wanted badly to talk to her. He had to talk to *somebody,* and she was the only one who would understand.

The train started up just as an uptown train creaked into the station across the tracks. Alex looked out the window and saw more DREEMZ. It would take the Transit Authority a long time to buff them off of all the trains. Years maybe. And he'd be looking at them every day until they disappeared. Would he ever get used to them? Or would they be a constant reminder of Paulie? All the more reason to find his killer. Quickly. Or get out of town, to someplace where they'd never even heard of subways.

He tried to picture himself tooling along a California highway in a fine small car, a blonde California girl sitting next to him, tanned and laughing in the wind. But the highway kept turning into the Belt Parkway and the girl kept looking like Edie, brown-haired and freckled. And the only car he could conjure up was an NYPD patrol car. No, that would never work. He couldn't run away from it. Couldn't even make himself think about it seriously.

He leaned his head against the window and closed his eyes. Change at Fifty-ninth Street for the D train and then home. If he didn't fall asleep and ride this junkheap all the way down to South Ferry. He opened his eyes and struggled to keep them open. The train rocked along, stopping every few minutes as the street numbers crept down through the hundreds. Alex fought his drowsiness, wishing he had something to read. There were pages of newspapers scattered on the floor, but that wasn't what he wanted. It was all bad news, even the comics.

He tried reading the ads on the subway cards. About half of them were in Spanish. *"Aprenda inglés,"* and *"Victima de hemorroides."* Easy to figure those out. He wished he'd paid more attention to learning Spanish in school. It would have come in handy in the police. But he hadn't known that then.

At Fifty-ninth Street, there was a pay phone attached to one of the blue-painted platform pillars. He called Edie again. She answered on the first ring, and his heart began thumping in his chest just as it had when Juice came at him out of the shadows of the front porch. Funny, how love and danger had the same effect.

"Edie?" he said.

"Oh, Alex. Did you call a while ago? I was in the shower and by the time I heard it ringing and got to it, it stopped."

"Yeah. That was me. Can I come over?"

"If you don't mind that my hair's wet. It takes forever to dry."

Alex laughed drily. "Stop being cute, Edie. I've seen you with wet hair before."

"Oh. I thought we were going back to being just pals. I was planning to go to bed early."

"Fine with me. I'm tired, too. I almost fell asleep on the subway."

Edie giggled, then tried to sound exasperated. "Where are you, Alex?"

"Fifty-ninth Street. I can be there in half an hour."

"How did your meeting go?"

"What meeting?"

"Don't *you* be cute."

"Tell you when I get there."

"You will? What brought that on? I thought you were being the strong silent type."

"Edie, do you want me to come over or not?"

"Yes, Alex."

"I'll pick up something to eat."

"I've eaten already."

There was a newspaper and candy stand on the platform, just about to close up for the night. He bought himself a bag of peanuts and stared for a few moments at the skin magazines on display, remembering when, as a teen-ager, he'd had a stack of them stashed under his bed. Paulie, just a kid then, had got into them one day and Alex had yelled at

133

him and thrown him out of his room. He realized now it was because Paulie'd made him feel ashamed of himself. The magazines, with their pictures of naked women in blatantly erotic poses, had seemed disgusting in Paulie's young hands.

"You want something else?" The old news vendor was waiting patiently for him to finish staring so he could pull down the shutters and go home.

Alex said, "No," and started to walk away. But then he stopped and snatched a late edition of the *Post* from the depleted stack at the front of the stand. Something on it had caught his eye. Just a few words down in the corner of the front page.

GRAFFITI DEATH CALLED MURDER. PAGE 8.

He turned quickly to page eight, but learned little more than what Frank Bruno had told him. The autopsy report had come in. The reason his brother's leg had looked peculiar was that a bullet had shattered his tibia. He had to think for a minute before he realized that meant his shinbone. But that couldn't have killed him. All it could do was immobilize him. Poor Paulie. Some maniac taking potshots at him, and not being able to run away. The report didn't say anything at all about the wound on his head. And it didn't say what Bruno and Farley were doing, didn't mention them at all. All it said was, "Police did not rule out the possibility of homicide." God, he hoped Paulie was unconscious when that train ran over him. Imagine him lying there with a broken leg *watching* the thing come at him.

A D train pulled in and Alex got on, remembering as the doors closed that he still hadn't reached his mother to tell her he'd be late. She'd be worried about him, but she ought to know by now that he could take care of himself. He'd give her a call from Edie's place. He opened his bag of peanuts and settled down for the long ride out to Brooklyn.

Edie's hair was still damp when he got there, carrying a hero sandwich and a pint of chocolate ice cream. The ice cream was a peace offering. It was her favorite flavor.

"You didn't have to do that," she said. "I could have made you a sandwich."

He handed her the newspaper and said, "Look at that."

While Edie read, Alex went to the phone. "Mind if I call my mother?"

She nodded absently.

But there was no answer at home. That was strange, for both of them to be out. His father often went out at night; he had friends he played poker with, or he just didn't bother to say where he was going. But his mother was always home. She never went anywhere.

Edie tossed the newspaper aside. "Is that all the news?" she asked. "It doesn't say much. What happened this afternoon? You disappeared. Nobody knew where you went. Beatty told me two detectives came and got you right out of the locker room."

Alex unwrapped his hero sandwich and took a bite. Now that he was here with Edie, he didn't know where to begin or how much to tell her. He chewed, swallowed and then muttered, "They told me to stay out of it." He took another bite.

"Who?" Edie demanded. "Did you meet with the graffiti writers or not?"

"Bruno and Farley. The detectives. So it's definitely a homicide and they're definitely investigating, but they don't want anything from me except who were my brother's friends and who could have hated him enough to kill him. Bruno did all the questioning. Farley just sat there with his nose in a book and made snide remarks."

Edie reached across the table and pulled a slice of salami from his sandwich. "What about the graffiti writers? What

135

did they have to say?" She folded the salami and put it into her mouth.

He put down his sandwich and reached for her hands. Holding both of them, he looked searchingly into her face. "Edie," he said, "if I tell you about this, you've got to promise not to tell anyone else and not to bug me about getting involved in whatever I decide to do."

She pulled her hands away and stood up. In her fleecy pink bathrobe, with her long hair lying damply on her shoulders and her scrubbed face shining, she looked like a little girl. But a serious little girl with an air of determination about her. "No, Alex," she said. "I can't promise you that. If that's what you really want, you might as well leave right now."

Alex fought with his conflicting impulses. The urge to get up and stalk out into the night was strong. But he recognized it as childish and self-defeating. The opposite side of the coin was his desire to crawl into Edie's bed, pull the covers over his head and forget the whole thing. But he knew that five minutes of that would be all he could stand. He'd be right back where he was now, searching for a way to walk the tightrope between Bruno and the graffiti writers, while making sure that Paulie's death did not go unavenged.

He looked up at Edie, but couldn't bring himself to utter a word.

Her face softened. "Is it so hard to trust me, Alex? Or is it because I'm a woman and you think you ought to protect me?"

He shook his head, but then he said, "A little of that. But that's not the whole thing. There's something else I haven't told you. Something my mother told me last night. It's so unreal, I can't make myself believe it. But I guess it's true, or why would she have said it? It seems my father isn't my

136

father after all. I probably shouldn't be telling you. It's been her secret all these years. Their secret. She says he knows. I wish she hadn't told me. It's been on my mind all day, underneath everything else."

Edie moved her chair closer to Alex's and sat down again. "You've had a lot to think about, haven't you?" she said. "All right, I'll try to make it easy for you. A compromise. No promises, but I'll keep whatever you tell me to myself unless you tell me otherwise or you get yourself into a dangerous situation and there's no other way."

"And you won't ask to come along if I have to go see them again?"

"I'll try to restrain myself."

"No tricks, Edie. I don't want you following me around or doing something on your own."

"Okay. Okay."

"There's not all that much to tell."

"There may be more than you think. Not just what they said. Your impressions. The killer could be one of them, you know."

"Do you think I haven't thought of that? He could have been right there, in that room, laughing at me. But I really don't believe that. What I do believe is that they're scared. Especially the four who'd been shot at before Paulie. They were there. They put on a lot of bravado, but underneath it all I think they're terrified. What I'm afraid of is that they'll psyche each other up to the point where they go gunning for this guy themselves. They talked a lot about that. And the fact that some of them think it's the police hunting them down."

"Could they be right about that?"

"Edie!"

"I'm serious, Alex. Cops go haywire just like anybody

137

else. Maybe even more than anybody else. It's worth thinking about."

"Okay. I'll think about it. But it doesn't smell right to me. For one thing, a cop wouldn't miss as often as this guy has. As one of the kids said, he couldn't shoot for shit. It wasn't a bullet that killed Paulie. It was a train."

"What kind of person would sneak around subway yards at night and shoot at people?" Edie mused.

"A nut," said Alex.

"Yes, but what kind of nut? What's his particular brand of craziness?"

"Maybe he's a train buff. Someone who loves the subways and hates to see the trains marked up."

"Could anybody love the subway that much?" Edie answered her own question. "I suppose so. I've heard of stranger hobbies. But this goes way beyond collecting Barbie dolls. Get back to the graffiti writers. What else did you learn about them?"

"There was a guy with a deep voice. He sounded older than the rest, like a ringleader. They listen to him, but I don't think he can control them."

Edie picked up on it right away. "What do you mean 'sounded?' Couldn't you see him?"

"I couldn't see any of them. I couldn't even see where I was."

Edie sucked in a sharp breath. "What did they do? Blindfold you?"

"Just about. They used dark glasses. Lenses painted black. I couldn't see a thing except around the edges and not much of that. There wasn't a whole lot of light in the place."

"Oh, Alex! You let them get away with that?"

"I didn't have much choice, Edie. Now who's talking about being a hero? You'd have done the same."

"I don't know. I can't stand not being able to see where I am. It scares me more than anything. That's why I always keep the bathroom light on at night."

"I've been meaning to talk to you about that. I thought it was because you liked to wake up and admire the gorgeous hunk in your bed. You shouldn't disillusion me like that."

"Were you scared?"

"Of having you admire me?"

"No, dummy. Of not being able to see them."

"To tell you the truth, yes. At first. But it's amazing how much you can pick up on just by listening and by letting yourself kind of absorb what's going on. I was never in any danger, not even when they started shouting and stomping."

"They did what!"

"When I told them I'd already talked to the police. I figured I had to tell them that. They'd know the way the police work. This way, they know I'm not going to lie to them about being questioned." Alex had finished off his sandwich and was looking around in the kitchen for something else to eat. "Want some of this ice cream?" he asked.

"What a question," she answered. "I thought it was all for me. Make some coffee, too. Please."

Alex filled the kettle and put it on the stove. He split the pint of chocolate ice cream between two dishes and carried them over to the table. He went back to the kitchen area, got out two coffee mugs, and spooned instant coffee into them. Edie's apartment was bigger than his own, but not by much. If they ever did move in together, they'd probably have to find a bigger place. But all of that was on hold. He wouldn't even be able to spend the night here as he often did on Friday nights. Pretty soon, he'd have to get on home and see how his mother was doing. He wondered where she could have gone. Probably to one of the neighbors. She had some good friends in the neighborhood. They'd want to cheer her up, do what they could for her. When the kettle boiled, he made the coffee and carried the mugs to the table.

"There's just one other thing I learned," he said as he sat down and started eating his ice cream. "One of them goes by the graffiti name of Mellow. If I could find out his real name and where he lives, I might be able to get him alone. He sounded pretty young. Without his friends around, he might be willing to talk to me."

"What about the one who met you in the playground this morning?"

"Juice? No. Juice isn't giving anything away. And, for now, he's my only contact with the rest of them. I don't want to jeopardize that. So that's all I know."

"You're right," said Edie. "It's not much. You know what I'd do if I were you?"

"No. What?"

"This." She got up and put her arms around his neck. Curled herself into his lap. Kissed him long and thoroughly.

"M-m-m," he said finally. "Very tasty. Next time, I'll get butter pecan. It's getting late. I'd better be going."

"You're leaving?"

"I told my mother I'd be staying there for a few days. It's the least I can do for her."

"Oh, yeah. Well, okay." Edie sounded disappointed.

"Besides," he added, "I want to find out what Bruno talked to her about. Maybe he told her something he didn't tell me."

"Keep in touch," said Edie, watching him zip up his jacket. "If I get any bright ideas, I'll give you a call."

Alex hugged her and inhaled the sweet smell of her clean

140

hair. "Don't sound so miserable. I'll be back, probably tomorrow."

"I'm not miserable," Edie protested. "It's just that I don't like feeling helpless."

"Neither do I." He kissed her lightly on the forehead. "Good night, Edie."

"Good night, Alex." She stood in the open doorway of her apartment and watched him run down the stairs. "Thanks for the ice cream," she called after him.

14

It was getting to be weird, coming home every night and the house dark as if nobody lived there. He glanced at his wristwatch by the light of a streetlamp. Not quite midnight but late enough for both of them to be asleep. Snow had begun to fall, light, bright flakes that fluttered down through the still, cold night. He let himself in quietly and switched on the light in the front hall.

His mother's new stormcoat was draped over the "hall chair that nobody liked." She'd bought the chair cheap at an auction years ago, but it was so ugly it killed every room she tried it out in, so she'd put it in the hall for people to sit on when they were putting on their boots or galoshes. Only nobody ever did. All it did was collect dust and coats that were thrown down in a hurry. Alex felt a twinge of sadness for the failure of his mother's small economies.

He picked up the coat and hung it in the hall closet. It wasn't like her to throw her own coat down there. Especially not a new one that she was so proud of. She must be sleeping, Alex thought. Good for her. She needs it. He hung his jacket up next to her coat.

He tiptoed up the stairs to the darkened second floor. The door to his parents' bedroom was ajar. He peeked in, just to be sure she was all right. A shaft of light from the hall fell across the bed. It was empty. The striped bedspread had been carelessly pulled into place and the blankets beneath made ripples on the surface. A sloppy job, not like her at all. He opened the door wider and walked into the room. No one. The room was cold and felt abandoned.

Where could she be?

He hurried back downstairs, this time not bothering to walk on tiptoes. He called her name. He turned on the lights in the living room. She hadn't fallen asleep on the couch. He tore through the dining room and kitchen, not really expecting to find her there. He went down into the cellar but found nothing that didn't belong there. Dusty old junk.

Worried, he climbed the stairs again. The bathroom door was closed. People committed suicide in bathrooms. Slit their wrists. Drowned themselves in bathtubs. Hanged themselves from shower rods. With these deadly visions clamoring in his mind and urging haste, he knocked on the bathroom door. When there was no answer, he opened it and barged in, prepared for the worst. There was no one there.

He turned the light on to be sure. Looked behind the shower curtain. Stared at his own white face in the mirror. Please let me find her, he begged his agonized image. Please let her be okay. Don't let this happen.

He tore his eyes away from his own hypnotic glare and that's when he saw it. There on the rim of the sink. An empty prescription vial. He picked it up and read the label. "D. Carlson. One, as needed, for sleeplessness." One. But the vial was empty. For sleeplessness. How long had she been without sleep? How long would she sleep if she'd swallowed them all?

Clutching the vial, he ran out into the hall. Across from

the bathroom, the door to Paulie's room was closed. He knew, suddenly, that she was in there, holed up with her grief and dying from it. He twisted the knob and pushed. The door was locked.

"Ma!" he shouted. "Ma! Are you in there?" He pounded on the door.

There was no answer.

He backed off across the hall and threw himself against the door. It didn't budge. The house was old, the doors solid. The lock held firm.

Somewhere, there had to be a key. Years ago, after Paulie had locked himself in one of the attic rooms and refused to come out, she'd collected all the keys and put them away. He had a dim recollection of a large metal key ring with all those long skinny gray keys dangling from it. But there wasn't time to look for it. Anyway, she probably had it with her on the other side of the door.

He forced himself to think. What other way was there to get into the room? There were windows, but no fire escape. His own room had French doors and a little balcony overlooking the backyard, but not Paulie's. But Paulie used to climb out his window and sit on the porch roof, smoking joints and gazing at the stars. And the porch roof wrapped around from the side to the front of the house and ran under the windows of his parents' room.

That was the way in. The only way. He ran back into his parents' room and flung open the side window. A cold wind rushed into the room, but Alex didn't feel it. He thrust one long leg over the windowsill and felt with his foot for the shingles of the porch roof. The roof sloped down away from the window. He gained a purchase with one foot and drew his other leg through the open window. Standing there, he felt a sprinkling of snowflakes melting on his face. The shingles were lightly dusted with snow and slippery.

He inched his way along, clinging to the side of the house, leaning inward away from the slope of the roof. Below, the concrete driveway leading to the garage glimmered under a quickly gathering accumulation of snow. Step by step, slowly in the dark, slipping and catching himself, he edged toward Paulie's window. So close, he wanted to run for it; so far, it seemed to take a thousand years. The snow was falling faster, piling up on the shingles in streaks that were treacherous underfoot.

When he finally gripped the window frame, the muscles of his legs were cramped from the effort of his slow crawl. He braced himself and tried to insert his fingers between the upper and lower sashes to push the lower one up. The space was too narrow. He peered through the glass. The windowshade was down. The window was locked. Without a knife or a length of flat metal, he'd never be able to open it.

There was another window further on at the very edge of the porch roof, but it was no doubt locked, too. And time was passing too quickly. He'd have to break the window.

Gripping the windowframe with both hands, he let his body swing back and raised one foot. If his hands slipped, if only one hand slipped, he'd wind up flat on the driveway below. He slammed his foot against the windowpane, felt it shudder and then give way. There was hardly any sound, a faint shattering of glass inside the room. Nothing more.

Jagged shards of glass remained quivering, still attached to the sash. He pried two of the largest pieces loose and tossed them through the window into the room. Then he crawled through the window, pushing the shade aside, and heard the crunch of glass beneath his feet as he landed on the floor.

The room was utterly dark. He groped his way into it, bumping into furniture in his haste to get to the other side of the room and the light switch.

When the light came on, she was there, sprawled on Paulie's bed, fully dressed, eyes closed, mouth open. He couldn't tell if she was breathing.

"Ma," he whispered, and shook her.

She felt limp under his hands, but she was warm.

He knelt beside the bed and listened for her breath. He searched for a pulse in her wrist. He laid a hand lightly on her chest, hoping for a heartbeat. It was there! Faint and slow, but steady. She was alive!

He stood up and shook her again, tried to make her sit up. He propped her against the pillows and spoke to her, coaxing her to wake up. When he took his hands away, she flopped sideways, her head hanging over the edge of the bed.

He'd have to get her out of this room. Cold water and hot coffee. That's what she needed. He unlocked the door; the old key ring with all its old keys was hanging from the lock. He picked her up and carried her into the bathroom. She seemed so light and small, a fragile weight that could at any moment drift out of his arms and away forever.

Gently, he put her down in the bathtub. Her eyes were still closed, but her breathing had become irregular and harsh. He wondered if he ought to take off her clothes, but decided to spare her that embarrassment. Better to ruin a skirt than have her wake up naked under his eyes. He took off her shoes and placed them side by side on the tile floor.

"Ma," he said, "please forgive me for this."

And then he turned on the cold shower full force.

She lay there, under the drumming water, not moving, her clothes drenched, her hair plastered to her skull. Alex reached down to feel for her heartbeat once again. Could she have gone off, without a murmur, before he'd had a chance to do what he could to save her? A cold, wet hand gripped his.

146

"Ma!" he cried.

She made a sound. It wasn't a word, or even a groan. Just a small weak sound somewhere deep inside her throat. Alex rejoiced. He held her hand in both of his, unmindful of the cold water soaking his shirt and splashing down on his head.

"Can you sit up, Ma?" He tried to pull her into a sitting position.

Her head waggled from side to side. He couldn't tell whether she meant no, or was simply trying to escape the water raining down into her face. He turned the shower off.

She sighed. Her eyelids flickered, parted, and then fell closed again. A long shudder passed through her body. "Cold," she murmured. Her lips were blue.

Alex wrapped her in towels. She shivered spasmodically and her teeth chattered against each other. As he wrapped a towel around her head, he felt her eyes on his face. He avoided them, putting off the moment of explanation.

"Can you get up?" he asked.

Again a sound, not a word. But she was sitting up, bracing herself against the sides of the tub.

"That's right," he encouraged her. "Upsy-daisy. Want to get out of there?"

"I'm all wet," she moaned. "What did you do?"

"What did *you* do?" he countered. "Never mind. We'll talk about that later. First things first. How about some dry clothes?"

"I feel sick," she gasped. "Get out of here." He tried to help her out of the tub, but she pushed him away. "Out, I said. And close the door."

He did as she told him, but stayed close to the door, listening first to her soft fumblings and then to her painful retching. Good, he thought. The best thing. She'll get rid of

147

it all. But it was hard, listening to those sounds and not being able to help her.

At last, the door opened a crack. Her voice came through it, weak and raspy. "Alex? You there?"

"Yeah, Ma. How're you doing?"

"Get my bathrobe, will you? It's in my closet. And my slippers."

He went into the bedroom where a drift of snow had accumulated on the floor under the open window. He closed the window. The snow would just have to lie there and melt. He'd mop it up later. Her old flannel bathrobe was hanging on a hook inside the closet, the slippers on the floor beneath it. He took them and handed them in to her through the partly opened bathroom door.

"If you're okay, I'll go down and make some coffee," he said.

"I'm not okay, but coffee sounds good. I need something hot. I've never been so cold in my life."

Down in the kitchen, he filled the old electric percolator and plugged it in. He considered dialing 911 and getting an ambulance to take her to the hospital. But before he could do it, she appeared like a wraith in the kitchen doorway.

"Ma," he said, "you should have waited. I would have brought the coffee up to you. You should be in bed."

"No, I shouldn't," she said. "I should be walking around, pacing back and forth. One, two, three, four. One, two, three, four. Isn't that what you do with stupid people who take too many pills? Is the coffee ready?"

"Almost. You want to talk about it?"

"You're all wet, Alex. You'll catch a cold. Take that shirt off and put this on." She handed him an old sweater of Theo's that was hanging on a hook by the back door.

"Don't worry about me," said Alex. "Let me worry about you for a change." But he did as she told him. The sweater smelled of Theo's cigarettes and old disappointments.

He looked in the cupboard and got down her favorite coffee cup and saucer, the one with bright yellow daisies inside and out.

She paced back and forth behind him, slow then fast then slowing down again. He heard her counting her steps. Her voice sounded weary and her footsteps dragged.

He poured the coffee. "Sit down, Ma," he said. "The coffee's ready." He put the cup on the kitchen table and pulled out her chair for her.

"Do you think I should?" she asked. "Shouldn't I keep on walking?"

"Sit down for a little while. You can walk some more later."

She collapsed into the chair, her hands lying loosely in her lap. Her face was pale, the skin tight and almost transparent. "Alex," she said, "I'm sorry."

"Don't, Ma. You don't need to apologize to me."

"It was a stupid thing to do. I feel awful. Everything aches. My head, everything."

"Why did you do it? You don't have to tell me if you don't want to."

"Why? I don't know. It must have seemed like a good idea. I can't really remember deciding to do it. I guess everything just got too much and the pills were there. And I took them."

"How many?"

"There weren't a lot left. Five or six."

"How's the coffee?" She hadn't tasted it yet. Alex poured himself a cup and sat down next to her.

"The coffee?" She sipped. "It's good. Strong. I guess I'm a big pain in the neck."

149

"Was it because those detectives came here today?" Alex asked. "Was it rough for you?"

She looked at him sharply. "What do you mean, rough?"

"You know, did they ask you hard questions? Did they make you talk about Paulie?"

"Oh, that. Sure. But I didn't mind that. I didn't exactly enjoy it, but I know it needs to be done. Did they talk to you too?"

Alex nodded. "Two of them. Frank Bruno and a guy named Farley. They said they'd talked to you and Pop."

She nodded. "They came early this morning. Right after you called. Your father . . ." she hesitated. "He hadn't even shaved yet." She sipped at her coffee again and shuddered. "This stuff is really strong."

"Drink it, Ma. It'll do you good."

"Keep me awake all night," she objected, and then she gave a short, bitter laugh. "I guess that's what it's supposed to do. Oh, Alex, I had the notion that there was nothing left to live for. But here you are, telling me you think I ought to stick around for a while."

"Damn right," said Alex. "Who else thinks I'm the greatest?"

She smiled and touched his cheek gently with her fingertips. "Do you remember how we used to go to the library, the three of us?"

"Yeah. I'd read to Paulie in the children's room and you'd go off and get lost."

"I didn't get lost," she said. "I used to read a lot in those days. I'd come back with five or six books, and the two of you would be sitting there, looking like angels."

"Some angels!" Alex said. "He used to kick me in the shins under the table."

"I went there today," said Dorothy. "I hadn't been there for years. I went into the children's room and just sat there

150

for a while. I found one of the books that Paulie used to love, the one about Little Bear."

"There were three or four of those," said Alex. "I always had to read him the same one over and over."

"I sat there looking at it. I guess I cried some. Must have scared the librarian. And then all of a sudden nothing seemed to matter anymore. I don't know how I got home. I remember thinking how easy it would be to just jump in front of a Flatbush Avenue bus. When I got home, it was so lonely here, so empty. Nobody to talk to. Nobody to do anything for."

"Where was Pop?"

She shrugged. "Who knows? He comes, he goes. He doesn't say anything. You know how he is. You won't tell him about this, will you?"

"Not if you don't want me to. But why shouldn't he know?"

"Maybe I'm embarrassed. Maybe I just don't want to give him something else to worry about. He was pretty awful with those detectives. Especially when they wanted to search the house. He didn't want to let them. I told them to go ahead and he didn't like that much."

"What were they looking for?"

Dorothy shrugged. "I don't know. They took Paulie's sketchbooks. I made them promise to give them back." Her voice quavered and she looked as if she might cry. "I want to keep them," she said, "to remember him by."

Alex stood up. "I'd better do something about that window," he said. "Some cardboard or plywood, if there's any around."

"What window?" she asked.

"In Paulie's room. I had to break the window to get in."

"Oh, Alex," she sighed. "I'm sorry you had to do that.

151

I'm sorry for so many things. But it's too late to be sorry, isn't it?"

"Didn't you tell me we shouldn't blame each other? I think that goes for ourselves, too. Don't blame yourself, Ma. You couldn't know what would happen." He headed for the door to the basement. "I'll take a look downstairs and see if there's something I can put over the window."

"I think there's some sheetrock left over from the time your father put the ceiling in the garage. That might work."

"Good idea," he said, running down the stairs.

"I'll get the window man to come in tomorrow," she called after him. "I'll tell your father somebody threw a rock."

Lies, Alex thought as he rummaged through the junk stored in the basement. Why couldn't she stop calling him "your father"? But what else could she call him? And how many other lies had they lived with over the years? Wouldn't it be better to get everything out in the open, no matter how much it hurt? But he couldn't suggest that to her now. Maybe in a few days, they'd be able to sit down together, the three of them, and really talk about it all. Maybe by then, he'd have found out something about Paulie's killer. If he could at least offer that to Theo, it might go a long way toward helping him deal with his loss. After all, Paulie was Theo's only son. No wonder he was in a rage.

He found the sheetrock, dusty and warped, stacked up behind the window screens that Theo always put up in the spring and took down in the fall. In a few months, it would be spring again and everything would be different. This year, he'd help put up the screens.

15

"Another graffiti writer got shot last night."

It was Saturday morning, and they were sitting in Frank Bruno's car, parked on a side street not far from the house.

"Dead?" Alex whispered.

"Not dead," said Bruno. "I'm going out to see him. Want to come along?"

"Me?" said Alex. "Why me? I thought you didn't want me to get involved."

"I changed my mind. Farley's got the weekend off, and I thought I might as well use some local talent. Anyway, you are involved. I got an anonymous telephone tip last night. Guy said, 'Doesn't that kid Dreemz have a brother?' What do you think of that?"

Alex stared into Bruno's impassive face. The man gave no indication of what he was thinking. "Someone's trying to say I killed my brother?" he asked.

Bruno nodded gravely.

"Do you believe that?" Alex asked.

"Doesn't matter what I believe. I think about a lot of things, but I only believe what I can prove. If you did do it, I'll find out. You can believe that."

Alex had slept late that morning. When he finally got

153

downstairs, he found Frank Bruno sitting at the kitchen table drinking coffee with his mother and father. They all turned to stare at him when he walked into the room. The moment was uncomfortable, as if they'd been talking about him. Then his mother had started to hustle up some breakfast for him, and Theo had launched into one of his lectures about people who sleep their lives away. Bruno had just sat there, taking it all in and smiling that smile of his.

Alex had wanted to ask his mother how she was feeling this morning, but he didn't dare. She looked okay, a little pale but she was putting on a good show. And he wanted to ask Theo why he couldn't stick around more and take care of her now when she really needed him, but that would only provoke an argument. Not the sort of thing to do with Bruno for an audience.

He ate his eggs and listened while his mother talked about Paulie and Theo threw in an occasional comment. He was surprised that she was able to talk so freely to Bruno. It was almost as if they were old friends talking over something that had happened years ago. If it was some kind of cop technique, it sure wasn't anything they taught at the Academy.

And he was surprised, too, when Bruno asked him to go for a ride. "It might take a while," he'd said. "I hope you haven't got other plans."

They'd all laughed politely when Theo, joking, said, "You're not gonna arrest this guy, are you? That's no way to treat a rookie cop."

It wasn't much of a joke, but now it was even less of a laughing matter.

Alex stared out the window of the car and wondered what Bruno was leading up to. The little street with its bare trees and winter-stained houses looked dismal and shabby, just about the way he felt. How could anybody think he'd killed Paulie? Who could think that? Bruno had said it was an anonymous tip. Maybe one of the graffiti writers was trying to shift the blame onto him. That meant one of them was guilty. Or maybe there was no tip at all. Bruno could have made the whole thing up, just to get his reaction.

"Is that all the guy said?" he asked. "Just doesn't that kid Dreemz have a brother? Nothing else?"

"That's all," said Bruno. "He hung up before I could ask him what he meant. Somebody got an ax to grind with you?"

"Not that I know of."

"You wouldn't happen to own a gun, would you?"

"No!" Alex was about to say he wished he did own one, but he had to be careful what he told Bruno. Even his denial was too loud, too emphatic. He toned it down when he added, "We don't get our service revolvers until graduation."

"Oh, right, right," said Bruno. "I forgot. They used to hand them out on the first day at the Academy. That's when I got mine. Never been without it since. But that was over twenty years ago. Things change. So how come your father was telling me something about a rifle that used to be around the house? He even showed me where it used to be kept, but it wasn't there."

"A rifle?" Alex's mouth was suddenly dry. There had been a rifle, years ago. He must have been about eleven or twelve when Theo had brought it home. And then there'd been a hunting trip, either that year or a year later. In the fall. He couldn't remember where they'd gone, only that it had been cold and dark, and he'd been excited to be there, the only boy among the men, his father's friends. They hadn't caught anything, hadn't even seen a buck, although he remembered hearing noises that might have been an animal. He'd been frightened by the noises, but tried hard not to show his fear. After that, Theo lost interest in hunting and years later his mother had brought the gun down from the attic and asked him to get rid of it.

"I don't care what you do with it," she'd said. "Sell it or give it away, and don't tell me anything about it. I just don't want it around the house. Too many accidents happen with guns and I don't want Paulie to get his hands on it. Your father'll never miss it. I don't think he even remembers it. If he ever asks, I'll just tell him I don't know what happened to it."

But Alex hadn't gotten rid of it. He hadn't felt right about selling it and could think of no one to give it to. Besides, it was a pretty nice gun. Who knows, maybe someday they might want to go hunting again. As long as it wasn't in the house, his mother would be satisfied. And he knew of a perfect hiding place for it, where no one would ever think of looking. Theo had just put the new ceiling into the garage, some panels of sheetrock laid over strips of lath. They weren't even nailed down. It had been a simple matter to slide one of the panels aside and slip the rifle into the dark cavity between the ceiling and the roof. And then he'd forgotten all about it.

Until now. Bruno was watching him, waiting for his answer.

"Yes," he said. "There was a rifle once. It was my father's. I don't know what happened to it."

"He doesn't either. Your mother thought you might know."

So they *had* been talking about him when he walked into the kitchen. "She said I knew?"

"No. She just said maybe I should ask you about it. I would have asked you anyway. And you don't know."

"No."

"A mystery," said Bruno. "I wonder why your father brought it up."

156

"Did you ask him if there was a gun in the house?"

Bruno nodded.

"Well, that's why. He was telling you the truth. You reminded him of it. But nobody's seen it for years and nobody knows where it is. Maybe somebody stole it."

"Have you ever had a robbery?"

"No. What I meant was, Paulie could have taken it and sold it when he was doing grass. He did some pretty strange things back then. He took a camera of mine once. I never saw it again." Forgive me, Paulie, Alex said to himself. It's rotten of me to bring up that old stuff. As soon as I get home, I'll check out the garage and really get rid of it.

"Kid brothers, huh? They can really be a pain." Bruno reached across Alex to open the glove compartment. "You mind looking at some pictures?"

"Of what?"

"Oh, just this kid that was shot last night. Maybe he was a friend of your brother's. I thought you might recognize him."

"I didn't know any of Paulie's friends. I told you that yesterday."

"So you did. Well, take a look anyway." He shoved a sheaf of Polaroids into Alex's hands. "He came into Coney Island Hospital, walking if you can believe it with a bullet in his chest, a little after midnight. Told some wild story about a sniper in the subway yard before he conked out. They operated on him right away, so we have the bullet, but we haven't been able to talk to him yet. Could be he got shot by the same guy who did your brother."

Alex stared at the photographs. There were six of them, different angles of the same young black face. The eyes were closed, and the face looked peaceful. Except for the IV bottle hanging just behind his head, the boy might have been sleeping in his own bed.

"What's his name?" Alex asked.

"He didn't give one," said Bruno. "He didn't have any identification on him."

"What about his graffiti name? His tag?"

Bruno shook his head. "The Coney Island police picked up a shopping bag in the subway yard. Paint cans, a sketchbook, a tuna fish sandwich. If it belongs to the kid, then maybe there's something in his story."

"What tag does he write in the book?"

"Beats me," said Bruno. "I can't make it out. Just a lot of lines and colors going off in all directions. Wanna take a shot at it?" He reached into the back seat and handed Alex a black sketchbook just like the ones he'd seen his brother working in.

Alex opened the book. Across the first page and the inside cover, a tag screamed its anger at being young, black, male, poor, and unknown in the city. Its arrows, angles, and stabbing lines thrust across the two pages, doubled back on each other and interlocked in a puzzle that disguised the name while blazing a welter of colors that stung the eye. Alex gazed at it, trying to make out the individual letters.

"It's wild-style," he said. "That's for sure."

"Yeah," said Bruno. "But what does it say?"

"Give me a minute." Alex paged through the book, looking for an unfinished sketch where the letters would be easier to read. Paulie could have read it in a flash. He knew all the styles, all the tags. In a way, Alex could almost understand why the ghetto kids did graffiti. It was their way of saying to the monster city, "Hey! Look at me! I'm here! Pay some attention to me!" But why Paulie? Why did he have to do it? Didn't he have a home, a family? Okay, so it wasn't a penthouse on Park Avenue, and maybe things got a little sticky sometimes. But it was home. What had he wanted from life that made him so lost and lonely he had to advertise himself on the subways?

158

Toward the back of the book, Alex opened to a page that made him stop. There it was. DREEMZ. In Paulie's own style, bright and clear, magenta and green with yellow highlights. He'd seen in Paulie's books the way the other graffiti writers signed their tags for their friends. So this kid, whoever he was, knew Paulie. He looked up at Bruno. "This is my brother's tag," he said.

"Yeah," said Bruno. "I recognize it. We've been looking at his books. There's some things in them maybe you can tell us about. But what about this kid? Any luck?"

Alex went back to the front of the book and stared at the chaotic tag. It was so carefully done. It must have taken hours, each letter and its relationship to the others planned and meticulously drawn. But the whole was virtually indecipherable. Alex tried once again to isolate the letters. If he could figure out two or three, he might be able to guess at the whole word. The last one, that could be a C or a G or maybe even an O. It wasn't exactly round, but it was fat and could be either closed or open. Hard to tell with that arrow slashing across it. The two letters before it looked more or less identical, tall and spiky, angling toward the top of the page. Might be a pair of I's. But I's didn't usually go in pairs. Maybe they weren't the same letters. A tag could end in IC as in MAGIC, or IO as in ROLIO. Alex got out a ballpoint pen and wrote down the two possibilities. They didn't look right in his small, neat printing. Although that first letter, come to think of it, could really be an M. Either that or an N and an I close together. Could it be NITRO? He wrote it down and looked at it. Wrong again. The R didn't belong. But the longer he stared at the tag, the more it was beginning to reveal itself.

"What do you think?" Bruno asked. "Make any sense to you?"

"It's beginning to. Just give me a few more minutes."

159

"Take your time," said Bruno. "If the kid dies, I'd like to have some idea where to start looking for his parents."

Alex bent over the book again. Say the tag started with an M, then skip over the next part which was really a mess. Next came the two tall letters. Maybe they were L's. M something LL and maybe an O. MOLLO? MELLO? Holy Christ! MELLO! The kid at the meeting who'd said, "I write Mello," before the deep voice had cut him off. Alex had heard it as "mellow" the way it was spelled, but graffiti writers seldom wrote their tags the way they were spelled. And here it was, right before his eyes. MELLO. Wild-style. MELLO in the hospital at Coney Island with a bullet hole in his chest.

And what the hell could he tell Bruno about it? Nothing. He hadn't even seen the kid, just heard his voice. He glanced at the Polaroids. The face looked so young. Twelve or thirteen. Fourteen at the oldest.

Slowly, Alex printed MELLO on his list of possibilities. "I think that's it," he said. "MELLO. M-E-L-L-O. That's the best I can do with it."

Bruno peered over his shoulder. "More than I can see in that scribble. Well, we'll soon find out."

He started the car and pulled away from the curb. Bruno drove fast but carefully, always in control of the machine. His car was designed for speed, a red Trans Am. Alex thought it was a bit flashy for a man who dressed so conservatively, a man who must have been about his father's age, late forties or so. But he was learning that Frank Bruno was full of contradictions. Tough as a two-dollar steak one minute and almost philosophical the next.

As they swung onto Ocean Parkway, Alex got another surprise. Bruno flipped on a tape deck and soaring violin music filled the car coming from speakers located somewhere in the back.

160

"You like music?" Bruno asked.

"Uh, yeah. But I don't know much about this kind. What is it?"

"Tchaikovsky. My father played the violin, but he didn't know much about this kind either. Guinea weddings and church fairs, everybody wanting to hear "Come Back to Sorrento" so they could cry on each other's shoulders about the old country and feel glad they were here instead of there. If he'd stuck to his fiddle, he'd have lasted longer."

"What happened to him?" Alex asked.

"Maybe I'll tell you about that sometime. Tell me about your mother. What's she like?"

Alex was stumped. How do you tell a police detective who's investigating your brother's murder what your mother is like? "Why do you want to know that?" he asked.

"Just background. That's all. You never know when some stray piece of information might turn out to be useful."

"Well," said Alex, gazing out the window at the apartment buildings that lined the broad straight boulevard all the way through Brooklyn to the ocean, "she's forty-four years old, weighs about a hundred and thirty and thinks that's too much because she's short." Alex paused, at a loss what to say next. There was so much and yet so little that would make any difference one way or the other to the investigation.

"Go on," said Bruno. "Tell me how she feels about you going into the police."

"She doesn't like it much, but she doesn't hassle me about it. She's afraid I'll get shot by some crazy dope addict. I keep telling her that most cops never get anywhere near a shootout. Never even get to use their guns except on the pistol range."

"True enough," said Bruno. "But there are other ways of

getting hurt. Just dealing with slime and sleaze day after day can hurt."

"I guess she'd be happier if I was an accountant, something nice and safe and clean."

"What about your brother? What would she have liked him to be?"

"Oh, an artist. She always wanted him to study art. I think he would have done it, too, sooner or later. He wasn't stupid. He would have figured out that graffiti wasn't enough to last him all his life." Alex sucked in a deep breath and let it out again. "I guess it was, though, huh?"

"That reminds me," said Bruno. "Get my briefcase out of the back seat and open it up."

Alex reached for the black leather bag, a smaller, classier version of his own recruit's satchel, and dragged it over the back of the seat onto his lap.

"Open it up," said Bruno.

Alex hesitated, wondering what kind of trick Bruno had planned for him now.

"Go ahead. Open it. There's nothing personal in it."

Alex opened the briefcase and breathed easier. Nothing in it but three sketchbooks.

"They're your brother's," said Bruno. "Your mother let us have them. We'll get them back to her, but there might be something in them that could help us out. How about you take a look?"

Alex pulled a sketchbook out of the briefcase and opened it on his lap.

"That's the one he had with him in the yard," Bruno remarked.

Alex's fingers faltered slightly as he turned the pages. He almost expected to find traces of blood in the book, but there wasn't any. Nothing but page after page of Paulie's drawings. Pages of DREEMZ and pages of the scenes of destruction that he'd imagined and set down so carefully. Crumbling walls and burning buildings, laughing skulls, prancing skeletons, red-eyed voracious rats, maggots feasting on dead babies. For the first time, Alex wondered if his brother had been a little bit crazy. It wasn't exactly sane to have this kind of stuff eating away at your brain. It was, in fact, kind of spooky, looking at all of these sick drawings of death and realizing that he'd never really known the person who made them. His brother. Was this the way Paulie had seen his own life? A battleground littered with blasted hopes and the rotting corpses of dreams?

He turned a page and came to a piece captioned ADAM AND EVE II. Paulie in a cheerful frame of mind, but still trying to get his message across. He read the bubble-letter words at the top of the drawing. "NO GOD. NO SNAKES. NO NUKES. JUST US. DREEMZ." It was the unfinished piece he'd seen on the train. Paulie's last piece. Alex examined the drawing carefully, looking for some clue as to what had been on his brother's mind the night he'd been killed. But the two figures, ADAM and EVE, told him nothing he didn't already know. Paulie thought the world's troubles could be cured if everybody loved each other. Maybe he was right, but it would never happen. Not in his lifetime or anybody else's. Paulie hadn't lived long enough to find that out.

"This is the piece he was working on when he was killed. He didn't finish it."

"Oh, yeah?" said Bruno. "How do you know?"

"I saw it," said Alex. "On a train. That morning. Before we knew what had happened. I wondered why he hadn't finished it."

"Well, that's interesting," said Bruno. "But it doesn't tell us anything, does it?"

"No," said Alex. "But wait a minute. What if we find

163

that car? Maybe he wrote something on it. It went by too fast for me to see more than a big DREEMZ on one side and this on the other. He hadn't finished the message. But maybe he had time to write down a name or something."

"You think he knew who shot him?"

"I don't know, but isn't it worth trying?"

Bruno reached over and patted his knee. "Yeah, Alex. It is. We'll do it. I like the way you think. You'll make a good cop someday. Now see if there's anything else in those books that'll give us an edge when we talk to this kid."

They were getting near the ocean. Even with the windows closed, Alex could smell the faint briny odor that in summer meant Nathan's hot dogs, rides on the Cyclone, and the beach crammed with bikinis. He pulled out another sketchbook and quickly flipped through the pages, looking for the graffiti tags of other writers who'd signed pages for his brother. JUICE was there, several times, and MELLO once. There were BLITZ and SHAM and D-COY. MISS BEE. HONOR 17. About a dozen more, some of them unreadable. He listed the ones he could read on a blank page, and wondered which of them had been in the room with him the other night. Was Miss Bee the girl who'd met him at the Ninety-sixth Street station and dragged him to the meeting place? Her tag was yellow and black striped, the colors of a honeybee, but crudely drawn. Paulie would have considered her a toy.

And then there was Mello. If the kid in the hospital was Mello, Alex would be in trouble. Not with Bruno, but with the graffiti writers. Mello would certainly recognize him and tell the others, and that would be the end of their trust in him. But there was no way he could get out of it now.

Bruno pulled into the hospital parking lot. "Find anything?" he asked.

"Only this." Alex showed him the list of tags.

164

Bruno merely glanced at the list. "Try to remember them. If he mentions any of them, remember that, too. And any that aren't on that list. We'll have to talk to all of them. We may have to round up all the graffiti writers in the city."

"But there are hundreds," Alex protested. "Maybe even thousands."

"Nobody ever said it was easy. These kids are an endangered species. I don't want any more of them winding up in the morgue."

"You think it's a sniper?" Alex asked. "Somebody picking them off one by one?"

"Could be," said Bruno. "Let's go see what Mello has to say for himself." He got out of the car.

Alex put the sketchbooks back into the briefcase and tossed it into the back seat. As he walked beside Frank Bruno across the parking lot and into the hospital, he briefly yearned for happier days when going to Coney Island meant only a day of fun in the sun and maybe picking up one of those bikinis.

16

Mello's room had a window looking out over the ocean, but he wasn't enjoying the view. He was too busy throwing up into the kidney-shaped steel basin that a nurse held under his chin.

Alex sat on the windowsill and stared out at the heaving dark water, flecked with small whitecaps. In the distance, the skeletal framework of the Cyclone reared against the sky. One summer long ago, he'd taken Paulie for a ride on the giant roller coaster. One ride had turned into ten, and both of them were rubber-legged and laughing hysterically when they finally got off. Although his back was turned to the boy in the high hospital bed, he heard clearly every retch and moan. The boy was miserable and obviously in pain.

Out of the corner of his eye, he saw Bruno standing at the foot of the bed, just waiting.

He heard the nurse murmur, "Okay now, honeyboy. This is water. Just rinse your mouth out, but don't swallow any or you'll be bringing it right back up. In a little while, I'll give you some ice to suck on." She spoke with a faint Jamaican lilt.

The boy made a sound that was somewhere between a sigh and a whimper.

166

"He's all yours," said the nurse. "Call me if you have any trouble with him. He tries to be so very tough. But go easy on him. He's a very sick boy."

"He's not in danger, is he?" asked Bruno.

"No. He'll live. He's too obstreperous not to. But right now he's got a grand pain in the chest and a big headache. Not to mention a stomach that wants to jump through the roof. I pity his poor mother and that other one's mother. If my son ever did that graffiti, I would beat his bottom for him, no matter he is considerably bigger than I am."

Alex turned away from the ocean view to watch the nurse march primly from the room. Small and trim and starched, she made no sound in her crepe-soled white shoes. At the door, she turned and spoke to Mello.

"Behave yourself, young man," she said. "These gentlemen are here to help you. You talk politely to them. None of your poison mouth." Her round dark face managed to look stern despite the soft, wide mouth and gentle eyes that seemed more accustomed to smiling. She closed the door behind her softly.

From the bed came a hoarse croak that suggested she commit obscenities upon herself.

Bruno dragged a chair to the side of the bed. Alex remained perched on the windowsill. Mello lay absolutely still, his head centered on the pillow, his eyes closed.

"You write a mean tag, Mello," said Bruno softly.

The boy didn't move except for a faint fluttering of his eyelids.

"We're not transit cops," said Bruno. "We don't care what you were doing in the yard."

The eyelids flickered again.

Bruno insistently pursued the flickers. "Nobody's safe, Mello, until we catch this guy. Don't you want to help us?"

A pink tongue darted out from between the dry lips and just as quickly disappeared.

"Did you see him, Mello? Can you tell us what he looked like?"

The lips moved, as if the boy were tasting his words before he spoke them. His eyes stayed closed. His voice, when it finally came, was weak and pitiful. "I'm so thirsty, man. Can I have a Dr. Pepper?"

"Not now," said Bruno. "You heard the nurse. We'll send you a case when you're feeling better."

The boy grinned. "Make that a case of Heineken. I get outta here, I'm gonna party." He shifted in the bed, then winced and groaned. "Oh, shit! That hurts. You sure you're not transit?"

"Homicide," said Bruno. "That's what this is about. You were lucky, but your friend Dreemz wasn't. Murder's a lot more serious than defacing public property."

"Maybe I seen something. Maybe not." The voice was a little stronger, not quite so pitiful. "If the transits come and get me, can you call them off?"

Bruno laughed. "Trying to make a deal? How old are you, Mello?"

"Fourteen." The boy stumbled over the word. "I be fourteen next month. I almost didn't make it, huh?" He sounded awed at his brush with death.

"That's right," said Bruno. "But I wouldn't go around bragging about it."

"Too true," said the boy. "That way, somebody get the bright idea to try again."

"Who?" said Bruno. "Who might try again?"

The boy's eyes still remained closed. Alex watched his face closely. The voice was certainly the same as the one he'd heard in the room. There was no doubt about that. But without a chance to look into his eyes, it would be hard to tell if he lied.

The boy tossed his head from side to side on the pillow

168

"I didn't mean nobody special," he moaned. "Whoever it is that's doing it. Some freak. I don't know who. I guess it's time to retire and stop doing that shit. But I don't know what I be doing instead. All my friends . . ." And then he went silent again.

"Your friends?" Bruno prompted.

No answer.

"What's your real name?"

"You gonna call my momma?" came a whisper from the bed.

"She's got to know where you are sooner or later. Don't you want her to come and see you?"

"Yeah. That be real nice. If only she won't cry. I can't stand it when she cries over me. You tell her to bring me some Dr. Pepper, okay?"

"What's her name?" Bruno asked.

"She don't know I write Mello. You gonna tell her that?"

"She'll find out anyway."

"Yeah." The boy sighed and moved one hand to rest tenderly on his chest. "They give me something for the pain, but it don't help much." Tears rolled out from beneath his closed eyelids. "I didn't do nothing to that motherfucker. What'd he have to do this to me for?"

"What if he does it to somebody else?" Bruno asked. "You were lucky. Did you see him?"

"I seen somebody. You gonna call my momma or not? Tell her to bring me some bananas and grapes. They won't give me nothing to eat here. I'm getting hungry. I didn't even get to eat my sandwich last night. You call her. Tell her to don't be mad at me. And don't cry. I'll die if she cries."

"What's her name, Mello?"

Reluctantly, the boy said, "My momma's name is Mrs.

169

Jessie Wheeler." And he gave a phone number which Bruno jotted down in his notebook.

Alex did his best to memorize it. He might need it some time.

"I'll need one more thing, Mello," said Bruno. "What's *your* name?"

"Daniel," the boy whispered. "She calls me Dandy, but don't you tell nobody else that."

Bruno nodded to Alex to stay in the room and hurried out. When he was gone, Alex slid off the windowsill and moved over to the bedside chair.

"Hi, Mello," he said. "Remember me?"

Mello's eyes flew open. "I seen you," he said. "I seen you when you come in. You thought I was too sick to notice. What you doing with that shithead cop?"

"Investigating my brother's murder. Did you think they'd leave me out of it? He dragged me along because my brother's tag was in your book. He thought I might have seen you with him."

"Blitz ain't gonna like it. He ain't gonna like nothing about this whole thing."

"Blitz is the boss, huh?"

Mello groaned. "Don't tell him I said that, huh? He'll whip my ass good. He's a fucking maniac when he gets mad. No telling what he'll do when he finds out I got shot."

"Maybe he'll be ready to talk to Bruno."

"No way! Is that his name, the dude who's calling my momma?"

"Frank Bruno. He's a homicide detective. You're lucky his partner isn't here today. He hates graffiti writers."

"How do I know this one doesn't? He talks real nice, but I don't trust no kind of cops. Especially the ones that talk real nice. They all a bunch of motherfuckers."

170

"Daniel, you've got no choice," said Alex. "Bruno isn't going to give up. I've seen enough of him to know that. And don't let him fool you. He's being nice to you because right now, you're a victim. He's being nice to my family because of Paulie. But he's determined to get what he wants. And he wants to get this killer. So you might as well tell him what you know or you'll never see the end of him. The guy sticks like Crazy Glue. He was waiting for me when I got up this morning. I don't think he even sleeps."

Mello stared at the ceiling. "I want my momma," he said. Tears brimmed up in his eyes and rolled into his ears. He wiped them away with the edge of his sheet. "Fuck! I never thought anything like this would happen. Even when it happened to Dreemz, I never thought it would happen to me. I'm scared, Alex. I'm real scared. They weren't just talking about guns the other night. Some of them already have guns. Blitz, he's got a gun. What if it's one of them? They're supposed to be my friends, but how do I know?"

"That's what you have to tell Bruno. Or do you want me to tell him?"

"No! I mean, don't you tell him none of this. I'll think about it. Can I have some water, please?"

Alex poured water from a plastic pitcher into a paper cup. "The nurse said you shouldn't drink anything yet."

"She wants me to die of thirst. I'd rather die from throwing up. But I'll spit it out. I promise."

While Alex helped the boy rinse his mouth and held the basin for him to spit into, the door opened and Bruno returned.

"Your mother's on her way," he said. "Do I need to tell you she was up all night waiting for you to get home?"

"She got nothing else to do," said Mello. "Did you tell her not to cry all over me when she gets here?"

Bruno stood over the bed and glared down at the cring-

171

ing boy. "If you're such a badass, suppose we stop all this tap dancing and play a little hardball. Did you see anybody in the yard last night?"

"Yeah. I saw somebody."

"Who was it?"

"How should I know? He didn't introduce hisself."

"What did he look like?"

"Big, man. He was a fucking giant."

Bruno motioned to Alex. "Stand over there, near the window." Then he turned back to Mello. "How big? Was he that big?"

"Bigger. He had a coat on."

"Alex. Put your coat on."

Alex put on his down jacket and zipped it up, wondering if Bruno was up to another one of his tricks, trying to get Mello to say that he was the man he'd seen in the yard.

"Bigger than that even. I couldn't see him too good. It was dark. He was about as big as you. Maybe it was you."

"Sure." Bruno's fierce smile flashed across his face. "I spend all my free time prowling subway yards. Listen, twerp. If I shot at you, you wouldn't be lying here in this nice hospital bed, and your mother would be more than just worried about you. Now, get serious. Did you see his face? Could you tell if he was black or white?"

"Too dark."

"Where was he?"

"Oh, shit. You want to know how it was? I wasn't gonna go out last night at all. But then I got a call from . . . never mind who from . . . said, 'Meet me in the Coney Island yard, I got a chill new piece I want to get up and you gotta help me.' I said, 'Man, it's cold outside.' And he said, 'Never too cold.' So I said okay. So I went. So I'm there in the yard, minding my own business, waiting for the dude with the piece to show up. I found just the right car for us

172

to work on, all clean, not a mark on it, and I'm sitting down right next to it and I'm getting ready to eat my sandwich. Then I hear this noise, like maybe it's a guard coming around, so I stand up and look around, and way down the line I see this monster thing walking toward me on top of the cars. Well, I know what happened to Dreemz and I think, 'Uh-oh. Time to get lost.' So I start walking backwards 'cause I don't want to turn my back on that thing coming at me. And I'm going as quiet as I can. I want to get to the end of the cars and then run like hell. But he sees me and I see him seeing me. And I swear his eyes was shining red like cigarettes in the dark at the movies. The next thing I know there's a big blam! and I get knocked on my ass and there's blood all over the front of me. I didn't feel a thing except like it knocked the wind out of me. I didn't pass out or nothing. But I couldn't get right up. So then I hear him running tromp, tromp, tromp on top of the cars. And then he's gone. And that's about when it started in hurting, so I came on over here."

"Did your friend ever show up?" Bruno asked.

"He's not my friend. He's just some guy I know."

"What's his name?"

"You guys got a real thing about knowing everybody's name."

"Why did he call you?"

"I told you. To help him get his piece up."

"Yeah. But why you? It sounds to me like a set-up. Get you out there alone and blow you away."

Mello glanced at Alex. Alex turned away and looked out the window. Mello said, "Nah. Juice wouldn't do a thing like that."

Alex whirled around and stared at Mello. Mello shrugged.

Bruno said, "Isn't that one of the names on your list, Alex?"

"It's one of the tags in my brother's book. I don't know who it is, though."

Mello smiled and closed his eyes.

"Who's Juice?" Bruno demanded. He shook Mello until his head bounced on the pillow. "What's his name? Where does he live?"

The boy let out a howl. "Help!" he shouted. "He's beating up on me! Nurse! *Owwww*! It hurts!" His finger stabbed at the call buzzer lying on his pillow.

The door flew open, and the little Jamaican nurse marched in.

"Get him outta here!" Mello yelled. "Police brutality! He punched me in the chest. I think it's bleeding. Oh, God, it hurts. Call the doctor. I'm dying. I want my momma." Mello tossed and writhed on the bed until the coverlet slipped off and his thin brown legs were exposed beneath the short white hospital gown.

The nurse strode up to the bed and stood, arms folded across her chest, watching Mello. His eyes were closed again, and he was breathing hard, but he sported a triumphant smirk.

The nurse waited, scowling. Mello opened his eyes a slit, saw the expression on her face, and smiled ingratiatingly. "I got to pee," he whispered.

"That should be your only problem, honeyboy," she snapped.

She whipped open the bedside cabinet and held a steel urinal for him while he managed to produce a meager trickle. Then she covered him up again and straightened his pillow. "Anything else?" she asked.

He shook his head. "Only get these cops outta here and don't let them come back. They been getting me nervous."

"You deserve to be nervous. I don't know why they bother with a silly little boy like you anyway."

"Don't be mean, sister," Mello pleaded. "You want me to get better, don't you?"

"I am not your sister. So mind your manners with me."

"Well, fuck off then. My momma's coming. She'll make some noise around here if I tell her I been mistreated."

"Tell away," said the nurse. "I have been dealing with mommas like yours for too long to be intimidated. You don't know what mistreated is, honeyboy, but if you don't start behaving properly you are very likely to find out." She turned to Bruno. "Are you finished with this naughty infant?"

Bruno nodded. "For now. We may have to come back. I'll be checking in to see how he's getting along. I'd like to talk with you privately. Alex, you wait here."

Mello waved an upraised middle finger behind their backs as they left. Then he motioned to Alex to come and sit on the bed.

"Sit down, bro. Sit down." He moved his legs to make room.

Alex perched on the bed and waited to find out what the boy was up to next. If Juice had really made a date to meet him in the yard, there were questions he should be asking. Was that why Bruno had left him there alone with Mello, to try to find out the things that Mello wouldn't tell him? It would be nice to know how far he should go on his own.

Mello tugged at his arm. Alex leaned closer to hear the boy's conspiratorial whisper.

"I won't tell Blitz you showed up here with that cop if you don't tell him I let on that Juice was supposed to be with me last night."

"Okay," said Alex.

"And don't you go telling Juice neither."

"I won't. But did he really ask you to meet him or were you just bullshitting?"

Mello nodded seriously, his brown eyes wide and guileless. Alex wanted to believe him, but if what he said were true, it meant that Juice could have had something to do with Paulie's death. Blitz, too, if he was the leader, the dude with the deep voice who'd shut Mello up. Could they have tried to silence Mello for good because they couldn't trust him to keep his mouth shut? But what about the other writers who'd been shot at? It didn't make sense for them to be shooting at each other like that. Or was it all a show, put on for his benefit, to get him on their side and through him distract the police into looking for a sniper that didn't exist?

"Is Blitz a big guy?" Alex asked.

"Oh, yeah. Bigger than you. Bigger than him." He jerked his head toward the door. "But don't you go getting any ideas about Blitz. He wouldn't off any of us. He tries to protect us, man."

"And you're sure the guy in the yard was big? After all, you were on the ground and he was on top of the car. He could have looked bigger than he was from where you were standing."

Mello thought about that for a moment and nodded. "Yeah, could be," he agreed, "but he was still humongous. He was like something out of a horror movie."

"So that lets Juice out. Juice isn't much bigger than you are."

"Hey! Juice is my friend. He asked me to be his writing partner now that Dreemz is gone. That's why I went last night. Nobody ever asked me to be partners with him before."

"But he didn't show up last night."

"I live closer to the yard than he does."

"He told me he was real tight with my brother. Did they ever have any fights?"

176

"I wouldn't know about that."

"You mean you know, but you're not saying?"

"Don't ask me that. I told you everything I know about last night. I ain't telling you any more. You getting worse than that other guy. Besides, I don't feel so good."

Alex stood up. "Can I get you anything?"

Mello shook his head weakly. "Just go away and leave me alone. Ask that nurse to come here. Tell her please. Tell her I promise to be nice. I don't want to die."

"You won't die, Mello. Like she said, you're too obstreperous."

177

17

Alex asked Frank Bruno to drop him off at his own apartment. He hadn't been there for a couple of days, and he needed to be alone to think about the things that Mello had told him and everything else that was buzzing around in his head. When they left the hospital, Bruno had quizzed him about the time he'd spent alone with Mello, but Alex had denied learning anything more except that the kid felt threatened and was afraid the sniper would try to get him again.

"That's only natural under the circumstances," Bruno had said. "He won't be feeling safe for a long, long time. I've already ordered a police guard for him."

"Do you believe the sniper would actually come into the hospital?" Alex asked.

"No. But I want to know who visits Dandy-boy Mello, and I don't want him checking himself out unofficially. That kid knows something he's not telling. It could have nothing to do with the investigation. It's probably just some low-level shenanigans that would get him and his pals into family court, but whatever it is, I want to know about it. That's all police work is, Alex. Knowing everything there is to know and putting it together in a way that makes sense and gives you an edge on the opposition."

The opposition. Alex felt lousy about keeping things from Bruno. The guy was coming on like his "rabbi," confiding in him, teaching him, and letting him in on a little piece of the action. He wondered what had made him change his mind about that. Of course, it could be that this was Bruno's way of keeping tabs on him. Alex couldn't forget what Bruno had suggested about brothers killing brothers. Bruno probably hadn't forgotten it either. But there was a big difference in his attitude now. Alex couldn't quite put his finger on it. It was almost as if Bruno had taken on some kind of unofficial responsibility for him. Alex was uncomfortable with the burden that involved, even as he welcomed the opportunity to watch a real pro at work.

When Bruno dropped him off outside his building, he'd said, "See you around, son. Call me if you get any inspirations, no matter how off-the-wall they might seem."

Alex had promised to do just that, but it was a relief to get away from the man, to get away from everybody, and just hang loose in his own place until he could figure out what to do next.

His midget-sized refrigerator was practically empty, and he was starving. He found a package of frozen minestrone in the ice-cube compartment and put on a pot of water to boil. One of these days he'd really learn how to cook instead of living off deli food or heating up frozen things that never were enough to satisfy his monster appetite. There was a half-empty box of saltines in the cupboard and a jar of peanut butter. Some lunch.

While he was waiting for the soup in its plastic pouch to heat in the boiling water, the phone rang. He leaped for it, answering it on the first ring. It could be Juice, who by now, would have heard about Mello, maybe even talked to him.

But the voice that came over the phone was hoarse and nasal, hardly recognizable.

"Richie, is that you?" Alex asked. "You sound terrible."

"Yeah, it's me. I feel terrible. What's new with you?"

"Oh, God, Richie! I hardly know where to start. I haven't seen you since, when? Thursday morning."

"Yeah, well, that's why I'm calling. I been trying to get you since yesterday. I just want to tell you I'm real sorry about your brother. Is there anything I can do?"

"I don't think so. But thanks. How're you doing? What did the doctor say?"

"Strep throat. He gave me twenty-eight different kinds of medicine and told me to stay in bed. None of it's doing any good and some of it's giving me the trots. And I'm going stir-crazy from staying home. It's the pits. But here I am moaning about myself, and you've got big trouble. I heard another graffiti writer got shot last night, some kid out in Brooklyn."

"Yeah," said Alex. "He's in the hospital. I went out to see him with one of the detectives that's handling the case."

"Holy shit!" said Maldonado. "You mean they're letting you work on it? I thought that was against the rules."

"It is. And I'm not really working on it. This kid knew my brother and they thought maybe I could identify him if he conked out or refused to give his name. I never saw him before in my life."

"Sounds to me like some citizen's gone crazy and thinks he can wipe out graffiti by shooting some of the kids who do it. They should round up all the writers and warn them to stay out of the yards. I could probably help them do that. I know a lot of them. I know the yards like the back of my hand. I used to do that shit myself."

"You?"

"Don't sound so surprised. Every young stud in the

180

Bronx does graffiti one time or another. And not just the Bronx. All over. They even come in from Staten Island and New Jersey to do it. I did it more than most. I used to write ROBOT, and I almost got to be 'King of the Woodlawn Express' just because I got my tag up so much. But I wasn't any good at it. There were some real artists around in those days, and I was no artist. So I gave it up. But old ROBOT had some fame. Maybe some of the kids remember me. They'd listen to another writer, even a retired one, before they'd listen to a cop."

"You really want to help, Richie?"

"Bet your ass. Ain't we buddies? Besides, I don't think it's right these kids should get shot for doing graffiti. How else can they get a little adventure in their grungy lives? They can't go surfing or even get out of the city to see what the rest of world looks like, except on TV. I'd like to get my hands on the animal who's doing it."

"You and me both, Richie." Alex was tempted to tell Maldonado everything that had happened in the last two days. But he knew his friend wouldn't be content to stay home and nurse his sore throat if he thought there was something happening. "That kid in the hospital. He writes MELLO. You know him?"

"Nah. The TV said he was only fourteen. He wouldn't have been around when I was active."

"What about a guy who writes BLITZ?"

"Oh, him. Yeah. I know him. I thought he'd be retired by now. He's around twenty-three, twenty-four. Old, like us. Big guy. Black. Lives over on the west side, or he did when I knew him. Why?"

"Oh, just asking."

"Hey, Alex. This is Richie you're talking to, not some goofball tourist. What's going down?"

"Nothing, Richie. Honest. It's just that Blitz's tag

181

showed up in one of my brother's piecing books, and this Detective Bruno's been asking me about all of Paulie's friends. That's all."

"You'd tell me if it was something else?"

"I'd tell you."

"I wish I could believe you. Because if you're thinking about getting mixed up with Blitz, I gotta tell you that's a wrong-o thing to do. The guy's scary. Loco in the coco. He used to walk around like a one-man arsenal. Anybody disagreed with him, he'd pull out a gun or a knife and no more disagreement. Protection, he said. For himself and his friends. So everybody wanted to be his friend. He used to take a machete into the yards with him. Said it was for the dogs. If one of them attacked him, he said he'd cut its head right off. But there was only ever one yard with dogs, out in Corona, and I don't think he ever went out there. But how do I know? I been out of it too long."

"How long since you've seen him?" Alex asked.

"Oh, it's gotta be three years, maybe four."

"Could it be someone else is using his tag?"

"Could be, but when they do that, they usually put a number after it. Like BLITZ 2. A sign of respect. But I really don't think anybody'd use his tag. They'd be too scared."

"I can't see my brother hanging out with somebody that crazy. Paulie was into things like peace and everybody loving everybody else. My mother used to call him the last of the hippies."

"Yeah, well, maybe old Blitz has changed. But just in case he didn't, you better warn that detective what to expect if he goes making house calls."

"Do you remember where on the West Side he lived?"

"Way up, off of Broadway someplace. I can't remember the street."

"Thanks, Richie. I gotta go now."

"Hey, wait a minute. Something tells me you been jerking me around. You think Blitz killed your brother? You think you're gonna go after him by yourself? You're the crazy one."

"Richie, shut up."

"Don't do it, Alex. Tell the detective what you think. Let him handle it. That's his job."

"Richie, calm down. I'm not going to do anything stupid. I'm just trying to find out as much as I can. That's what police work is all about." Alex grimaced as he realized he was echoing what Bruno had told him.

"Oh, shit! Why don't I believe you?" Maldonado's voice was a plaintive moan.

"Because you're too suspicious. Isn't it time for your medicine?"

"It's always time for my medicine. If I find out you went off on your own and didn't take me with you, I swear to God, old buddy, I'll break your kneecaps. You hear me?"

"Goodbye, Richie."

Alex hung up in the midst of another burst of moans and protests. So Blitz was a big, tough hulk who carried a machete into the yards. And guns. Paulie'd been found on the track, so everybody assumed he'd been run over by a train. But suppose he'd had some kind of argument with this Blitz? He'd have been no match for a guy like that. Alex assumed that the autopsy would have shown whether or not a machete or some other kind of weapon had been used, but he hadn't thought to ask Bruno about that. He hadn't known what to ask, for Christ's sake! But Bruno knew, and hadn't told him. Which just went to prove that Bruno was right when he'd said that the more you knew, the better you were able to deal with the opposition. Well, now he knew something, and the next time he was anywhere near Blitz he'd keep that knowledge well in mind.

He went back to the stove and found that the water had boiled away and the plastic soup package was stuck to the side of the pot. He stuck a knife into the package, and the hot soup spurted out in a geyser that splattered his hand and spewed all over the top of the stove. At that moment, the doorbell rang.

"Damn!" he muttered, wrapping his hand in the damp dishcloth. He raced across the room to the intercom and barked into it, "Who is it?"

Edie's voice came through, faint and tinny. "It's me. Can I come up?"

He pressed the buzzer that unlocked the downstairs door, and then raced back to the stove where he made furious swipes at cleaning up the mess. When Edie knocked at the apartment door, he'd succeeded only in smearing the soup all over everything he touched.

He opened the door, and there she was, smiling at him uncertainly over two huge grocery sacks. "I was just passing by," she said.

"Come on in."

"I really was just passing by. Is something burning?"

"Just my lunch."

She walked past him and looked around for a place to park the bags.

"Put them on the bed," Alex told her. "I guess things are a bit messy. I just got home a little while ago."

"Your mother said you went off with some detective." Edie put the bags on the unmade bed and turned to look at him. Her questions remained unspoken, but they were there in her eyes.

"You called my mother?" he asked.

"I was trying to call you. She answered the phone."

"What else did she tell you?"

"Nothing else. She asked me if I thought you were okay."

"What did you say?"

"What do you think I said? I told her as far as I knew you were doing fine. What's wrong, Alex? Why the interrogation?"

Alex shrugged, trying not to feel that Edie'd gone behind his back to try to find out what he was doing. "I guess I just don't like you talking to my mother like that."

"What was I supposed to do? Hang up on her? Look, we talked for maybe five minutes. Most of it wasn't even about you. She told me how she always hoped your brother would go to art school. Is that so terrible? Alex, I think she needs somebody to talk to. She sounds so lonely."

"Well, I don't want you electing yourself." Alex knew she was staring at him, but he avoided meeting her gaze. He was doing this all wrong, but he couldn't seem to stop the words from coming out of his mouth.

"Are we having some kind of fight, Alex?" she asked. "Because if we are, I don't know what it's about. Would you mind telling me?" She walked hesitantly toward him and reached out to touch his hand.

He pulled away from her and threw himself into the single armchair, a derelict piece of furniture retrieved from the attic at home. "Edie, I think you'd better leave before I say something I don't want to say."

"No," she said. "I want to know what's going on with you." She perched on the arm of the chair and laid one arm across its back, careful not to touch him. "I've never seen you like this."

Alex exploded. "Christ, Edie! I've never *been* like this. How do you think it feels to have your brother dead and your mother trying to commit suicide?"

"What!" Edie took his face in her hands and forced him to look at her. "But I talked to her only this morning. Like I said, she sounded lonely, but that's all. Spill it, pardner. Is that what's eating at you, or is it something else?"

Alex gripped her hands and pulled them away from his face. Until this whole thing was over, there'd be no room for Edie. No easy comforts. He'd have to reach into himself and find the strength and the hardness to see it through. Alone. If he let himself wallow in her sympathy, he'd be weakened and distracted from the job he had to do. No way he could explain that to her.

"Isn't that enough?" he said. "I'm sorry, Edie. I shouldn't have laid that on you. It's not your problem."

"It is if I want it to be," she retorted. "You're my main problem, and if something's bothering you, it bothers me, too."

He shook his head wearily. "Go home, Edie. I don't want to talk about this anymore."

"Okay," she said. "We won't talk about it. Don't you want to know what I have in the bags?" She got up and went over to the bed where she started pulling packages out of the grocery bags. "Look, Alex. Here's a steak and some of that garlic bread you like. Want me to make some lunch?"

"I'm not hungry."

"That'll be the day. There's salad and chocolate cake and I even got some vino to go with it." She went to the tiny kitchen area and viewed the mess on the stove. "It sure beats scorched soup and peanut butter. I was going to invite you over for dinner, but we might as well have it now. Nothing like a good meal to chase the blues away. You know what I think, Alex? I think I'm going to have to teach you how to cook. Every cop should know how to cook. You never know when it'll come in handy. Firemen learn how to cook. I was talking to this guy once, a fireman, and he said the meals in the firehouse were better than anything he ever ate in a restaurant."

"Edie, you're babbling. Cut it out."

She whirled on him. "Okay, Mr. Macho Big-Shot! You don't have to listen to me. Who am I? Just some girl you like to sleep with and have around for fun. But when something important happens, it's, 'Edie, go home,' and 'I don't want to talk about it.' I feel sorry for you, Alex, and not because of your brother. I feel sorry because you haven't got the faintest idea how to be a human being." She stalked across the room and snatched up her coat and shoulder bag. "You can keep the groceries," she snarled at him, brushing the tears away from her face. "I hope you choke on them."

"Edie, Edie." Alex moved swiftly to get between her and the door. "I'm sorry if I hurt your feelings. I don't want you to go away angry."

"Hah! Don't go away mad, just go away. Is that it? Well, I'm going, no fear. Get out of my way." She tried to push past him, but he caught her and held her.

"When it's all over, Edie, we'll work it out. I promise."

"When what's all over? Do you think you can shut me out and expect me to be waiting patiently on the sidelines of whatever it is you're up to? Not this lady. Either you tell me what's going on or don't bother to tell me anything ever again."

Alex stared mutely into her angry face. There was so damned much going on, he didn't even know how to explain it to himself, let alone to her. He hadn't meant to blurt out the news about his mother's suicide attempt. It must have shaken him up more than he realized. When the phone rang, he let go of Edie and dashed for it. But before he answered it, he said, "Please go now, Edie. And try to understand."

Edie stood by the door with her arms folded across her chest and an immovable expression on her face. "Answer it, Alex," she said.

The phone rang twice, three times.

Edie said, "It must be important, or you wouldn't want me to leave."

Alex picked up the receiver and said, "Hello."

He recognized the voice at once, deep and slow and menacing. It said, "Hello there, brother of Dreemz. How do you like the latest news bulletin?"

"If you mean Mello, I don't like it."

"I hear you been out to see him. You and some detective."

"That's right. And I hear you go by the name of Blitz." Alex glanced at Edie, who was still standing by the door, listening intently.

"Who told you that? My little homeboy been telling tales again?"

"He's scared, Blitz. And he's been hurt pretty bad. But he's still alive and I want to see him stay that way. Him and all the others."

"Me, too, man. This development has us all in an uproar. We got to have another meeting. You up for that?"

"When?"

"Tomorrow morning. Eight o'clock. The bandshell in Central Park. You know the place?"

"I know it."

"You better be alone. No detectives."

"Right."

"And nobody else. Just you. Then we'll decide."

"Decide what?"

"What we gonna do. You and me, and all the rest. Stay cool, man." The phone went dead.

Alex hung up and said to Edie, "You might as well take your coat off and stay a while."

188

"Who's Blitz?" Edie asked. "One of the graffiti writers?"

"You got it. Do you think you could possibly just let it go at that?"

Edie sighed. "I'll try. But it won't be easy. When are you meeting him? Just tell me that and I won't bug you about it anymore."

"I think I could eat that steak now."

"Are you asking me to cook it?"

"I think so. Unless you want me to."

"Tell you what." Edie took her coat off and tossed it on the bed. "I'll do the steak and you do the salad. Where are you meeting him?"

"Uh-uh. No more questions. Let's get to work, woman. I'm starving." Alex began washing the salad greens the way he'd seen his mother do.

"Well, maybe I've got some news for you," said Edie, as she lit the broiler and unwrapped the steak. "Richie's wife's had an abortion. She sure didn't waste any time."

"How do you know?"

"Talked to him this morning. He's pretty sick, with his throat and now this."

"Well, I talked to him just a little while ago and he didn't say a word about it."

"That's Richie. You're only macho once in a while, but with Richie it's a full-time occupation. It's okay for him to tell me. I'm just a girl. But he'd never tell another guy he'd flunked out in the wife and baby department."

"It's just as well," said Alex. "She's been nothing but trouble for him."

"Shows how much you know. Richie really wanted that baby. Now, he's talking about dropping out so Idalinda'll come back and they can try again."

"What a mess," said Alex. "Richie won't do it, will he?"

"I don't know," said Edie. "I think I'll go up and see him

tomorrow. Give him a little moral support. Want to come along?"

Alex hesitated. He owed it to Richie to try to help him out, but he had things to do tomorrow and no idea what the morning would lead to. "I'll call you tomorrow, okay?"

Edie gave him a searching look, then dropped the steak onto the hot broiler rack. "This'll only take a few minutes. How about opening the wine? Sure, Alex. Call me tomorrow. I'll probably go in the afternoon."

Alex poured the wine and handed her a glass. She took it and raised it to his. "Good hunting," she said. "And now I promise to stop bugging you. Just don't make me sorry I ever met you."

18

After Edie left, Alex made a slapdash effort at cleaning up his apartment. But his mind wasn't on scrubbing the john or capturing the dust mice piled up under the bed. If his mother saw the way he lived, she'd have a fit. At least normally she'd have a fit, but nothing was normal now. After twenty minutes of trying to organize the place into some appearance of order, he put on his jacket and headed for the subway.

He needed action, and if there was nothing else he could do this afternoon, he could at least get rid of the rifle hidden in the garage. Maybe he wouldn't actually get rid of it. If he could think of some way of getting it over to his own place, it might come in handy pretty soon. He couldn't shake the mental image of Blitz as Richie Maldonado described him, big and mean and bristling with guns.

When he got to the house, he found his mother up in Paulie's room. A new windowpane had been installed, and she was in the midst of sorting through Paulie's belongings.

"I don't know what to do with all this," she said, indicating several cartons full of spray paint cans and marking pens. "The clothes I can give to the Salvation Army, but I don't think they'd want that stuff."

"Do you have to do that right now?" Alex asked. "Can't it wait a while?"

"What for?" she asked. "To remind me that Paulie's not coming back? Anyway, I want to use the room." She began taking clothes off the hangers in the closet. "I'll never understand why he wouldn't wear nice clothes. Look at this jacket. Brand new. I gave it to him for his birthday. He never put it on once. Do you think it'd fit you, Alex?"

Alex shook his head. "Too small," he said. It was a good jacket and it probably would have fit, but it would have been too hard for him to wear it, always remembering that it had once been Paulie's. "What are you going to do with the room?"

"Oh, I don't know. I've never had a room that was all my own. I could put my sewing machine in here. Maybe I'll sleep in here sometimes. I've been thinking that this place is going to be too big for just Theo and me. Where did you and that detective go this morning?"

"Just for a ride." Alex wandered around the room, looking at his brother's treasures, collected over his short lifetime. Graffiti drawings and rock star posters covered the walls. The bookshelves were full of books on yoga and macrobiotic food alongside Paulie's earlier enthusiasms: science fiction; Dungeons and Dragons; chess; poetry; R. Crumb comics. On top of the bookcase, an ancient battered teddy bear sat next to a blue glass bong. Alex wondered if his mother realized the bong was pot-smoking paraphernalia and not just a pretty glass object.

"Is that all?" she asked. "I thought he was going to take you to see that boy who got shot last night."

"He told you that?"

She smiled. "We had a nice long talk before you came down. He seems pretty decent for a detective."

"He's okay. Why did Pop tell him about that old rifle?"

192

"What difference does it make? You got rid of it, didn't you? I'd forgotten all about it until Mr. Bruno started asking about guns. And then Theo told him before I could think of anything else to say. I couldn't very well tell him the truth in front of Theo, could I?"

"Why does he always have to be protected from the truth? Wouldn't it be better to be honest with him?" Alex realized he sounded like a sanctimonious prig, especially after the way he'd refused to tell Edie the whole truth about his own activities, but he'd begun to feel that his entire life was built on one big lie with a lot of little ones piled on top of that.

His mother sighed. "Someday, Alex, you'll understand that the truth hurts. And when Theo hurts, he gets mad. Then you and I and . . . everybody get hurt. So it's not worth it."

"But isn't it better to take the hurt and get over it?" he persisted. "These lies just hang around for years, poisoning everything."

"Do you feel poisoned?" she asked.

"Yeah. I do. I feel like I've swallowed something that I can't digest and it's eating away at me. I don't know how to act around him anymore, how to talk to him. I don't even know what to call him. I keep on calling him Pop, but every time I say it, it's like another dose of poison in my gut. I'm glad you told me, but it'll be a long time before I feel right about it. Maybe never, unless we get it out in the open so he knows I know and we can both be natural about it."

"I wouldn't do that just yet," said Dorothy. "He's having a pretty rough time of it right now. Has it occurred to you that Paulie was his only son? Sure, he'll go on treating you as his son, but Paulie was the only child of his own flesh. I'm worried about him. I don't know what he's thinking

193

and I don't know where he goes. He just gets in the car and drives off. Comes back hours later. For all I know, he's just driving around out there right now, trying to get rid of his grief."

Alex picked up one of Paulie's books. He'd never been much of a reader, but this one, *A Clockwork Orange,* had been made into a movie, a pretty strange movie. If he read it, he might get a better idea of what had gone on in Paulie's mind. "Mind if I borrow this?" he said.

"Keep it. Keep anything of his you like. You should have something to remember him by."

"Christ, Ma! Do you think I could ever forget?"

She looked so stricken, he dropped the book and went and put his arms around her. "I'm sorry, Ma. I didn't mean it the way it sounded. I guess we're all edgy. Especially with that lunatic out prowling the yards, looking for more kids to murder."

"What was he like?" she asked. "The one in the hospital? Is he like Paulie?"

"No. Not a bit. I don't think there's another one on the face of the earth quite like Paulie. Have you told Pop about last night?"

She looked up at him, her eyes warning him not to go too far. "What about last night?"

"Aren't you going to tell him?"

"There's nothing to tell." She went back to the closet and hauled out another armload of clothes.

"Well, what did you tell him about the window?"

"He didn't ask. The window man came, did his work, and left."

"It's not like him. He always has something to say."

"I know," said Dorothy. "That's why I'm worried. He's being too quiet."

"I'd feel a lot better if *he* did a little worrying once in a

194

while. About you. Doesn't it bother you that he doesn't give a shit how you feel?"

"I can take care of myself."

"Sure you can. Like last night."

"That was a mistake. It's over. It'll never happen again. I'm going to forget it ever happened, and so are you. I never want to hear about it again." Her face had gone closed and stern.

Alex knew the conversation, such as it was, was over. If Theo was out driving around, this would be a good time to go out to the garage to retrieve the rifle. All he needed was a few minutes alone out there. But he'd need something to carry it in. A duffel bag would do nicely, and he could fill it up with other things to disguise the shape.

"Maybe I will take that jacket after all," he said. "After all, Paulie never wore it. Is there anything else of his that I could wear?"

"Take your pick," his mother said, piling another armload of clothes on the bed. "They're all practically brand-new. I'd rather see you wear them than some stranger."

Alex put together a heap of Paulie's clothes. It didn't matter what he took; he'd never wear them. "Is there a suitcase around, or a duffel bag? I'll need something to carry these in."

"Take a look in the attic. There ought to be something up there. While you're at it, take those boxes up. I ought to throw them away, but if I put them out on the street, I just know some kids'll pick them up and we'll have spray paint all over the neighborhood."

Alex picked up one of the boxes and headed for the attic stairs. It had been years since he'd been up there. The last time was when he'd moved into his apartment and raided the attic for odds and ends to furnish it. The attic was his mother's dumping ground for things she couldn't bear to throw away, which was almost everything that had out-worn its usefulness or served as a remembrance of past events. It was a warren of small, low-ceilinged rooms, some with oddly shaped closets that had been fitted in under the eaves of the sloping roof. There was even a small, old-fashioned bathroom up there which no one ever used. Alex supposed that when the house was built, eighty or ninety years ago, there were servants or poor relations who lived in those tiny rooms. When he was very young, he'd imag-ined that the attic was haunted. He would lie in his bed at night and listen for ghostly footsteps or the creak of a door above his head. But all he ever really heard was the occa-sional scampering of mice.

He opened the door of one of the tiny rooms and went in. There, in the corner, was the closet where the rifle had been stored before he'd hidden it in the garage. He put the box of spray paint down on the floor and opened the closet door. Of course, the gun wasn't there. But he remembered ex-actly where it had been, propped up at the back of the closet, its long barrel pointed toward the overhead shelf. And his father had brought Frank Bruno up here and shown him the room and the closet and the empty space where the rifle had been. Was there no part of their life that wouldn't come under Bruno's implacable scrutiny? Did he have to see this pitiful collection of junk, his mother's hoardings?

Alex slammed the closet door and prowled the room, and the other tiny rooms, until he found what he was looking for. An old canvas bag that was long enough to hold the rifle and wide enough for him to stuff it with all those clothes of Paulie's. With the bag under his arm, he ran down the stairs all the way to the first floor and out the back door.

The garage was empty, and its door was open. He rolled

it down and switched on the interior light. The ladder was in its usual place, leaning against the back wall. He opened it up and placed it under the panel he'd moved once before. He climbed the ladder and paused at the top, listening for the sound of a car in the driveway. If Theo should come home and find him with the rifle in his hands, there'd be explanations and probably another argument. But he'd have to take that risk. He shoved the panel aside and groped in the dark space above the ceiling.

His fingertips touched the gritty top surface of the panel and brushed against things that might have been dried leaves or dead bugs. He groped further, squinting into the darkness. Where was it? He could have sworn he hadn't shoved it any further back than his arm could reach. He shoved the panel further aside and leaned into the opening. His fingers touched the wall but nothing else. A sprinkling of gritty dust fell on his neck.

As he replaced the panel, he thought he might have been mistaken about which side of the garage he'd used to hide the rifle. It was a while ago, and he'd never had any reason to see if it was still there. He climbed down the ladder, moved it to the opposite side, and repeated his gropings in the dark, dusty overhead space—with precisely the same result. The rifle was gone.

He'd told Bruno it might have been stolen, that Paulie might have taken it and sold it for money to buy pot. Could he have been right without knowing it? But how would Paulie have found it? Might as well ask how Columbus found America. He just kept on going, and Paulie could have just kept on poking around the place looking for something he could trade for grass. It was gone, though, and that was the important thing. He wouldn't have to worry anymore about Bruno finding it.

He put the ladder away and rolled up the garage door,

just in time to see Theo's old green Pontiac roll into the driveway. The car stopped just short of the garage, and Theo got out.

Alex was shocked at his appearance. In daylight, he seemed to have aged ten years or more. His shoulders sagged, and the lines in his face drooped into mournful shadows.

He said, "Ah, Alex," and then seemed to forget what he intended to say.

Alex said, "Yeah, Pop."

"Oh, nothing. Nice day, isn't it?"

"Not bad. Where've you been?"

"What? Oh, I went to get some . . .". But he couldn't seem to remember what he'd gone to get or if he'd gotten it. "Never mind."

Alex urgently wanted to put his arm around the old man and tell him it didn't matter. He wanted to say, "You're the only father I've ever known, and that's good enough for me." But he didn't, and the moment passed.

Theo was staring past him into the garage. "What were you doing in there?" he asked diffidently, almost as if he didn't expect an answer.

Alex said the first thing that came into his head. "I was looking at Paulie's bicycle. It's a good bike. I could use it." Another lie, he thought. One lie breeds another and another until you can't tell the truth from the lies.

Theo's head began nodding as if it would never stop. "Take it," he said. "Take it, take it, take it. Take it away. Take it to Timbuktu." Then he laughed. "That's a joke, son."

Alex moved cautiously closer. "Come in the house, Pop," he urged. "I'll put the car away."

Theo pushed him away. "No!" he shouted. "Don't you touch it. I'll put it away. Go back where you belong."

Alex watched Theo climb back into the car and drive it slowly into the garage. He waited a few minutes and when Theo didn't come out, he went into the garage and found him still sitting in the driver's seat, staring through the windshield at the wall. He knocked on the side window and beckoned to Theo.

"Come on, Pop. Let's go inside."

Theo rolled down the window and said, "You go. I'll come along soon." Then he rolled the window back up.

Alex reluctantly went back into the house, but stood by the kitchen window where he could keep an eye on the garage. The old man really was having a rough time of it. No wonder his mother was worried. If Theo cracked up, and that's what it looked like, there'd be plenty to worry about.

After a few minutes, Theo slouched out of the garage, looked around suspiciously, then rolled down the garage door and locked it. Alex, not wanting to be caught spying on him, ran back upstairs to Paulie's room and said to his mother, "Pop's home. Why didn't you tell me he was acting so strange?"

"I thought I did." She dropped what she was doing and hurried out of the room, calling, "Theo, Theo, here I am."

Alex slumped down on Paulie's bed and buried his face in his hands. "What next?" he muttered. "What the hell next?"

19

The bandshell was deserted. Alex had arrived early, before eight o'clock, clutching a container of black coffee he'd picked up at a coffee shop near the subway exit.

For most of the night, he'd lain awake in his old room at the back of the house, listening for the sound of footsteps or any other sound that would mean Theo was heading out for one of his aimless drives or in some other way teetering on the brink. But all he heard were a few muffled sobs that seemed to come from Paulie's room.

Theo had scarcely touched his dinner and had gone to bed early, pleading exhaustion. Dorothy had fussed over him, excessively it seemed to Alex, since she looked no less exhausted, and once Theo was asleep had gone to bed herself in Paulie's room.

When she said goodnight to Alex, he gripped her hand and said, "Please don't lock the door."

"I won't," she promised.

He'd left the house early, before either of them were up, but not too early for the church bells that were ringing from one end of Brooklyn to the other. Alex seldom noticed things like church bells, but all of his senses, through lack of sleep, were raw and receptive and the bells jangled annoyingly in his head long after he'd boarded the subway on his way to meet Blitz.

He'd ridden the train to Columbus Circle and then walked the desolate wintry paths of Central Park, wondering if what he was setting out to do this morning would ease things for his mother and for Theo, or would only make their situation more unbearable. It all depended on what he learned from Blitz, and what he did with the knowledge. If it led to the capture of Paulie's killer, it might help Theo get a grip on himself, which in turn would give his mother one less thing to worry about. On the other hand, it could backfire on him, get him in trouble with Frank Bruno, and possibly dismissed from the Academy. That would be bad enough, but there was one other possibility he couldn't discount. Blitz could be every bit as dangerous and crazy as Maldonado had pictured him. He could have asked Alex to meet him alone in the park, practically deserted at this hour on a chill February morning, in order to set him up for target practice. Blitz could be the subway yard sniper. For what reason, Alex couldn't fathom. Yet. But if he was, if Alex was able to prove it to himself, he vowed he'd make him pay for Paulie's death and for all the turmoil and grief he'd caused.

He sat on the rim of the bandshell's stage and sipped at his coffee, cool now from his walk across the park but strong and bitter enough to keep him alert while he waited for Blitz to show. The weak lemon-tinged sunlight crept westward across the park, glancing dully off the leafless branches of trees and losing itself in the dark green slats of vacant benches. In the summer, the benches, the paths, the lawns would be swarming with people, but this morning anyone who had any sense was home in bed.

He thought about Edie home in bed, sleeping, with her long, brown hair tangled on the pillow. At the Academy,

201

she kept her hair pulled back in a tight knot on her neck, but when they were alone together, she let it flow loose. It always smelled so clean and good, and he hoped that he'd be able, once again, to take it in his hands and bury his face in it.

Hunched inside his down jacket, he sipped his coffee and waited. He waited and watched. If anyone approached the bandshell from the north, west, or south, he would see them. If someone came from behind the bandshell, he wouldn't have as much warning but would still be able to move quickly enough to get on equal terms. He realized he was a sitting duck for anyone firing from a distance, but if Blitz was the sniper, and if, as the graffiti writers claimed, the sniper was a lousy shot, there was at least a fifty-fifty chance he'd miss. Besides, he told himself, the sniper liked to work sneakily at night, in deserted subway yards, against unsuspecting children, not in broad daylight in Central Park where anybody could come along at any moment and see him.

In the distance, he saw a flash of blue and white and breathed a little easier. The Central Park Precinct patrolled the park at all hours. He hoped they'd keep on patrolling, but keep their distance and not spook Blitz into a no-show. He glanced at his wristwatch. Ten after eight. What was keeping him?

"Hello, brother of Dreemz."

He was standing at the side of the bandshell, near the steps, leaning against the curving wall, arms folded across his massive chest, smiling, as if he'd been standing there since daybreak.

"Hello, Blitz," said Alex.

He was tall, well over six feet, and everything about him was broad, his face, his shoulders, his chest. Even his thighs in baggy camouflage trousers swelled the coarse cloth with broad muscles. He wore an old navy pea jacket, and his eyes were hidden by flashing sunglasses.

Alex stood up. The stage was raised about four feet from the level of the pavement where Blitz stood. Blitz tilted his head back and grinned up at Alex.

"You early," he said.

"And you're late," said Alex.

Blitz shook his head slowly. "Not late," he said. "Just careful. I been waiting to see if you really alone. I seen you come mooching across the park. So far I don't see nobody else. You got anybody hiding in the bushes?"

"No," said Alex. "How about you?"

Blitz laughed. "I might, and I might not." He vaulted up onto the stage and thrust his face close to Alex's. "How come a couple of police came around my place last night? You have anything to do with that?"

"What did they want?" Alex asked.

"I know when not to be home. I figured they'd be coming around sooner or later. But I got friends on the street. They say these two blue boys been asking around about me. Wanting to know do I have a job and who my friends are and shit like that. You been spreading my fame in the wrong places?"

"No," said Alex. "But your tag was in my brother's piecing book. In Mello's, too. They'd follow up on something like that." Alex mentally filed away the information that Bruno had uniformed cops out checking up on the graffiti writers.

Blitz sat down on the rim of the stage, letting his long legs dangle over the edge, and gazed out across the park. "Be springtime soon," he said dreamily. "I like springtime. Don't you?"

"Sure," said Alex, sitting down beside him. "Who doesn't? But what's that got to do with anything?"

"Springtime is when the graffiti writers really get going. Some of them keep at it all through the winter, but everybody gets out there when the weather warms up. It's only natural."

"Maybe you ought to do something about that," Alex suggested.

Blitz flashed his sunglasses in Alex's direction. "What you got in mind?"

"Keep them out of the yards. That way nobody gets hurt."

Blitz laid a heavy hand on Alex's shoulder. "You fail to understand the graffiti mind, my man. Nobody, not even a psycho sniper, can keep them out of the yards. They got to do it. And if there's danger in it, then they got to do it even more."

"Is that why Juice asked Mello to meet him in the Coney Island yard?"

"Say what? Who told you that?"

"Mello. And then Juice never showed up."

"Did you tell that to your cop friends?"

"No. But that doesn't keep me from thinking about it."

"And what you be thinking?"

"I think I don't understand why Juice would set up a kid like Mello. They're supposed to be friends. Mello said Juice asked him to be his writing partner. You got any ideas about that?"

Blitz frowned. "Not as weird as yours, brother of Dreemz. You think Juice be the one doing it?"

"I don't know," said Alex. "I'm only saying what it looks like to me. It could be Juice, or it could be somebody else. Some other graffiti writer, and Juice was just doing what he was told. Mello said he saw the guy. Said he was real big." Alex eyed Blitz from head to toe. "Juice isn't exactly gigantic."

"I hear you," said Blitz. "And I don't like what I hear. You trying to turn us against each other, by any chance? You got some wildass notion that I be the sniper?"

"Tell me why I shouldn't think that."

"Tell you shit!" Blitz exclaimed. "I don't have to prove nothing to you. I don't even need you. You not doing me any good. All you do is talk a lot of crazy cop crap." He stood up and started walking off the stage.

"You got a reputation, Blitz," Alex called after him.

Blitz stood still, his broad back revealing nothing to Alex. "I hear you're a big man in the weapons department."

Blitz's right hand plunged into the pocket of his coat. Slowly, he turned and faced Alex.

Alex remained sitting on the rim of the stage. Despite the faint, mocking smile on his face, he wondered just how far he could go in taunting Blitz. The other night he'd been at a disadvantage, but this morning he was determined to establish equality between them, if not a slight edge. There was no strategy behind what he was doing. Nothing but an instinctive sense of what might work. "Mello's just a baby," he said. "It doesn't take much to be a big man among a bunch of babies. It doesn't take much guts to shoot them down like animals."

Blitz slowly drew his hand out of his pocket.

To his great relief, Alex saw that it was empty. "You're right about one thing," he said. "You don't have to prove anything to me. I came here this morning because, no matter what I might think about you, I still want to find out who killed my brother. If that means listening to a lot of hype, I can stand it up to a point. But let's not overdo it. I'm willing to accept that you're a big man in graffiti. Now, let's get beyond that and figure out what we can do together."

Blitz stood his ground. "It hurts me, man, that you

205

would think I would harm my little homeboy Mello. I don't blame you for thinking I might've offed your brother, even though I didn't. After all, he was a white child, and cops just naturally go looking for the ace of spades."

"Cut the bullshit," Alex said. "Why did you drag me out here? Did you have something in mind, or are we just here to blow smoke at each other?"

"How would you like it if I said I thought you been shooting up the yards to make it look like your brother was just one out of a whole lot? And then you try to blame it on somebody else. Like me."

"Where'd you get that idea? It's crazy."

"No crazier than what you been laying on me."

"Well," said Alex. "Where do we go from here?"

"The way I see it," said Blitz, sitting down again next to Alex, "is we're stuck with each other. I don't trust you and you don't trust me, but other than that, we're fine. Did you think I was about pull a gun on you?"

"The thought did occur to me."

"You were right." Blitz reached into his right-hand pocket and pulled out a revolver. He cradled it in two hands and passed it over to Alex. "Nice piece, isn't it?"

"It's a Police Special. Where'd you get it?"

"Took it off a rookie cop. You should have seen his face."

Alex handed the gun back, but Blitz refused it. "Keep it, man. I brought it for you. It's part of my plan."

"It's about time we got down to it," said Alex. "What's your plan?"

"First put the gun away. We don't want to cause any consternation here in the park."

Alex unzipped his jacket and thrust the barrel of the revolver into the waistband of his jeans, first checking to be sure the safety was on.

"You ain't gonna blow your nuts off. It's not loaded,"

206

said Blitz. "Do you think I'm whacked out enough to walk around with a loaded gun in my pocket?"

"From what I hear, yes."

"I'd like to know who's been spreading lies about me. Was it Mello? That little vandal would sooner tell lies than eat. But I love him like my own son. Just don't believe a word he says."

"Who should I believe? You?" Alex zipped his jacket up, relishing the heavy bulge of the gun against his ribs. Even unloaded, its weight gave him an extraordinary sense of power.

"I guess you have to," said Blitz. "Now watch this."

He stood up and faced out into the park. With two fingers in his mouth, he let go with a long piercing whistle.

They came from behind the bandshell, from among the naked trees, and out of the small brick building that housed the men's and women's toilets. Several zoomed up on bicycles. They were tall, short, and in-between. Most were black, but there were a number of whites and Hispanics among them. All were young, but not as young as Mello. There was one girl, not the same girl who'd led Alex to the west side apartment. They clustered around the bandshell, gazing up at Blitz and glancing curiously at Alex. There was an alert shyness about them, like a herd of deer, trustful for the moment but ready to dance away and disappear at the slightest hint of danger. There were about twenty-five or thirty of them.

Juice strutted up to the bandshell and grinned up at Alex. "How do you like this army?" he crowed. "We gonna get that fucker." The sun glinted off the knife he flourished like a dueling blade. "I'm gonna cut my tag in his guts."

"Put it away," said Blitz softly.

The knife disappeared and Juice faded back into the crowd.

207

Blitz surveyed his crew as if he were taking attendance. Then, satisfied, he smiled and said, "Sit down, everybody. This is a council of war. The Free Bombers Ink is about to take action."

The writers cheered and settled down on the cold pavement, forming a tight semicircle at the foot of the stage. Alex stood up and looked down into their eager faces. This is a game to them, he thought. They're nothing but children. Almost grown and streetwise, but still children. If Blitz's plan meant getting them involved, putting them in any kind of danger, he wanted nothing to do with it.

He started to protest, but Blitz grabbed his arm and raised it high. "Some of you know this guy," he said. "He's not one of us, but he's Dreemz's brother and he's gonna be helping us stop this graffiti sniper."

There were scattered cheers and a smattering of applause.

"His name is Alex," Blitz went on, "and he's going to cop school. He's not a cop yet, but he will be."

The cheers turned to boos and catcalls. Blitz raised his hand for silence.

"Alex and me," he said, "we've come to an understanding. We're in this together, for as long as it takes. That goes for you, too, as long as you're part of the Free Bombers Ink. Anybody doesn't like it, now's the time to split." He paused and waited.

No one left, but the girl stood up and shouted a question. "How do we know he's not a spy?"

Blitz chuckled. "You see too many movies, Tasha. Real spies wouldn't waste their time on graffiti. Now, listen, everybody. This is what we're gonna do. Pulse, where are you?"

A very short, very thin boy with thick glasses stood up and delivered a mock salute. "Yo, I be here."

"I want you to go up to the Writers' Corner this afternoon and tell everybody you see to stay out of the yards for the next week or so. Tell them to spread the word."

A groan went up from the crowd, and a voice shouted, "Does that mean us, too? No bombing?"

"That's what it means," said Blitz. "It's getting too dangerous. Mello's lucky to be alive. Tasha, I got a job for you."

The girl stood up again and raised a clenched fist. In a peculiar way, she reminded Alex of Edie. Her serious brown face bore the same expression of determination he'd seen on Edie's face when she was holding her own in a dispute over women's role in police work. There were still some cops who thought women shouldn't be on the force at all, and not all of them were old-timers. Some of the recruits gave the women a hard time.

"You'll be our communications center," Blitz told her. "That means sticking by your phone and reporting to me whenever there's anything to report."

"That sucks," said Tasha. "What are all the rest of you gonna be doing?"

"It's an important job, Tasha," said Blitz. "I wouldn't trust it to anybody but you."

"But that means I'll have to stay home," she protested.

"It does mean that."

"While you guys go out and have all the fun."

"That's the way it is," said Blitz. "Will you do it, or do you want to leave now?"

"I'll do it. I'll do it," she grumbled. "But I don't like it."

"Now, the rest of you," Blitz went on. "Anybody who has connections with other writing crews, you can pass the word what we're doing and they can join in if they want to. Kraze, you're in with the Rolling Thunder Writers. You tell them what's going down. And Sham, you get in touch with the Crazy Inside Artists. But be sure to tell them they should talk to me before they do anything, or else stay out of the yards. We don't want any cases of mistaken identity."

"What we gonna do, Blitz?" came a shout from the rear of the group. "We gonna waste this asshole?"

"We gotta find him first, don't we?" said Blitz. "This is what we gonna do. Juice is my lieutenant. He sticks with me."

Juice stood up and took a bow.

"Kraze, Big-1, Temper, and Sham—you're group leaders. Just you four for now. We may need more groups later on. Choose up your teams, no more than five or six. You'll go out on patrol. A different yard each night. Tonight I want you to cover Baychester, Concourse, Mosholu, and the Ghost Yard."

"Yo!" shouted one boy. "I get the Ghost Yard. I ain't scared of no ghost. I'm a Ghostbuster! I see that sucker, I bust him!"

The group erupted into groans and guffaws, and another boy shouted, "You couldn't bust nothing but your mama's titty!"

The two dove at each other and scuffled outside the semicircle until Blitz jumped down from the stage and dragged them apart. He knocked their heads together and sent them sprawling. "In case you hadn't noticed," he told them, "we're not playing games. That goes for all of you. Dreemz is dead and Mello's in the hospital with a hole in his chest. Anybody thinks this is a game better go home and play with himself. Got that?"

The group nodded and murmured among themselves. A fat boy held up his hand and whispered timidly, "My sister's getting married this afternoon. I got to go to the reception. It'll last all night."

Blitz patted him on the head and smiled. "Kiss the bride for me."

Then he leaped back up onto the stage and looked them all over. "I've got one final thing to say. None of you has to do this. If anybody wants to drop out, I don't mind. There's no shame. But if you do go out on patrol, here are the rules. One, no writing. Leave your spray paint at home. Two, stay outside the yards. Get yourself a spot where you can see what's happening inside. Spread out so you can cover the whole yard. If you see anything, get in touch with Tasha. Above all, if you see the sniper, don't try to tackle him. Don't even get close to him. He's got a gun and you don't. If he starts shooting, call the police or flag down a police car if you can find one. I mean that. But only if he starts shooting. We don't want a bunch of false alarms all over the place. Finally, if you spot any writers going in to bomb, try to stop them. They might not want to listen to you, but try to stop them anyway. We don't need any more targets. Is that clear? Any questions?"

"Why can't we have guns? I thought we was gonna waste this turkey."

"Suppose you waste the wrong turkey," said Blitz. "A yard bum or another writer. All we're gonna do for now is watch. It isn't gonna be easy and it isn't gonna be fun, but nobody else is doing it so we'll have to."

"So we see this guy," said another boy, "and we call Tasha and she calls you. All that takes time. What are we supposed to do while we're waiting for you to do whatever you're gonna do?"

"Good question," said Blitz. "You try to get a good look at him without getting too close. Don't let him see you. If he has a car, get the license number. If you see he's about to do something, make a lot of noise and scare him off. But don't anybody try to be a hero. That's a good way to wind up dead. Anything else?"

Tasha stood up again and pointed at Alex. "What's he gonna be doing? The baby cop?"

Blitz scowled and said, "You're out of order."

But Tasha ran up to the stage and persisted. "You always say cops don't understand us. Now you're sucking up to one. What's the big secret?"

"That's between him and me, little sister. You do your job and we'll do ours. That's all you need to know. Don't forget, it's his brother that's dead."

"Yeah. Well, I'm sorry about that." She looked up at Alex and said, "I did a top-to-bottom whole car for Dreemz. I liked him a lot. It's the one with my trademark on it. A heart with wings. Did you see it?"

"No," said Alex, "but I'll be looking for it."

"Better hurry," said Tasha, "before it gets buffed."

"Fuck the buff," said the fat boy whose sister was getting married. He inched up to the stage and beckoned to Alex.

Alex jumped down to listen to him. The boy couldn't seem to speak above a timid whisper.

"How do you get into that police school?" he asked.

"You have to take a test," said Alex.

"Shee–it! I never passed no test in my life."

"You can study for it. It's hard, but not impossible."

"I bet they don't let a whole lot of blacks in."

"Don't kid yourself," said Alex. "They got all kinds. Isn't the police commissioner black?"

"Yeah. But that's different."

"He had to start somewhere."

"How do you study for it?"

"There are books. I could lend you mine."

The boy's voice became even fainter. "I don't read so good."

"How old are you?" Alex asked.

"Sixteen," said the boy.

212

"Well, you got two years to work on it. And lose a little weight while you're at it. There are weight limits. You have to pass a physical."

"I don't know," the boy muttered. "I always been heavy. My momma says it runs in the family."

Alex shrugged. "It's up to you. But if you're serious, I'll help you."

The graffiti writers had begun to drift away and the fat boy scurried to catch up with a small group that was heading west across the park. The others scattered in all directions. Only Juice, Tasha, and the four who had been named group leaders remained behind, talking earnestly with Blitz. Alex stayed apart, but tuned in to their conversation.

The boy called Kraze stuttered badly when he spoke. "My folks are away. We could meet up at my place tonight. We could go up there right now and have some breakfast."

Blitz grinned and shook his head. "I don't want some nosy Park Avenue doorman asking questions or remembering my face. No. It'll have to be the storefront. Six o'clock tonight. That'll give us enough time to get to the yards by eight. The sniper's never done anything before eleven or midnight, but he probably spends some time scouting around before he makes his move. We want to get out there before he does."

Alex studied Kraze's pale, acne-ridden face, his long white fingers with dirt-encrusted fingernails. The boy's clothes were no different from anyone else's, surplus army pants, well-worn running shoes, a down jacket much like his own, but ragged and stained. A few of the writers had been stylishly dressed, in bright colors, their jackets and trousers clean and new-looking. But this boy, who lived in a building guarded by a doorman, looked shabbier than Paulie at his most outrageously ragged. Alex wondered why a rich kid would go to such extremes to look poor, and why

213

he was more at home in the world of graffiti than in his own world. If Alex could figure that out, he might learn something about his own brother. Maybe he could get Kraze alone sometime and talk to him about it.

Blitz continued to issue instructions. "Temper, you take the Ghost Yard since you want it so much. But if you start any trouble up there, if I hear one word about a fight or you losing your cool, you'll be off the team and I don't want to see your face again. You hear me?"

"I hear you," Temper muttered, "but what if I can't get nobody to go with me? Everybody be scared shit of that Ghost Yard excepting me."

"That's your problem. You wanted it, you got it."

"What's the Ghost Yard?" Alex asked.

"Don't you know nothing, man?" Temper crowed. "Two Hundred-and-seventh Street. They tell that a writer got killed there once years ago and he be buried underneath the tracks. They say it be his ghost that walks and makes all kinds of spooky noises. I hear some shrieking and moaning up there sometimes, but it don't be nothing but the wind coming off the river. Leastways, that's what I think. I never seen no ghost."

"Okay," said Blitz. "That's just a story to scare babies. Kraze, I want you to take Baychester. Big-1 gets the Concourse, and Sham gets Mosholu. Tell your teams to meet you there at eight o'clock and keep watching until one. Report anything you see to Tasha. If you don't see anything by one o'clock, go on home. We gonna keep doing this until we don't have to do it anymore. We meet every night at the storefront before we go out. That's it."

Tasha, her dark eyes challenging, said, "How come we ain't watching the yards where he's hit before? Except for Gun Hill, he's hit the same places two or three times."

"Two reasons," said Blitz. "The cops know about Gun

Hill Road and Coney Island. Chances are pretty good they'll be covering that territory. We don't want to risk drawing their attention. They don't know about 241st Street, but the sniper's likely to get cautious now. I been trying to put myself in his place and I think what he'll do is try out some new turf. So far, we've only got four teams, but when word gets around what we're doing and more writers join in, we'll be able to cover every yard in the city. Okay?"

"Okay," said Tasha. "But you still didn't say what you and Juice and Alex are gonna be doing."

"I haven't decided yet. For tonight, we may just go from yard to yard and try to psych the situation out."

"Check up on us, you mean," said Temper.

"That, too," said Blitz.

"How do I get in touch with you?" Tasha asked.

"I'll call you every hour or so. Make sure everybody has your phone number. You guys, be sure you have quarters in your pockets and spot yourselves a telephone as close to the yard as possible. You're getting too smart, Tasha. Next thing I know, you'll be taking over the Free Bombers Ink."

"Not me," Tasha retorted. "I'm retiring after this is over. I got better things to do. You can keep on playing the game if you want to, but I'm planning to get me a scholarship. Someday, I'm going to be Harlem's gift to Yale University." She tossed her head and set her beaded cornrows jangling about her ears.

"No shit!" said the boy called Sham. "What you want to do that for? You too foxy to go busting your head over a bunch of books."

"Foxy don't last forever," she said. "Besides, I got to get to be a lawyer so I can get you out of jail when you been busted for the ten thousandth time and they throw away the key. You gonna be so glad you knew me way back when."

"Hoo! Listen to the lady!" Temper cried. "She got delusions of going big-time. She think going to some honky school gonna turn her white overnight. I bet she think she gonna be president!"

"Why not?" said Tasha dreamily. "It could happen."

"Yeah," said Big-1. "It could happen. Just like I could get a job downtown anywhere but in the mailroom. Face it, Tash, you ain't ever gonna get away from what you are. Why fight it?"

"Ah, leave her alone," said Kraze. "It's all bullshit, but if that's what she wants to do, she should do it. She can go in my place. That's all my old man talks about. When am I gonna straighten up and do the right thing so I can go to Yale and be a big-shot lawyer just like him? I keep telling him never, but he doesn't believe me. If he'd let me go to film school, though . . ." The boy trailed off wistfully. Then suddenly, he flared with enthusiasm. "Hey! I just had a great idea! Suppose I take my minicam along? Wouldn't it be great if I could get shots of the sniper in action?"

"It's a thought," said Blitz. "You just do that."

"But what would I do about lights?" the boy mused. "Well, I'll figure something out."

"You guys cut along now," said Blitz. "See you later at the storefront. Don't be late."

The five graffiti writers, chattering excitedly among themselves, strolled off across the paved area in front of the bandshell and then split up to join the small groups that were waiting for them in the distance. Tasha turned to smile and wave, and blew a kiss toward Blitz. Then she ran off alone toward the other side of the park.

"She's right, you know," said Alex.

"About what?" Blitz asked.

"Why are you sending these so-called patrols to yards where nothing's happened? I'd do it the other way around. The guy seems to have a pattern."

216

"You really want to know?" Blitz asked. "You haven't figured that out yet? I thought you were smart."

"Tell me," said Alex.

"So they don't get hurt. I got to keep them busy and feeling important so they don't go off and do something stupid on their own. I been thinking about this whole situation, trying to figure out why it's happening. First I thought it was just members of the FBI, Free Bombers Ink, who were getting shot at, and it was some rival crew doing it. But your brother worked with two or three other crews, and so do the others. Mello's the only one who hasn't branched out yet. So it's not that. And it doesn't look like a race thing. The guy might be crazy, but he's an equal opportunity killer. Some of the kids think it's a cop. It could be, but I doubt it. Even a bad cop doesn't do shit like this. He'll go for money or dope and he'll get nasty if you cross him, but there's no profit in this. The only handle I can get on it is these three yards. Why does he go back to the same places? Maybe they're the only ones he knows or knows how to get into. One thing they all have in common. You can see them from the trains going by. But they're not the only ones. And we don't know yet if he's hit on any other yards. That's why I want to hear from the other writing crews and from the independents. We don't have enough information."

"There's something else I haven't figured out yet," said Alex.

"What's that?" Blitz asked.

"Why you care."

"What makes you think I do?"

"It's obvious. And I don't mean just about the sniper. You care about those kids, what happens to them. You didn't say much when Tasha was talking about going to college and the guys were ranking on her. But I was watch-

217

ing you. You were proud of her. I heard things about you, Blitz. You're not exactly what I expected."

"Who'd you hear from?"

"A guy I know. Someone who used to do graffiti. Someone who knew you a while back."

"Don't believe everything you hear. A while back isn't now. Hey, let's cut the cackle. You and me's got one more thing to do. Juice, get your ass up here!"

Juice, who'd been industriously inscribing his tag on the side of the bandshell, put his wide black marker away and loped up onto the stage. "Yeah, Blitz," he said eagerly. "You got something for me to do?"

"You go out bombing last night despite what I told you?"

"Me? No way!" Exaggerated disbelief widened his eyes and offended innocence pursed his lips. "Why would I do that?"

"What about the night before?"

"Home in bed," said Juice. "Sleeping like a baby."

"Any idea why Mello went out by himself?"

Juice shrugged elaborately, waving helpless hands like broken wings in the air. "No, Blitz. He just don't listen to nobody."

"Okay. That's all. Don't you have a job to go to?"

"Oh, yeah. I forgot. Don't seem right, going out there without old Dreemz. But I'm changing the mural and putting him in it. It's almost like he's working on it alongside me. See you later."

Juice ran off and then came back. He said to Alex, "You don't mind if I put Dreemz in my mural? It's gonna be real chill."

"I don't mind," said Alex. "I'd like to see it when it's finished."

"Okay!" said Juice. He ran off again, leaping as he went to grab at the lower branches of the trees along the path.

218

"What do you think?" said Blitz. "Do you believe him?"

"I don't know," said Alex. "Why would Mello put him on the spot? He has to realize that by saying Juice called him, he was practically accusing him of being the sniper."

"Mello's still just a kid. He doesn't think much beyond the moment. He knew he wasn't supposed to be in the yard. If he could blame that on Juice, he'd come off more like an innocent victim. Did he tell the cop that story?"

"No," Alex admitted. "We were alone together for a few minutes. That's when he told me."

"I think he was having you on," said Blitz. "Seeing how far he could go with you."

"Maybe," said Alex doubtfully. "But I don't want to dismiss what he said so easily."

"That's why I'm keeping Juice with us tonight," said Blitz. "I can't believe he'd do it, but I want to be sure. He's one of the talented ones, but he doesn't realize it yet. Oh, he knows he's good, but he can't see beyond graffiti yet. Maybe this job'll help. He's painting a mural for a community center out in Williamsburg and getting paid for it. Your brother had talent, too. They were working on the mural together. Juice wanted to give it up without his partner to help, but now, well, you heard him. He's going to dedicate it to Dreemz."

"Did you get him the job?" Alex asked.

"You ask too many questions."

"Isn't that what a cop's supposed to do? So you got him the job and you've been encouraging Tasha to get an education. What else have you been doing? Are you some kind of self-appointed social worker? Have gun, will counsel? I don't understand you."

"You don't have to. But maybe I'll explain it to you someday. Just say I got my reasons. Here." Blitz handed Alex a slip of paper. "Come to this address at five-thirty. It's the storefront, kind of a clubhouse for the kids. You and me got some business to conduct before they get there. Bring the gun and don't be late. I got to go now. I see the blue boys are congregating."

A couple of police cars had pulled up and parked opposite the bandshell. The men in them seemed to be doing nothing at all, not even looking their way, but Alex knew that attitude could be deceptive. When he turned back to say goodbye, Blitz had vanished.

Alex jumped down from the stage and walked toward the police cars. One of the cops got out and started walking toward him. Alex stopped and waited. The cop turned around and went back to the car, but didn't get in. He leaned against the door and said something to his partner through the open window. Alex started walking again, slowly. The cop watched him.

Alex decided to walk right past them and see what happened. When he got to within fifty feet of them, the door of the second car swung open. At that moment, a familiar red Trans Am raced around the curving lane and screeched to a halt behind the two police cars. Frank Bruno leaped out and ran toward him. His face was fierce with anger and he shouted as he ran.

"What the fuck do you think you're doing? What are you, some kind of Rambo-nut? You got a shitload of explaining to do, and it better be good." He shoved Alex toward the car with a bruising grip on his arm. "Get in," he ordered.

Without a word, Alex got in and Bruno slammed the door on him.

Bruno stalked over to the police cars and talked rapidly to the uniformed man standing beside the first car. Then he listened while the cop seemed to be giving some kind of report. Alex watched, wishing he could hear what was going on. It would be an understatement to say that Bruno

220

was mad. But was he mad enough to get Alex disciplined out of the Academy? At least, he wanted an explanation. Alex hoped he could make it good enough. And he wondered why the cops had let Blitz get away. They could have stopped him if they wanted to. Had Bruno been having him watched? That meant he still considered Alex a suspect. God, what a mess!

When Bruno came back and got in the car, Alex braced himself for a reaming out.

Instead, Bruno favored him with his menacing, wolfish grin and said, "Nice going, son. Now give. What have you got?" He started the car and cut around in front of the blue and whites, heading out of the park.

"Where are we going?" Alex asked.

"You'll find out. I'm asking you for a report of your tour of duty."

"What!"

"If I can't keep you out of it, I'm damn well gonna use whatever you can tell me. This isn't official. It's between you and me. But if you screw up, it'll get official real quick. *Capisce*?"

"Yeah. I think so. But how did you know where I was?"

"I didn't. It was Blitz we were trailing. When I heard he was in the park with a gang of young punks, I asked for descriptions. One of them was so obviously you, I decided to come on over and see what you were up to."

"I didn't see anybody watching us."

Bruno laughed. "You didn't see the old wino flaked out in front of the men's room? He's one of our best undercover men."

"Even Blitz didn't spot him."

"By the way," said Bruno, "if that gun is giving you a pain in the gut, you can take it out and get comfortable.

221

The only thing we didn't get is a tape recording of the conversation. I hope you've got a good memory."

Alex unzipped his jacket and pulled out the revolver. "What do you want me to do with this?"

"Keep it," said Bruno. "You've had a few lessons, haven't you?"

"Yeah," said Alex. "Two."

"It's enough."

"Then you don't think I had anything to do with these shootings?"

"I didn't say that."

"But you trust me with a gun."

"Let's just say I'm taking a calculated risk. For which I expect to get something of value in return. Now stop with the questions and start with the answers. What's our friend Blitz cooking up?"

They were out of the park and cruising down Fifth Avenue. Traffic was light and the sidewalks empty of all but a few pedestrians. Even St. Patrick's Cathedral, on a Sunday morning, drew only a scattering of the faithful. Alex glanced at his wristwatch. Not yet ten o'clock. A long time until six. A lot could happen between now and then. If he told Bruno of Blitz's plan to patrol the yards, would Bruno put a stop to it? Or would he let them go ahead, even support them, unofficially, of course? And how could he get assurance of that before giving away what he knew?

"Blitz is a funny guy," he began.

"I know that," Bruno interrupted. "He's got a rap sheet going back quite a few years. Nothing recent, though. His name, by the way, is Gregory Harlan Gaines. What's so funny about him to you?"

"Let me say one thing right off," said Alex. "I don't think he's the sniper. I went there this morning nine-tenths convinced he was. But after listening to the way he deals with those kids, I don't think so anymore. He's trying to straighten them out and get them to do something with their lives."

"How touching," said Bruno. "You mean to say he's given up street-brawling and apartment-stripping for a life of good works?"

"I mean he really cares about those kids, and they listen to him because he talks their language. He wants to find this sniper just as much as we do."

"Then let him come and tell us what he thinks."

"You know he won't do that. Isn't that why you've been having him followed?"

"I could have him picked up anytime I want to."

"Then why don't you?"

"Why don't you quit apologizing for him and tell me what he's up to?"

They turned off of Fifth Avenue at Forty-second Street, heading east. As they stopped for a red light in front of Grand Central Station, Alex thought about jumping out of the car and dashing down into the subway. But that would merely postpone Bruno's questions, not eliminate them.

"If I tell you, will you leave him alone?" Alex asked. "Let me work this through with him?"

"How can I answer that unless I know what it is?"

"Who else have you got that's as close to him as I am? All you can do is follow him or arrest him. I can talk to him. Can't you trust me enough to believe that if I find out anything at all incriminating, I'll pass it on to you?"

"Trust me!" echoed Bruno. "Famous last words."

"You're ready enough to use what I can tell you about this morning. Why not give me a little more time? What can it hurt?"

"It can hurt you!" Bruno muttered angrily. "Think I want your mother to have something else to grieve over?"

223

"Leave her out of it. She's got nothing to do with this."

"You're right," said Bruno. "I must be getting soft-headed in my old age. Okay, son. You've got it. Stick with Blitz. But just remember, I'll be watching both of you. I've got eyes and ears in places you never dreamed of. And put that gun away. I'd hate it if some Brownie stopped us on a weapons charge."

Alex shoved the gun into his pocket and glanced out the window. There were none of the brown-uniformed Traffic Police in sight, but of course there wouldn't be on a Sunday morning.

"And you won't arrest Blitz or even haul him in for questioning?" he asked.

"Not unless I've got a good reason to."

"Okay, then. Here's what's happening." As they turned onto the East River Drive, Alex outlined the plan to patrol the subway yards.

Bruno listened and nodded thoughtfully. When Alex finished, he said, "Not bad. And it fits in with something I've been thinking of."

"What's that?" Alex asked.

But Bruno flipped on the tape deck and once again, violin music swelled and capered in the small car. Soon, the Brooklyn Bridge loomed up against the sky, and the car swerved onto its approach ramp.

20

"Here we are," said Bruno, jockeying the Trans Am into the only parking space on the narrow side street in South Brooklyn. "My ancestral home. If you don't count a little village in Sicily a long time ago, before I was born."

Alex peered out at the small three-story brick building. There were thousands like it all over Brooklyn, rows of them here in the section called Red Hook. He said, "Looks like you've got your own parking space reserved."

"Damn right," said Bruno. "Every Sunday. I grew up here. We lived on the top floor then. Three little rented rooms. Years ago, I wanted to buy my mother a house in the country. She didn't want to leave the neighborhood, so I bought her this one. She's happy. She has a little garden in the back. Grows her own tomatoes, peppers, arugula, some roses. Hey, let's go in."

Alex got out of the car and waited while Bruno locked it up and set the alarm. "Even here," Bruno said, "I have to be careful. Especially here. Everybody in the neighborhood knows this is a cop's mother's house and this is a cop's car. But the temptation is too great for some wiseguys. Makes them big men with their girlfriends to steal a cop's car or a cop's tape deck."

"Do you live here?" Alex asked.

"Not for a long time. It's no good for a grown man to live with his mother. She'd love it if I would, but she'd worry about me too much. Wives and mothers, they worry. Well, I haven't got a wife, and I visit my mother on Sundays unless I'm working."

"I thought we were working. I don't want to horn in on your visit."

Although Alex was fascinated by each new facet of himself that Frank Bruno revealed, he was reluctant to enter the little brick house and have to sit around and be polite to an old lady. There were too many other things he should be doing. When they'd crossed the Brooklyn Bridge and turned on to the Belt Parkway, he was so sure Bruno was driving him back to his parents' house, he started thinking about ways to draw Theo out of his misery and get him back on the track again. Even picking a fight with him would be better than watching him mope around the house like a zombie or go off in the car not knowing if he was in any kind of condition to be driving. He hadn't even noticed that they'd turned off the Parkway and plunged into the narrow old streets of Red Hook until Bruno had slowed the car and was ready to park it.

"Sometimes I combine business with pleasure," said Bruno. "Come on, Alex. I want you to meet my mother. You'll like her. And I know she's gonna like you."

Alex followed Bruno up the little stone stoop. Up and down the block, several people called out, "Hey, Franco! How's it going?" and waved. Bruno answered them and waved back. He unlocked the front door and walked into the house, calling out, "Mama! I'm here. I brought someone." Alex trailed along behind.

From the back of the house, a voice shouted, "Come in the kitchen."

Bruno ran through the narrow hallway. Alex followed slowly, peering through curtained arches at a living room crammed with furniture, a dark formal dining room with a lace cloth covering a polished table on which sat a bowl of artificial fruit. Why, he wondered, had Bruno brought him here? The man never did anything without a purpose, he was sure.

At the end of the hallway, a tiny, white-haired woman appeared, wiping her hands on her apron. Bruno picked her up and swung her around. "How's my sweetheart," he cried. "How's my beauty? Been breaking any hearts lately?"

"Franco!" she squealed. "Franco, put me down! You'll give me a heart attack!" But she was laughing and her lined face was flushed with pleasure.

Alex watched, transfixed. This was another Bruno, as different from the tough-talking street cop as that Bruno was different from the "rabbi" who'd taken him under his wing, the breaker of rules, the music lover. Alex realized he was watching a man who was not afraid to show his love. He realized, too, that he was envious.

"Come. Come." Bruno's mother was beckoning to him. On her feet, she was barely five feet tall. "Who did you bring me?" she asked her son. "Another giant? He's as tall as you are. But so skinny. We'll fix that up."

Alex came forward, feeling that the smile on his face was a silly grin. He held out his hand. The little woman took it and turned it palm up to peer at it. "Ah," she said. "A brave one. This one has the courage of a lion. And a long life, too. But some lessons to learn along the way. Courage isn't enough. You gotta be smart, too. What's your name?"

"Alex."

"A good name. Alex what?"

"Alex Carlson."

"What is that? German?"

"No. My father's people were Swedish."

"Huh. I thought Swedes were all blonds. You look Italian to me. Look at that hair, almost black. Look at those eyes, a girl could fall into them and drown. Anyway, for today you'll be Italian. Always on Sunday, I cook a big meal for my Franco and he eats like a pig. You'll see."

"Mama," said Bruno. "I only eat so much because you'll think I'm sick if I don't."

"Sure. I know. The food's no good here. Alex, you be the judge. Take your coat off. Have a glass of wine. Franco, open the wine. There's some olives, the kind you like."

She led the way into the kitchen, which was huge and almost entirely yellow. It stretched across the back of the house, its three south-facing windows glowing with sunlight filtered through filmy yellow curtains and rows of potted plants. The wallpaper bloomed with large yellow flowers. A round table in the middle of the room was covered with a yellow and white cloth and set with yellow dishes. All the appliances were a deep golden yellow. It was the most cheerful room that Alex had ever seen. In a way he couldn't explain, he felt at home.

In the midst of all the yellow, Bruno's mother darted about, taking their coats, pressing wine and tidbits of food on them, checking up on the pots bubbling on the stove, releasing wonderful fragrances from the oven.

"You like my kitchen?" she asked Alex. "My Franco did it for me. The old one was okay, but this, even Queen Elizabeth couldn't ask for better."

"Mama," said Bruno, "I don't think Queen Elizabeth spends much time in the kitchen."

"Why not? She's a grandmother, isn't she? More than I got."

"It's a nice kitchen, Mrs. Bruno," said Alex. "It's like summer in here. A garden full of . . . of daffodils." Alex wondered if the wine was making him goofy. He'd never said anything like that before. He glanced at Bruno to see if he'd noticed.

But Bruno was just smiling and sipping his wine.

"I like that," said the old woman. "A garden full of daffodils. For once, Franco, you've brought me a poet. Alex, you should see some of the donkeys he brings me. Don't deny it, Franco. Most of them behave as if they were brought up in a stable. No manners. Alex has good manners. I can tell. You're not a cop, are you, Alex? Cops don't talk about daffodils."

"He's a cop, Mama. Remember when I told you I wanted to join the department and you had a fit? Well, that's about where Alex is right now. He's learning to be a cop, and I think he's gonna be a good one."

"Ah, Alex. And what does your mother say about her son and this cop business? Does she like it? Tell the truth."

"No, Mrs. Bruno, she doesn't like it. But she doesn't say anything against it. She knows I want to do it more than anything in my life."

"Me, I'd be screaming my head off. Ask him. Ask my Franco if I didn't scream my head off. But it didn't do any good. You can call me Mama Angie. That's what everybody around here calls me. I gotta be Mama to the whole neighborhood because I only got this one son and he doesn't make any grandchildren for me. You got a girlfriend, Alex?"

Alex took a deep breath and plunged. "Yes, I do." Bruno probably knew all about Edie anyway and if he hadn't questioned her already, he'd no doubt do it first thing in the morning. "She's in the Police Academy too."

"Ah, a lady cop," said Mama Angie. "I've seen them. There's one walks around the neighborhood. A nice girl.

229

But kind of *bruta*. You know what I mean? Your girl is pretty?"

Alex looked at Bruno. "Yes, she's very pretty," he said.

"Mama thinks the local lady cop is ugly," said Bruno.

"Hey! I tell the truth. This one, she wears the pants, she wears the hat, she swings the billy club. And she's got a can on her like a sofa cushion. Buck teeth out to here." She bit her thumb and waved it a good two inches in front of her face. "And she's not Italian. We used to have a good Italian cop here. Ernani Monteleone. What ever happened to him, Franco?"

"He retired, Mama. I think he went to California to be with his kids."

"And what are you gonna do when you retire? You're not too old to have kids, you know. Get a nice young wife, you could have a dozen in ten years."

"Mama, cut it out. Alex doesn't need to hear this stuff."

"He doesn't know where babies come from?"

"Sure, I know, Mama Angie," said Alex. "But sometimes it's not easy to know when it's right to have a kid. Me and Edie, for instance, even if we got married, it'd be quite a while before we could even think about raising a family. And what kind of parents would we be, both of us cops?"

"I'm hungry," said Bruno. "Did we come all the way out here to talk about babies? Maybe we ought to send out for pizza."

"Ah, you're crazy, Franco." Mama Angie stood behind his chair and put her hands lovingly on his shoulders. "I talk a lot, I know. But this is the first time you brought me somebody worth talking to. Your mother must be very proud of you, Alex. Don't deny it. Don't say a word. It's time to eat."

The meal was wonderful. Alex ate until he thought he would burst. And then he ate some more. There was home-made pasta. Veal and peppers. Spicy sausages flavored with fennel seeds. Broccoli and mushrooms. A salad of sweet red onion and tomatoes. And Mama Angie kept remembering more delicacies for them to taste. She bobbed up and down, carrying dishes back and forth, and wouldn't hear of Alex's helping her do a thing. "It's a holiday for cops," she insisted. "All the saints wear badges today."

When it was over, she shooed them into the living room where comfortable old armchairs jostled a stiff, new cut-velvet living room suite. Bruno collapsed with a sigh into one of the old chairs, and Alex did the same.

"You've made her happy," said Bruno.

"I ate like a pig," said Alex.

"Exactly. Now we have to talk."

Mama Angie came in with a tray of coffee and dessert, an assortment of Italian pastries. "You both look like big important cops now. I don't want to hear cop talk." She put the tray down and went away.

Bruno handed Alex a tiny cup of black coffee and took one himself. "If you don't like expresso," he said, "I'll see if she has some of the other kind."

Alex took the cup and sipped. The coffee was hot and strong, but delicious. "What do you want to talk about?" he asked.

Bruno put his feet up on a hassock and closed his eyes. "It's a wild idea," he said, "and I haven't got it completely worked out yet, but do you think your friend Blitz and his buddies would be willing to act as decoys?"

"You mean go into the yards and wait for the sniper to take potshots at them? That's pretty dangerous."

"It wouldn't have to be. We'd be covering them." Bruno leaned forward and gazed intently at Alex. "But there's always the possibility of danger. I can't deny that."

231

"Most of them are just kids. Like Mello. I don't think it would be right."

Bruno slumped back in his chair again. "Yeah. Well, it was just an idea. I'll think of something else. We're already pulling the records on every known gun nut in the city. Maybe something'll turn up." He didn't sound very hopeful.

"I'll do it," Alex said. "And maybe I can talk Blitz into it. He's no kid, and it's just one step up from his plan to patrol the yards. But I thought you had him on the suspect list."

"You know something, Alex? You're very convincing. You've spent some time with Blitz, and you've got a different view of him from what his rap sheet shows. It doesn't happen often, but bad guys have been known to change. I'm willing to go along with your view, at least until it gets proved wrong. By rights, I should have hauled him in as soon as we identified him. We could still get him on an illegal weapons rap. But if he'll do this, he could be useful to us. I'll take the chance."

"I'll put it to him tonight," said Alex.

"Good," said Bruno. "Now tell me some more about your brother. Tell me how it was for the two of you, growing up and all that." He pushed the tray of dessert toward Alex. "Have a cannoli. She made them herself. You have to eat at least two."

"Why?" said Alex. "Why do you want to know all that? Why did you bring me here? Why did you change your mind about letting me work on the investigation?"

"Why?" said Bruno. "Because you remind me of myself when I was a young cop. Besides being a lousy violin player, my father was a low-level Mafia soldier. He thought he could outsmart the big guys, but just like with the music, he didn't have the talent for it. One day they fished him out of the Gowanus Canal. He should have stuck to his fid-

232

dle. You don't get killed for being a bad fiddler. When I was a rookie, I was so full of vengeance for my father, I wanted to shoot every *mafioso* I came across, and I did kill a few. It was a long time before I realized that all I was doing was becoming a bad cop and it was only a matter of time before I either got killed or booted off the force. I guess I'm trying to keep you from making the same mistake."

"I think you're a good cop," said Alex.

"Shut up and eat," said Bruno.

21

"A decoy, huh?" said Blitz. "Sounds interesting. But how do I know it's not some kind of trick? Certain members of New York's Finest would consider it a privilege to deprive me of my civil rights. Cops are like elephants. Long memories."

"It's no trick," said Alex. "Frank Bruno's a different kind of cop. You can trust him."

Blitz laughed. "What is he, some kind of wimp?"

"He's about as wimpy as you are," Alex retorted. "And twice as ugly when he gets mad."

"Just exactly how does this decoy work?" Blitz asked.

"I don't know that yet," said Alex. "He's working out the details. If you won't do it, I'll have to do it myself. Alone."

"You!" Blitz was scornful. "What do you know about the yards? This needs an expert."

"That's what I told him. Blitz is the expert."

"I don't want none of my crew taking part in this. I don't even want them to know about it. They're too young for cop games."

"Can I tell him you'll do it?" Alex asked.

"I'm thinking about it. I'll let you know later. Who knows? We might get lucky and find the sniper tonight.

Then nobody'd have to do no dumbshit decoy. Now let's get ready to go hunting."

They were in a back room at the storefront. Blitz unlocked a steel cabinet and brought out boxes of cartridges. On the shelves, Alex saw hard evidence that Maldonado hadn't been wrong when he'd called Blitz a walking arsenal. There were two rifles among the handguns and assorted knives. If Blitz had gone straight, what did he need with all the armament? Doubt flamed in Alex's mind.

"What do you do with all that stuff?" he asked.

Blitz grunted and handed him a fistful of cartridges. "Load up and let's see if anybody's here yet. You do know how to load a gun, don't you?"

Alex inserted the cartridges into the chamber the way he'd been taught at the firing range at Rodman's Neck. Both times he'd been out there, he'd done all right, but others had done better. Edie'd surprised him by knocking off several perfect rounds, and later confessed that her father had taught her to shoot when she was a child.

"Do you really think the sniper'll be out there tonight?" he asked Blitz.

"*Quién sabe, amigo?*" said Blitz. "I almost hope he doesn't show. The more I think about this decoy thing, the better I like it. Gives me an excuse to blow the sucker away without getting busted for it. You ready? Let's go."

Blitz locked the steel cabinet and pocketed the key. As they left the back room, he locked that, too. Then he led the way through a dark passage into the storefront's one big room that Alex had passed through when he'd arrived, but hadn't had time to examine.

Tasha was sitting at a long table, eating a hamburger and french fries. Beside her, Sham and Temper were working on their piecing books. Big-1 lay stretched out on a dilapidated sofa, apparently asleep. Juice paced up and down the long room, peering at shelves and into cardboard cartons as if he was looking for something. There was no sign of Kraze.

Blitz went to the long table and sat down at one end of it. Alex remained standing and gazed around at the walls. They were of bare brick that had been whitewashed and then painted with a series of enormous graffiti murals. In one of them a rampaging subway car, fanged and red-eyed, bore down on a cowering group of passengers waiting on a crumbling platform. In another, a fierce black panther charged up the steps of a subway entrance, blood dripping from its muzzle. The images seemed to leap from the walls, each of them shrieking a message of danger and destruction.

"How do you like our gallery?" Tasha asked him. "Better than a museum, huh?"

"I never saw anything like it," Alex said. And he meant it. The graffiti he saw daily on the trains was incomplete compared to this and usually worn and scarred. Even the pieces he'd seen in Paulie's piecing books lacked the impact of size.

"Damn right," said Tasha. "There isn't anything else like it. Not all in once place. This is where we do our best work. It's not the same as getting it up on the trains, but it lasts longer. Come and see the one your brother did."

She got up and led him through the clutter of battered drawing tables, moribund sofas leaking their stuffing, rusty birdcages, old tires, a doorless refrigerator filled with magazines and books and labeled "library,"—anything and everything that could be picked up on the streets of the city. And everywhere, on every flat surface, rows of paint cans and marking pens.

They stopped in front of a mural that took Alex's breath away. It was so full of joy and yet it was so simple, just two figures, young men, standing together side by side. But all around them Paulie had painted a garden of delightful things. Flowers, of course, trees laden with fruit, a stack of books in one corner, and in the other a grinning dog that looked suspiciously like Rocky, the silly mongrel they'd once had years ago. There were other clues in the picture, but the central figures, the two young men, were unmistakably meant to be himself and Paulie. He was the taller one, dark-haired and dark-eyed, and Paulie's long blond hair was a dead giveaway. But just in case there was any doubt, Paulie had painted a banner at the top of the mural on which he inscribed in bold red letters "BROTHERLY LOVE."

"Not bad, huh?" Blitz had come over to look at the mural with them. "Your brother really had it. He was good. He wasn't afraid to paint his heart out. Everybody respected him for it."

Alex turned away from the mural, glad to have seen it but saddened by the thought that he'd never lived up to Paulie's idea of what love between brothers was all about. "I wish I could take it off the wall and take it home with me," he said. "I wish my mother could see it."

"You could bring her here," said Tasha. "Would she come?"

"I'll photograph it for you," said Blitz. "Then you could have it blown up."

Alex shook his head. "Not now. First things first. Blitz, how about getting this thing started?"

"Okay. Okay. We're just trying to be nice. Ain't it just like a cop to be so ungrateful?"

"I'm not ungrateful. I just can't think about things like that until we put this sniper where he belongs."

"So let's do it," said Blitz. He strode back to the table and called everyone around.

Juice had finally found what he was looking for, a large cardboard carton which he carried over to the table and set down in front of Blitz.

"Where's Kraze?" Tasha asked. "He's always late. You can't depend on him. I don't think he should be in on this."

"What have you got against Kraze?" Blitz asked. "You're always ranking on him."

"He's not serious," said Tasha. "I don't trust him."

"Because he's white?"

"No." Tasha considered her answer thoughtfully. "I trusted Dreemz. So far, I have no reason not to trust Alex, except that he's a cop."

"Then what is it? If there's something we should know, let's hear it."

Tasha cast her eyes down and began picking splinters out of the table top. "I guess it's because he's got money. He can do anything he wants. How come he wants to hang out with us?"

"That's not sensible, Tash," Blitz chided her. "You're making us out to be some kind of lowlife. That's nigger thinking, and I know you don't think of yourself that way."

Tasha's head jerked up and her eyes flashed. "Watch your mouth, motherfucker. Don't you be calling me nigger."

"Is that the way you're going to talk when you get to Yale?"

"Bet your ass, honey. If anybody up there calls me nigger, they're gonna hear what it sounds like."

Temper giggled. "They throw you out," he gloated. "Then you come back here where you belong. I give you one week."

"And I give you five in the fucking mouth!" Tasha stood up and leaned across the table, brandishing her fist in Temper's face. But just as quickly, she sat down again and said, "Ah, shit, I haven't even got there yet, and you're wishing me to get thrown out. Some friends!"

Alex wondered how on earth his brother had fit in with this crowd. It wasn't that Paulie had been weak or unable to defend himself, but that his mind always seemed to be somewhere else, in some Utopian dream that didn't include ranking and wrangling. Yet, fit in he obviously had. These kids all seemed to regard him with something approaching awe.

"Let's get down to it," said Blitz. He stood up and began unloading equipment from the cardboard carton. Flashlights, binoculars equipped with night sights, lengths of rope, wire cutters. Alex wondered if they and the weapons locked up in the back room were stolen property. He was getting into something he hadn't anticipated, but there was no backing out now.

As Blitz passed the equipment around the table, the door at the front end of the room opened and Kraze charged toward them breathing heavily, his minicam dangling from a shoulder strap.

"Sorry I'm late," he panted. "There was this fantastic scene in the park. Two guys fencing in the twilight. Masks and everything, those white vests. I had to stop and try to get some footage. It'll fit right into my movie. The crazy things that happen in this city!"

Tasha rolled her eyes toward the tin ceiling. "How long is that movie of yours?" she asked. "Ten years?"

"Not that long," said Kraze seriously. "I've only been working on it for two." He smiled at her shyly. "You're in it, Tash. I've got you getting up your tag in the Graffiti Hall of Fame."

"What's that?" Alex asked.

Big-1, who rarely spoke, swelled with obvious pride as he answered. "It's the greatest," he said. "You gotta be invited to put your tag up there. It's a schoolyard. In Harlem. Big wall. Real chill. Dreemz is up there. Didn't he tell you? He was so proud."

Kraze slid into a chair next to Alex. "I've got some scenes of Dreemz in action," he confided. "If you ever want to see them, just say the word. There's one where he's hanging

239

down from the top of a car, painting upside-down. He was one crazy bomber."

"I'd like to see that sometime," said Alex.

"If it's not too much trouble," Blitz interrupted, "can we get started here? We still got some things to get down about tonight."

"What happens if nothing happens tonight?" Tasha asked.

"Then we keep on watching until something does happen," said Blitz. "But I got a feeling we won't have to watch forever. This guy's on a hot streak. It's like when a nuclear pile reaches critical mass. Nothing can stop it. I think he's reached a point where he can't stop. Mello got a look at him. Not a good look, and you know how Mello likes to make things sound better than they are, but he said the guy was as big as Godzilla and his eyes glowed in the dark. I take that to mean we're looking for a giant economy-size crazy."

"I been thinking, Blitz," said Sham. "I know you say we better off without no guns, and mostly I agree. But supposing one of us comes smack up against him and those eyes be glowing in the dark? What the fuck we supposed to do? Say 'please, mister, don't shoot me. I be nothing but a innocent child'?"

"He's right," said Tasha. "I think the patrols should have guns. The leaders anyway. Shoot him before he shoots them."

"Right," Kraze agreed. "'Gunfight in the Number Three Yard.' I could get it all in my movie."

"Wrong," said Blitz. "No cowboys in this operation. Nobody goes into the yards. The patrols do nothing but watch from the outside. That way nobody gets close enough to get hurt."

"Gonna be hard," said Big-1, "not going in. I got a piece I been working on. I'm ready to get it up."

"Save it," said Blitz. "No piecing until this is over."

240

Big-1 nodded glumly. "So I'm sitting up somewheres and I see a guy with a rifle sneaking around in the yard." He picked up a pair of binoculars and peered through it. "Yo! There he goes, and down there's a writer, all calm and peaceful, getting his piece up on a train. The guy takes aim." Big-1 put down the binoculars. "What am I supposed to do? Send somebody to call Tasha?"

"Yes," said Blitz. "And then you scream, yell, make noise." He threw a handful of police whistles onto the table. "Use these. Wake up the guards. If it's really that close, call the police."

"It don't seem right," said Temper. "We always trying not to wake up the guards."

"That's enough," said Blitz. "It's time to get going. Be careful and don't do anything stupid."

After the graffiti writers had left, Blitz said to Juice, "Where's the car?"

"Two blocks away. Closest I could get."

"Go get it. Drive it right up in front. Wait there until we come out. Take these with you." He handed Juice a pair of wire cutters.

"We going in the yards, Blitz?" Juice asked.

"If we have to. Get moving. We got a lot of territory to cover tonight."

"Hey, Alex," said Juice. "You gonna ride shotgun?" He aimed the wire cutters at the panther mural. "Blam! Blam! Gotcha!" He raced toward the front door, blasting at the walls along the way.

When he was gone, Blitz disappeared into the back room and came back carrying a rifle.

"What's that for?" Alex asked.

"Just in case," said Blitz.

Alex looked closely at the gun, trying to figure out if it was the one that was missing from the garage. Paulie could have taken it and brought it here.

"You ready, man?" said Blitz. "Let's go."

241

22

It was after two in the morning when Alex got home. He found Edie and his mother in the kitchen, drinking coffee. "What are you two doing?" he said. "Ganging up on me?"

"I invited Edith to come over," said Dorothy. "I thought it was time we got acquainted. We seem to have something in common."

"Yeah," said Alex. "It looks like a conspiracy to me."

"Nothing of the kind," said Edie. "We both like sitting home alone wondering where the hell our men are."

"Is Pop out again?" Alex asked his mother.

She nodded. "I keep thinking he'll fall asleep at the wheel. If only he'd talk to me about it. But you know him. The strong, silent type."

"Is that what you are, too, Alex?" Edie asked. "Strong and silent? Like father, like son?"

"Low blow," said Alex. "Come on, Edie. It's late. I'll take you home."

"Not necessary. I'll call a cab." She got up and looked around for the phone.

"In the hall," said Dorothy. "Thanks for coming over. I guess I really needed to talk to another woman. I'm glad you and Alex are . . . friends."

Edie bent and kissed Dorothy's cheek. Then she headed for the hall. Alex followed her.

"What's the matter with you?" he whispered as soon as they were out of the kitchen. "I said I would take you home, and I will. We need to get a few things straight between us."

"Not tonight, Alex. I'm too angry with you. Have you any idea what it does to her to suspect that something's going on with you and not know what it is?"

"Are you speaking for her or for yourself?"

"Both. But I can do something about it. She can't."

"What can you do?"

"I can tell you to get out of my life and stay out."

"Is that what you're telling me?"

"Don't push me, Alex. Just let me call the cab and go home." She picked up the phone and dialed.

Alex waited while she ordered the cab and when she hung up, he said, "You know why I can't tell you what I'm doing."

"The cab'll be here in fifteen minutes. If you don't mind, I think I'll go sit with your mother until it gets here. Incidentally, I didn't say anything to her about what you told me. Which wasn't much. Or anything I figured out for myself."

"What have you figured out?"

"Did you forget I was going up to see Richie today? You were supposed to call me."

"Yes. Yes, I forgot. I'm sorry."

"Richie had a few things to say. He thinks you're messing around with dynamite. He's about as pissed off with you as I am."

Alex groaned. "I don't know why you all can't just leave me alone. Everything's under control. I know what I'm doing."

243

"Sure you do," said Edie. "You're the Lone Ranger. But I have a funny feeling you're gonna find yourself up shit creek without a Tonto." She got her coat out of the hall closet and put it on. "Well, as they say, it's not my job. See you around, Alex."

She went back to the kitchen with Alex trailing glumly along behind her. Dorothy was gazing out the kitchen window toward the garage. Edie said, "The cab is on the way. You should go to bed."

Dorothy turned and smiled at her. "I know I should. But I wouldn't be able to sleep. It's funny how you always imagine the worst when you don't know, and then sometimes it turns out to be worse than you could possibly imagine."

"Ma," said Alex. "I'll stay up and wait for him. I want to talk to him anyway. Maybe I can get him to loosen up."

"Yes," said Dorothy. "Yes, maybe you can." She reached for their hands and, holding onto them, said, "Be good to each other. It's so easy to forget how important that is. Good night."

After Dorothy had gone upstairs, Edie said, "She thought we wanted to be alone together."

"Didn't we?" Alex asked. Tentatively, he put an arm around her. When she didn't object, he kissed her forehead lightly. "Please don't shut me out of your life."

Edie sighed. "It hurts, doesn't it? Alex, believe me, I don't want to hurt you and I'm not just trying to get back at you. But can't you see that if we're not honest with each other, we'll end up exactly where your mother and father are? Is that what you want?"

"No, of course not. If you could only give me a few more days, I promise I'll tell you everything."

"After it's all over," said Edie bitterly. "When there's nothing left to do. Richie told me all about this graffiti

244

writer named Blitz. He's got some ideas and he wants to talk to you."

"No more, Edie." He aimed a kiss at her lips, but she turned her head away.

A car honked loudly in the street in front of the house.

"There's the cab," she said. She grabbed her shoulder bag and walked swiftly toward the front door.

Alex hurried after her. "I'll see you tomorrow," he said.

"I guess you will," she said. "You know where I'll be." And then she was gone.

"I'll be there, too," he called out as the cab door slammed.

He stood in the open doorway and watched the cab pull away. Then he closed the door and wandered back through the house to the kitchen. There was still hot coffee in the pot. He poured himself a cup and sat down to wait for Theo.

23

"I don't care, Frank. It's another one of your crackpot ideas, and I don't like it." Larry Farley paced up and down the small, overheated room, bumping into the green metal desks and threatening to dislodge the stacks of files that covered each of them. "I don't see why we can't just do it the normal way."

Alex sat on a green leather psychiatrist's couch and wondered who needed it more—himself, Frank Bruno, or Farley, who looked about ready to pop. The couches were an old joke in the department. Some eager purchasing agent had got a great bargain years ago, a truckload of the damn things at a very good price. No one knew what to do with them, so they turned up in precinct houses all over the city. They were so uncomfortable, even drunks refused to pass out on them.

"My crackpot ideas get the job done," said Bruno. "I'm not saying don't do the normal stuff. That's necessary. But let's do this, too. If it works, we'll catch the sniper in the act and there won't be any opportunity for him to weasel out of it."

"If it works!" Farley shouted. "And what if it doesn't? What if somebody, say Alex here, gets killed in the process? You'd like that, wouldn't you?"

"No, I wouldn't. But what if the sniper keeps on shoot-

246

ing up the yards? I want to get the son-of-a-bitch before he does any more damage."

"Nobody got shot last night," said Farley.

"So, it was Sunday. He took the day off."

"Look, Frank. I've got a list of gun nuts. There's this wacky old guy out in one of the Coney Island projects who shoots seagulls from his window. There's a weird survivalist group in Staten Island. There's a convicted sniper out on parole in the Bronx. He went apeshit in Van Cortlandt Park a few years back over losing a softball game. Didn't kill anybody but he sure played hell with the outfield before they stopped him. And that's just a few."

"Any of them look any good?" Bruno asked.

Farley shrugged. "I'm going down the list and bringing in the hottest prospects. Then I'll go on to the not-so-hot ones. I know it's not likely to give us much and it takes time, but it has to be done. If we don't do it, and the sniper turns out to be somebody on this list, we'd look pretty dumb."

Bruno nodded. "Good. So you take care of that end, and I'll take care of the decoy and we'll see who gets there first." Bruno leaned back in his swivel chair and propped his feet on his desk. "Someday," he said, "I'm gonna dump all this paperwork in the sewer."

"I hope it backs up on you," said Farley. "I can't even take a couple of days off without you dreaming up some half-assed way to get us both hip-deep in manure." He charged out the door, muttering "stubborn bastard" and "guinea gonzo" just loudly enough for them both to hear.

"Larry's okay," Bruno said to Alex. "He just doesn't feel right unless he's knocking his head against a brick wall and yelling about it. But if there's anything to be found out his way, he's the one who'll find it. So what did you accomplish last night?"

"Looked for a needle in a haystack." Alex shook his

foggy head. Three hours sleep had left him more exhausted than no sleep at all. "Nobody saw anything. Blitz and Juice and I drove around to all the yards where the patrols were posted and then to a few others. There weren't even any graffiti writers out. Blitz got the word around and I guess they're all taking it to heart."

"That's good," said Bruno. "You still think Blitz is okay?"

"I don't know," said Alex. "He had a rifle with him in the car. I can't figure out if he's flaunting it in our faces or if he really thinks he needs it. Either way, he's dangerous. But he says he's willing to go along with us on the decoy."

"Nice work," said Bruno. "I'll let you know when we're ready to move. Can you get in touch with him?"

"I can go by the storefront, or I can call Tasha. I thought you guys had his address. He told me somebody came around to check him out."

"That's right. But if he didn't give it to you, I don't think you should try him there. I don't want him to get spooked. Okay, son. You better get on over to the Academy. I don't want you flunking out and using this for an excuse."

Alex stood up to leave, then remembered a question that had been bothering him. "How do you know which yard to set up the decoy in?"

"Why don't you let me worry about that?"

"I saw about eight yards last night, big ones and little ones. He could turn up anywhere. Blitz says he's likely to stick to the ones he knows, but what's to stop him from breaking new ground?"

"Blitz could be right. Did you ever try to put yourself in the mind of a killer?"

Alex shook his head.

"A guy like this, a random murderer who comes out of nowhere and kills for what seems to be no logical reason, nine times out of ten he's just begging to be caught. He wants to stop, but he can't. So he has to make it possible for someone else to stop him. He may not consciously point the way, but he'll be leaving little signposts behind him. That's why I don't think Farley's method is going to do the trick. It's based on logic and sheer hard work. Plugging away at detail. That's what Farley's good at. Me, I like to explore the illogical side of things."

"Have you found any of those signposts?" Alex asked.

"Maybe. Maybe not. Maybe I don't want to believe what's staring me in the face."

"What's that?" Alex asked in alarm. "You're not still thinking it could be me?"

"No, no. You were never a contender. Is Blitz planning to patrol the yards tonight?"

"Far as I know. But I don't know how long he can keep the kids interested. They got pretty bored last night."

"They won't be bored if this guy hits again. I'd be happy if they all stayed home and got their jollies from watching television."

Alex drifted toward the door, but was reluctant to leave. If there was anybody in the world he could have talked over his problems with, it was beginning to look like Frank Bruno. But what would Bruno think if he started unloading a lot of garbage about his love life and the way Theo was acting? Not to mention the strain on his mother. She was looking older and sadder by the minute. Bruno wouldn't be interested in any of that. He'd probably tell him get on with the job and forget everything else.

He said, "Should I check in with you before I leave tonight?"

"Good idea," said Bruno, "if I don't get in touch with you first." He picked up a newspaper and opened it to the sports page. "Can't wait for the baseball season to start. You like baseball, Alex? Mets or Yanks?"

"Yanks. I pitched a little in college." But baseball was pretty far down on the list of important things to consider,

249

and he didn't want to get into the inevitable discussion of whether or not there'd ever be a subway series. "I better get going. See you later."

On his way to the Academy, Alex wondered about those signposts Bruno had mentioned. Had one of them been the anonymous phone call he spoken of that morning in the car before they'd gone to see Mello? Had he tried to find out who the caller was? Bruno talked a lot, but when you came right down to it, he gave away very little of what he really knew.

He reached the Academy barely in time for roll call. Keeping up with Bruno was beginning to look like a twenty-four hour a day job. The guy never took a minute off, except for those Sunday afternoons in Red Hook. Who else would call up at six in the morning and tell him, not ask him, to be in his office in an hour? But he'd gone, after his mother had woken him up and he'd listened to Bruno say how essential it was that they find time to compare notes every day until the case was closed.

Sure, it made him feel important. Especially after the way he'd failed to make any kind of connection with Theo the night before. The old man had come staggering home at a quarter to three, fit for nothing but a quick beer and bed. He wasn't drunk. Alex had deliberately smelled his breath and found only the reek of too many cigarettes, nothing else. He'd helped him up to bed and after a few futile questions about where he'd been, had given up on getting any sensible answers. All Theo would say was, "Let's join the Navy and see the world." Over and over again. As if he were some kind of recruiting poster.

Alex could only suppose that Theo was trying to relive his life in some other time, when he was a young man and nothing horrible had happened to him. The best thing that could happen to him now would be a traffic accident. Nothing serious, but just enough to put him out of commission for a while.

Edie nodded at him distantly when he walked into the rollcall room. The other recruits swarmed around him, eager for news of the investigation, until the sergeant called them all to attention. Jim Beatty stood next to him and whispered, "What's bugging Edie? You two have a fight?"

Alex nodded and left it at that. There was nothing Beatty could do about it. Somehow, he got through his morning classes with only half his brain paying attention to the work. The other half was busy trying to envision what the decoy set-up would be like. Would he and Blitz be alone in one of those huge yards? Would Bruno stand for them being armed? Would Bruno himself be there? And what about extra manpower? If it was up to him, he'd have the yard surrounded with tear gas and riot guns, a fucking army, and blow the guy away the minute he showed. If he showed.

At the lunch break, he raced to the telephone and called Frank Bruno's number. Bruno wasn't there. Alex left no message. There wasn't anything to say.

Edie didn't turn up for lunch. Okay. So she was giving him the treatment. He ate with Beatty, the $3.95 special at the Chinese restaurant with a couple of glasses of seltzer to wash it down. His fortune cookie said, "Small events cast large shadows."

Beatty's constant concern about his own health dominated their conversation and, for once, Alex was happy to encourage his hypochondria. When he said, "I think I got what Maldonado's got," Alex was all sympathy.

"You should stay home," he said. "Remember what the sergeant told us. No point in infecting the entire Academy."

"Do you think so?" Beatty asked, worriedly. "Do you think I should go see the doctor?"

"I would if I were you. Catch it before it gets worse."

Edie was absent from the afternoon classes. Alex wondered about that. It wasn't like her to skip for no reason. But, of course, she might have a reason. More of the treatment. The silent treatment. Well, you could say he deserved it. But she was sure getting her point across. He missed her.

The day dragged on with Alex expecting at any moment to be jerked out of class by a call from Bruno. It was at the end of his sociology class, the last class of the day, that a message came that he was wanted on the phone in the sergeant's office. He raced down the corridor and snatched up the receiver.

"Bruno!" he shouted. "What's up? Is it tonight?"

But the voice that whispered in his ear wasn't Frank Bruno's. "You got Blitz so we got your girl friend. You want her back in one piece, you let Blitz go."

"What?" Alex tried to place the voice. "Is that you, Juice?"

"Damn right it's me. I should have known better than to trust a cop. They'll screw you every time."

"What happened?" Alex asked. "It's gotta be a mistake."

"No mistake," said Juice. "They picked him up this morning. Some asshole in a trenchcoat, trying to look like Columbo. I was there, man. I saw it."

"Where's Edie? What did you do to her?"

"We ain't done nothing to her yet. That ain't saying we won't. You better get Blitz sprung before we change our minds."

"Juice, believe me. I didn't know anything about it," Alex pleaded. "Tell me where she is. Let me speak to her." But the line had gone dead.

He dialed Frank Bruno's number and waited, fuming, while the phone rang unanswered. It had to be Farley, working down his list of gun nuts. Why hadn't it occurred to him that Blitz, with his rap sheet and his arsenal, would turn up on Farley's list? Why, for Christ's sake, hadn't it occurred to Bruno? Or maybe it had! He probably knew it all along. And now they had Edie! They must have come and picked her up right here at the Academy. Had they just grabbed her off the street? Or told her some story that convinced her to go with them? And where were they holding her? At the storefront? Probably not, but it was the only starting place he had. He still had the gun Blitz had given him, wrapped in a tee-shirt in the bottom of his satchel. If he had to, he'd blast his way in and make them tell him where she was. He was about to hang up the phone and hightail it on uptown, when Bruno answered, sounding irritated.

"Yeah? Who is it?"

"Bruno! It's me, Alex. What the hell's going on?"

"Oh, Alex." His voice softened. "I was just about to call you. Can you get over here right away?"

"No. I can't. You guys really fucked me over. You and Farley. You must really think I'm stupid."

"What are you talking about? We've got the decoy all set up for tonight. I need you."

"Sure. I suppose you need Blitz, too."

"Yes, I do. He's part of the plan."

"That's funny. That's really funny. Don't try to tell me you don't know what's happened, because I won't believe you."

"Alex." Bruno began to sound impatient. "I've gone to a lot of trouble to set this thing up. Now you're talking in riddles and what I'm hearing is that you want to back out."

"Back out!" Alex exclaimed. "Yeah. Yeah, I'm backing out. I've got something else to do tonight. I've got to find a friend of mine before something happens to her. And while I'm doing that, why don't you go take a look in your own cells. You might find something interesting."

"Talk straight," Bruno ordered. "What happened?"

The sergeant walked into his office and headed for the coffee pot on the windowsill.

"I can't talk any more," said Alex. "I trusted you. I'm not making any more mistakes like that." He hung up.

The sergeant peered at him over the rim of his coffee mug. "Everything okay, kid?" he asked. "Want some coffee?"

"Stuff it," said Alex. He stalked out of the office.

24

No one answered the door at the storefront. Alex banged
on it until his knuckles were raw. For all his Clint Eastwood
fantasies of blasting the lock with one shot and charging
into the place, he realized he couldn't do it on a busy Manhattan street without rousing the whole neighborhood and
drawing the attention of the local patrol cops. And yet, Edie
could be inside. Juice and the rest of them could be inside,
knowing that he'd be the only one banging on the door like
that. And laughing at him.

He stood in the doorway and looked up and down the
darkening street, hoping to spot one of the graffiti writers
hanging out nearby. It was a street of ancient tenements, as
yet untouched by the gentrification that was turning the
crummiest areas of Manhattan into trendy playgrounds for
young money. Any minute now, the brunch places and
health clubs would start springing up and the old railroad
flats would get chopped up into tiny apartments where you
couldn't sneeze without hearing "God bless you" from your
neighbor. He realized that he needed help.

But who was there to help him? Bruno was out. He'd
trusted the guy and look what happened. Even if Farley'd
been the one who'd actually arrested Blitz, Bruno had to

have known about it. He'd probably *told* Farley to go and do it. So, who else was there?

Maldonado. Of course.

But Richie was sick. Alex couldn't ask him to get sicker by coming out on a night that was turning colder and might even snow before morning.

Still, Richie knew his way around graffiti. He'd want to help, especially if he knew Edie was in any danger. If Alex didn't ask him, he'd be royally pissed off. And there wasn't anybody else.

Alex left the storefront doorway and walked down to the corner of Broadway. As he walked, he kept looking back over his shoulder. If there was anyone inside the storefront, they could have been waiting for him to leave so they could get away, dragging Edie with them. There was a phone on the corner. Alex hoped it hadn't been vandalized. He dropped in a quarter and dialed Maldonado's number, all the while keeping an eye on the storefront in the middle of the block.

Richie sounded a lot better. "Alex," he said. "What's happening? I think I'll be operational by tomorrow."

"What about tonight?" Alex asked.

"Hang tight," Maldonado said, after Alex had told him the whole story, leaving out only the dull insistent ache left by Bruno's duplicity. "I'll be there in half an hour. Where's this storefront?"

Alex gave him the address, adding, "You can't miss it. The windows are all painted with graffiti."

As he hung up, he spotted Tasha walking briskly toward the storefront from the other end of the block. He ran toward her and reached her just as she was unlocking the door.

"Let's go in," he said. He unzipped his jacket and laid a and loosely on the grip of the revolver that was stuck into the waistband of his jeans. Just in case.

She whirled and stared at him, her brown eyes angry.

255

Then she nodded and opened the door. "She's not here, if that's what you're thinking."

"If you don't mind, I'd like to make sure."

Tasha nodded again and flipped on the lights. "I don't like it," she said. "I voted against it. But the rest of them, they're off their nuts. They wouldn't listen."

Alex prowled the big room, looking behind the derelict furniture and under a tarpaulin that covered nothing but an ancient dress mannequin, naked and missing an arm. Tasha followed him into the back room where the locked steel cabinet had been broken open and its shelves swept clean.

Tasha shrugged. "I couldn't stop them. I told them it was dumb and Blitz wouldn't like it. I told them he'd been busted before and he knew how to take care of himself, but they want to be heroes. If I were you, I'd be pretty careful. They think you set him up."

"Where is she?" Alex demanded. "Where did they take her?"

"I don't know," said Tasha. "I haven't seen any of them since they took off in Blitz's car this morning."

"How did you know she wasn't here?"

"Because I've been hanging out here all day up until half an hour ago. I got hungry. I was hoping you'd turn up. We got to do something. Graffiti's one thing, but I don't want those numbnuts to get busted for kidnapping. That's serious shit. They're not thinking about how serious it is."

"Do you think I set him up?" Alex asked.

"Doesn't matter. See, I been thinking it over, trying to think like a lawyer. I gotta start doing that sooner or later. And what a lawyer does is listen to a whole lot of lies and then tries to get what he wants out of it. So you could be lying your head off, but we both want the same thing. What I don't know is how we're gonna get it. You got any ideas?"

Alex shook his head. "A friend of mine is on his way

here. He may have some ideas. Maybe you've heard of him. He used to write ROBOT."

"ROBOT!" Tasha exclaimed. "Wow! He's famous! But he's been retired for years. He used to be up all over the place when I was a kid. How come he's a friend of yours?"

"We got to be buddies in the Academy."

"Robot? A cop?" Tasha was incredulous. "I can't believe it. Do you think he'd sign my book for me?"

"No doubt about it," said Alex.

She ran back into the big room where she took a sketchbook from a shelf and put it on the long table. "I can't believe it," she said again. "Robot's the only one of the old-time kings I haven't got in here. This is my lucky day." She sat down in one of the rickety chairs but couldn't stay put.

"I hope it's Edie's lucky day," said Alex, collapsing onto the nearest seat-sprung sofa. "Where do you think they would have taken her?"

"They're probably driving around with her until it's dark. That's what they said they were going to do before I told them they were crazy. After that, they wouldn't tell me anything else." Tasha prowled the room, from the front door to the table and back again. "When do you think he'll get here?"

"It's dark now," Alex pointed out.

"I mean later. Real dark."

"And then what?"

"How should I know?" She sat down next to him on the sofa and clutched one of his hands. "What's he like? Robot? Is he good-looking?"

"No. He's a little runty guy, looks like E.T. He's even got a finger that lights up."

"Ah, come on, Alex. Tell me. Do you think he'll like me?"

"Sure. But do me a favor. Don't come on to him. Ask

him to sign your book. Fine. But give the guy a break. He's got troubles, too."

Tasha stood up and shook out her corn rows. The beads tinkled and seemed to give her a flash of dignity. "What the fuck makes you think I'd be coming on to him? I got better things to do. So do you. So let's do it."

"Right," said Alex. "So try to put yourself in their minds. What would Juice think of? What would he think was a safe hiding place?"

"Juice was real uptight. He's scared he's gonna get the blame for bringing you into it in the first place. It was his idea. To hold her hostage until they let Blitz go."

"But where? Didn't he say anything about that?"

"I don't think he'd figured that out. That's the way he is. He'll do something and then try to figure out what to do next. He's not logical. He can't see that one thing always leads to something else."

"Not logical," Alex repeated. And Bruno's words came back to him. "A guy like this, a random murderer who comes out of nowhere and kills for what seems to be no logical reason, nine times out of ten he's just begging to be caught." Was this Juice's signpost? Had he kidnapped Edie so that he'd be caught? But Juice was only a kid, Paulie's age. Still, he was a kid with a gun. And maybe this wasn't the first time he'd had one. "Tell me some more about Juice," he said. "All I know is that he and my brother were writing partners."

Tasha nodded. "They were real tight."

"Did they ever get mad at each other?"

"Oh, sometimes. But it was always over in a day or so. Your brother was such a sweet guy, nobody could stay mad at him for long. But he could be a real nutcake about some things."

"Like what?"

"Well, he hated it when Juice would go over one of his

258

pieces. Juice used to do it just to see how far he could go. Then when Dreemz would get mad, Juice would apologize all over the place and promise never to do it again. But he always did. He said he couldn't stand the way Dreemz was always so laid back."

"Did my brother ever do it to him?"

"What? Go over one of his pieces? Yeah, I think he did once. Not too long ago. Just to show him he could if he wanted to."

"What happened?"

"Nothing, I guess. I don't really know."

"What about Mello?"

"What about him?"

"Did he ever have a fight with Juice?"

"Wait a minute." She flung his hand away and went back to the table. "I don't think I like what you're getting at. Juice isn't the sniper."

"You're sure of that?"

"Sure I'm sure." Tasha opened her sketchbook and started turning the pages. "I've got Dondi in here, and Futura 2000, and all the kings. Blade and Dolores. I've even got Caine, but I didn't get that in person. Caine's been dead a long time. I had to buy it. I paid fifteen dollars for it. You're sure Robot's coming?"

"He'll be here. Who broke into the cabinet back there? Whose idea was that?"

Tasha turned pages in her sketchbook. "I even have an original Taki 183. You know how hard it is to get an original Taki?"

Alex got up from the sofa and walked over to Tasha. He took the book away from her and closed it. "I don't know, and I don't care. All I care about is first, finding Edie, and second finding who killed my brother. If Juice is the guy for both, it makes my life easier. Do you have any idea how much I don't care whose autograph you have in your album?" He slammed the book down on the table.

"I guess I do now," said Tasha. "He might be thinking of taking her to one of the yards. But it's too early for that. The trains are still running rush hour. He'd wait until they finish laying up for the night."

"What time is that?"

"Eleven, twelve o'clock. Will you stop asking me questions? I don't feel good about telling you all this."

"You'll feel a lot worse if anything happens to her."

Tasha slumped into a chair and put her head down on the table, cradling it in her arms.

"Does Juice have a favorite yard?"

No answer.

"Do any of the yards have good hiding places?"

Silence.

"Who was with him in the car?"

Tasha raised her head and groped in a pocket for a tissue. Her face was wet with tears. "Leave me alone," she sobbed.

There was a soft rapping at the door.

"Oh, shit!" she cried. "He's here. And look at me. Don't let him in yet."

Alex ran to the door and opened it. Maldonado slipped into the room, shivering. "Man, it's cold out there. Some night you picked. What's this place?"

"It's a clubhouse for graffiti writers," Alex told him in a low voice. "One of them's here. She's clammed up on me, but she's a fan of Robot, so maybe you can do something with her."

Maldonado peered down the long room, taking in the murals on the wall, but deliberately ignoring Tasha. "Oh, man!" he said loudly. "This is great. I wish we had a place like this when I was writing." He moved slowly along, stopping before each mural to examine it and comment on it.

Alex followed him, keeping an eye on Tasha. She sat with her back to them, doing something to her face.

When Maldonado reached the long table at the back of the room, he slid casually into a chair across from Tasha and said, "Hi. What do you write?"

"Tasha," she mumbled. "Heart with wings."

"I've seen you up," he said. "You've got good style, but you need to quit biting Seen. It's time for you to develop your own style. Is that your mural over there?" He nodded toward a picture of Howard the Duck on the end wall. "It's not bad. But it looks like Seen on an off day."

"Seen's great," said Tasha.

"I know he is," said Maldonado, "but you don't catch him copying anybody. That's what makes him great. What's going down here, Tasha?"

"Would you sign my book?" she asked.

"Let's do a little business first, Tasha. This is the real world we're talking about. I hear your friends did something stupid. Let's talk about that."

"I been talking about it. I don't want to talk about it anymore."

"I know," said Maldonado. "You feel like a fink. But think about how you'll feel if your friends do something really stupid to this lady, who happens to be a friend of mine, and they wind up in Attica."

"They won't wind up in Attica. They're too young."

"They'll get there sooner or later if you don't tell us what we need to know. Do you want to be responsible for that?"

"If I tell you, will you get Blitz out of jail?"

Maldonado looked at Alex.

"I'll make a phone call," Alex said. "That's all I can promise."

"And will you sign my book?" she asked Maldonado.

"Give it here."

She passed the book across the table. Maldonado took it

and held it closed in front of him. "Okay. Now give," he said.

Tasha held her head in both hands and stared down at the table as she spoke. "There's an old subway car in the 241st Street Yard. It's been there forever, off on one of the sidings. We go there a lot and just hang out. Nobody ever bothers us there. I heard Juice say they could maybe take her there tonight. But I don't know where they are now and he might think of some other place."

"I know the car," said Maldonado softly. "I used to hang out there myself. It says World's Fair on the front."

"That one," Tasha agreed. "It's real old."

"Who's in on it besides Juice?" Alex asked.

"Temper, he wouldn't miss a scene like this, Sham, and Kraze with his camera. Big-1 said it was getting too whacked out for him so he went home. I should have done the same."

"Did they all have guns?"

"You saw the closet in there. They cleaned it out. Blitz'll kill them when he hears about that. He don't like nobody messing with his equipment. Not even Juice."

"You didn't tell me about guns," Maldonado said to Alex. "What are we up against?"

"A couple of rifles, four or five hand guns, and four kids who think they're Sylvester Stallone."

"And who do we think we are? Dirty Harry?"

Alex pulled the revolver out of his jeans and laid it on the table. Maldonado grinned and pulled a Colt Combat Commander out of his coat pocket. "A relic of my misspent youth and my Uncle Hector's time in 'Nam," he said. "I thought we might run into something like this."

Tasha stared wide-eyed at the guns. "You're crazy, too," she muttered.

"Got a marker?" Maldonado asked. "I'll sign your book now."

Before they left the storefront, Alex tried to reach Bruno but the line was always busy. When it finally rang through a little before nine o'clock, no one answered. Despite his promise to Tasha, Alex was relieved. He didn't want to talk to Bruno, not tonight, not tomorrow, not ever again. Once Edie was safe, he'd think about whether or not he wanted to continue with his police training. He realized he'd been on the brink of setting Bruno up as some kind of ideal, some-one to pattern himself after. The trouble with ideals is that sooner or later they get smashed. He considered himself lucky that this one got smashed before it really had a chance to mean a hell of a lot.

Impatiently, he watched Maldonado draw his ROBOT tag in Tasha's book. Richie drew slowly and carefully, mut-tering about how out of practice he was. Tasha sat by his side, avidly following every stroke of his marking pen. Alex paced the room, plagued by visions of Edie lying bound and gagged on the floor of Blitz's car or, worse yet, in the trunk. If Bruno had answered the phone, he could have given him a complete description of the car, an old gray and white Impala with a sun roof and an I LOVE NEW YORK bumper sticker, and its license number. But would he have? It would have been the correct thing to do, and he could still do it simply by calling 911 and reporting a kidnapping. But what would happen to Edie if a patrol unit spotted the car and chased it down? No, better to do it this way. Just the two of them. And if Juice had the same respect for Robot that Tasha'd shown, it might be a way to get him to listen to them and let Edie go.

When Richie finally finished his piece, Tasha said to Alex, "One thing I didn't tell you. Juice said that even if they let Blitz go, he's gonna be coming after you. And that's all I've got to say. I'm going home now. No more graffiti for me. I've got better things to do with my life."

"Good for you," said Maldonado.

25

They rode the No. 2 train to the end of the line, 241st Street in the Bronx. Their footsteps echoed as they ran down the steel stairway from the elevated platform. The streets below were dark and deserted. Here and there, dirty puddles of melted snow had frozen into black ice. The cyclone fence that surrounded the yard lay a block away.

They walked along Furman Avenue where a long, low brick building marked the western boundary of the yard. Across the street, spindly naked trees and small shingled houses occupied the space between the yard and the elevated tracks on White Plains Road. Maldonado led the way along the quiet street.

"I haven't been here in years," he said. "There's a gate along here. Sometimes they forget to lock it."

Alex examined the cars parked along the street, but none was a gray and white Impala. When they reached the end of the building, a garage with offices of some sort, the fence continued and a view of the yard opened up before them. Alex gazed through the network of wires at an immense panorama of subway cars laid up for the night. He and Maldonado stood on a slight rise, looking down at the tracks. Widely spaced across the yard, flaring banks of mercury vapor lamps were set on tall stanchions, throwing deep shadows between the rows of trains while bathing their roofs in brightness. The yard extended southward as far as he could see, but toward the east it ended abruptly in a long row of workshops with slanted skylit roofs at the foot of a hill much higher than the rise on which they stood. At the extreme northern edge stood a tall square watchtower with lighted windows.

"They didn't forget," said Maldonado, tugging at the padlock that secured the double gate in the cyclone fence, "but I think maybe I can get this open. If not, we'll have to find a hole in the fence. There's always a hole in the fence. As fast as the workbums fix them, the writers make new ones." He pulled out a ring of keys and began trying them one after another on the lock. "Another relic of my glorious past," he said. "I've even got a key that unlocks the train doors. Every graffiti writer tries to get one of those. There." The lock sprang open, and Maldonado pushed the gate ajar.

Alex followed him into the yard and across a stretch of cracked pavement that ended at a steep incline leading down to the tracks below. They scrambled down the slope and into an area of darkness.

"So far, so good," breathed Maldonado. "Do you see anybody?"

"Not a soul," said Alex. "What about that watchtower? There must be somebody in there."

"Yeah. But they won't come out unless they have to. It's nice and cosy in there, and the yard's cold and dark. Let's go."

Walking softly, they skirted the tracks, keeping always in the shadows close to the base of the weedy, garbage-strewn slope.

"As I recall," Maldonado murmured, "that old World's Fair car is about a quarter of a mile down this way."

"How big is this yard?" Alex asked.

"It's one of the biggest. You say the sniper's been active here?"

"That's what a couple of the writers claim."

"Well, we'll have to keep an eye peeled for him, too. Watch out. There's a dead rat here. Frozen stiff."

Alex stepped over the rigid corpse and thought of Beatty. If he'd been with them, he'd be yelling about how he was going to come down with bubonic plague. The yard was eerie enough without imagining killer germs just waiting around to be inhaled. The silence was the worst thing about it. All Alex could hear was their own footsteps and the distant sound of traffic, humming along but muffled as if all the cars in New York City had been shifted to another plane of existence, right next door but invisible and barely within hearing distance. The long lines of subway cars, hundreds of them, were cold and silent in the night. Alex caught himself more than once looking over his shoulder, expecting to see the hulking red-eyed monster that Mello had described.

When Maldonado put a hand out and touched him, he sucked in a loud breath and jerked to a halt.

"Easy," said Maldonado. "We're getting close."

They stood in the shadows and Alex peered in the direction of Maldonado's pointing finger. At first, he could see nothing but a darker shadow. But then, as he stared, he began to make out glimmers of metal and the jagged edges of broken glass.

"That's it," Maldonado whispered. "It's been there ever since I can remember. It's a wreck inside and out, probably worse now than it was four years ago. They ought to put it out of its misery, melt it down for scrap. But as long as it's here, the kids are gonna use it. Nobody else does."

"It looks deserted," said Alex. "Maybe they're not here yet. Maybe they're not coming. Tasha could have been lying just to send us on a wild-goose chase. Or Juice could have changed his mind. They could have Edie halfway to Canada by now."

"Now, why would they do that?" said Maldonado. "Taking her out of the city wouldn't help their cause one bit. They probably don't even know where Canada is. Let's check it out."

They crept closer to the abandoned subway car. The smell of the yard, old and cold and metallic, filled Alex's nostrils and sent his mind reeling back to the night, only five nights before, that Paulie had gone out to paint his last piece. It was in a different yard, a smaller one, but from what he'd seen from Blitz's car last night, all the yards were pretty much the same, differing only in size. Tracks and trains, and the shadow of the sniper that now hung over all of them. What had Paulie seen that night? Why couldn't he have gotten away with nothing more than an injury as Mello had?

He looked back the way they had come and saw a fleeting movement on the hillside behind them. He tapped Maldonado's shoulder and pointed.

"What is it?" Maldonado whispered.

"I don't know. I thought I saw something."

They waited, watching, but there was nothing to see.

"It gets you sometimes," said Maldonado. "You start imagining things."

When they turned back to the subway car, now only forty or fifty feet away, they both saw a furtive flash of light through the window of the end door. It flared and was gone before they could be sure it had happened.

"Am I imagining things now?" Alex whispered.

"No. I saw it, too. Somebody's in there. That was a

flashlight or somebody lighting a cigarette. Quiet now. No more talking." Maldonado took a few cautious steps.

"Wait," said Alex. "What's our plan? If Edie's in there, I don't want any shooting."

"Let me go first," said Maldonado. "I can come on to them like just another writer. See what I can find out. You wait here."

"Richie, I can't wait here. I've got to know whether she's there or not. If she's not there, we've got to start all over again. Fast."

"I hear you. Okay. Come with me, but stay behind, out of sight. Or better yet, get under the train where they can't see you."

They walked the last few feet hunched over, keeping to the shadows as far as they could, then running across the open space between the hill and the car. As soon as they reached the car, Alex rolled under it. The crunch of broken glass sounded in his ears as loudly as a volley of machine gun fire. When he peered out from under the car, Maldonado had disappeared.

He waited for what seemed to be an hour, but he knew it was scarcely a minute. In that minute, in the darkness under the car, he listened for voices, footsteps, cries, anything that would bring him news of Edie's whereabouts. There was nothing. He wished he'd brought a bullhorn, tear gas, an army. He cursed Bruno for having let this happen, and himself for having been so stupidly trusting. When he could stand it no longer, he crawled out from under the car and stood up.

The car loomed above him. It was, for him, a new perspective. He'd seen plenty of subway cars, thousands of them, every day of his life, but he'd never before stood beside their giant wheels and realized the size and power and sheer weight of the brutes. Sure, there were bigger things on earth, but this was one of the things that had killed his brother. And now it was a prison for Edie. Even though it was an old dead car that would never roll again, he hated it.

But there wasn't time to stand around, doing nothing but hating a subway car. Where was Maldonado?

He crept along the side of the car. The windows were too far above his head for him to see through without scaling the sheer metal and somehow clinging to it. When he reached the end of the car, he climbed up onto the narrow platform and edged close to the window panel in the door. He peered cautiously through the opening. Although there was no glass between him and the interior of the car, he could see nothing in the darkness.

But he could smell. The distinctive odor of cigarette smoke. Juice smoked Kools. None of the other graffiti writers smoked, as far as he knew, unless it was funny cigarettes when they were hanging loose. And he could hear. A faint whispering that seemed to come all the way from the other end of the car. His impulse was to shove open the door and walk in, demanding Edie's freedom at gunpoint. He drew the revolver and gripped the handle of the door.

But then he remembered a lecture he'd attended on hostage negotiation. "Once you start the negotiation," the expert had said, "don't pull any surprises. You could ruin the whole thing and get the hostages killed."

Okay! But he'd feel a whole lot better if only he could know for sure that Edie was in there and that Maldonado was in control. He flattened himself beside the door, listening for just a single word that would tell him she was safe.

The shot, coming from somewhere in the immense yard, pinged off the metal next to his head. In the first split-second, he didn't realize what it was. Then, with the blast echoing in his ears, he knew. He crouched on the platform and stared out across the yard.

269

From inside the car, an uproar of angry voices and pounding footsteps erupted, stampeding down the length of the car. As the door was flung open, he leaped to the ground and hunkered down under the platform.

"What the fuck!" sounded above his head. He recognized the voice. Juice. "It's the blue balls! They're doing it to us! I'm gonna kill me a cop tonight! Starting with her!"

"Put the gun down." That was Maldonado. "Try to be smart, even if it hurts. Get back inside and lie on the floor. All of you. Get down and stay down."

Alex couldn't see what was happening above his head, but he could see out over the yard. The derelict car was shunted off on a siding some distance from the main tracks and at an angle to them. He was looking at the end cars of the nearest rows of trains, and he saw a shadowy figure slip out from between one row and dodge into the next.

"Who are you anyway?" Juice's voice sounded panicky. "You say you're Robot, but if you're retired from writing, what are you doing here? I think you're a cop, too."

Before Maldonado could answer, another shot rang out shattering one of the few remaining windows in the car.

"Oh, shit!" Juice cried, and the door slammed shut.

Alex slithered out from under the platform. The sniper was out there, just asking to be hunted down. But there was no way he could take off into the yard and leave Edie and Maldonado to cope with a bunch of panicky kids with nervous guns. He swung himself back up onto the platform and eased the door open.

"Juice," he whispered into the darkness, "listen to me. This is Alex. And that's the sniper out there. I'm going after him. Are you with me?"

Another shot hit the side of the car, inches away from Alex's shoulder. He walked into the darkness and closed the door behind him.

270

"No!" Juice screamed from the other end of the car. "You tell them cop friends of yours to bug off or I'm gonna blow your old lady away."

"Are you gonna let him get away, Juice?" Alex walked slowly down the length of the car, his eyes growing accustomed to the gloom. "Didn't you tell me you wanted to cut your tag into his guts? I think you're too chicken to go out there and face him like a man."

"Too right!" said another voice. "That's me. Call me chicken, but I ain't going out there. And I ain't up for shooting no lady cops neither. This is me, Temper, and I surrender." The boy came scampering down the car and threw himself at Alex's feet.

"Where's your gun?" Alex asked him.

"I give it to Robot already. I never wanted it in the first place, only Juice, he made me take it."

"Me, too. Me, too."

Two more of the grafitti writers came running down the car to stand behind Alex. Sham and Kraze.

"That's right," said Maldonado. "I've got all the guns except for Juice's. He doesn't seem to understand the right way to do things."

Alex could see that Maldonado was standing close to the opposite end of the car with his own gun trained on the shadows in the corner.

"Is Edie there?" Alex asked. "Is she okay?"

"She's here," Juice answered. "And she knows better than to make a move or a sound, unless I say it's okay. Tell them, bitch. Tell them what's sticking in your ear."

"It's a gun, Alex." Edie's voice was loud and clear. Not even a little bit edgy. She could have been answering a question in class. "From what I can tell, it's a nine millimeter automatic. And I think he's got another one in his pocket. He's pretty shaky. I doubt if he'd be much good against a sniper."

"Shut up!" Juice howled. "I'm just as good as any cop."

"Prove it," said Maldonado. "We're wasting time here. The guy could be halfway home by now."

Alex walked toward the end of the car, leaving the three graffiti writers huddled on the floor behind him. "Listen to me, Juice," he said. "I'll make a deal with you."

"No deals!" Juice shouted, but his voice wavered.

"Let her go, and we'll forget about this whole kidnapping thing." Alex could see Edie's white face glimmering in the dark corner of the car. She was sitting on the floor with her legs straight in front of her and her arms behind her back. "Is that all right with you, Edie?"

"Suits me. I hate to think of a scared young kid pulling twenty-five to life. Can you imagine what those first few years would be like? Nothing they like better in prison than fresh young meat."

"Stop it! Stop it!" Juice screamed. "I know what you're trying to do."

"Of course, if he lives through that," said Maldonado, "he can always look forward to getting out someday, when he's an old man. But not if he puts so much as a scratch on her. There's just no way out for him then."

"You don't scare me," said Juice. "But I'm deciding now. Okay. I've decided. Kidnapping is dumb boring shit. Too much sitting around keeping an eye on the prize. Not that she's such a prize. She's got a big mouth and she's uglier than a bulldog. You can have her." Juice came up out of the dark corner, his gun dangling loosely at his side.

Alex ran the rest of the way down the car and snatched the gun out of Juice's hand. "I ought to knock you into the middle of next week, you stupid shithead."

"Alex, Alex," said Edie laughing weakly. "Leave him

alone and get these ropes off me. My hands and feet are falling off."

Leaving Maldonado to search Juice for more weapons, Alex knelt beside Edie and cut through the ropes with his pocketknife. "Are you okay? Are you really okay? Because if you're not, I'll take it out of him, one way or the other."

"I'm really okay," Edie assured him, "as soon as I get some feeling back. Help me stand up, and then I'll be fine."

While Edie stomped around and shook her hands in the air to get the circulation going, Temper crept up to Alex and whispered, "Us three want to go home. How we gonna do that?"

"Just go," said Alex impatiently. "Nobody's stopping you."

"Only him out there." Temper nodded toward the immense yard outside the broken windows of the subway car. "What you gonna do about him?"

"He's probably gone by now. Have you ever heard of him sticking around after he's fired off a few shots?"

"No. But I don't want to find out different in person. Ain't you a cop? And ain't cops supposed to make things safe for us citizens?"

"Oh, that's cute. That's real cute," said Alex. "After the stunt you pulled, you expect me to make the world safe for you."

"I surrendered, didn't I?" Temper whined. "It wasn't my idea."

"He's right, Alex," said Maldonado. "We ought to get out there and check the place out."

"I know, I know. And I'm going. Me. Alone. You and Edie stay here and keep an eye on these young hoods. I don't want any of them romping around the yard while I'm out there. I might shoot one of them by mistake."

When Maldonado started to object, Edie interrupted.

"Let him go, Richie. Otherwise, he'll argue the point all night." She turned to Alex, and said, "It's your show. But we'll be covering you from the windows here. If you need us, yell. And if we see anything, anything at all, we're coming out. Is that clear?"

"Big mouth," Juice muttered from the corner where he sat slumped against the wall. "I wouldn't go out there if you paid me to. All we have to do is stay here until morning. He'll be gone by then. Cops are born stupid."

"Yeah, Juice," said Edie, "I think you're right. Why else would we take the crap we do from guys like you? Good luck, Alex. And be careful. I've got a few things to say to you when this is all over."

Alex gave her a fleeting smile, then turned and ran to the other end of the car where he cautiously let himself out the door and dropped to the gravel. He crouched under the platform for a few moments, scanning the yard. Then he ran toward the tracks and the rows of trains where he'd last seen the furtive figure slip into the shadows.

With his gun sweating in his bare hand, he reached the first of the long line of tracks. Instinctively, he realized that the way to stay alive was to keep the other guy guessing. When he dove into the darkness between the rows of trains where he'd seen the sniper disappear, he ricocheted haphazardly between the cars on either side. After he'd passed three or four of the silent subway cars, he stopped and tucked himself into the space between two of them and listened.

All quiet. Sure, why not? No reason for the guy to stick around. He'd probably done all the shooting he was going to do for tonight. And the graffiti writers were right about one thing. He was a lousy shot. Three misses.

Remembering Mello's no-doubt embellished tale of his own encounter, Alex glanced up and examined the roofs of the nearest cars. They glowed in the night, reflecting the light of the worklamps, but there was no gigantic figure on top of them. He was relieved to think that Juice had been in the World's Fair car when the shots were fired, and Blitz was safely in jail. He didn't want the sniper to be either one of them. They'd claimed to be Paulie's friends. It would have been horrible if he'd been killed by someone he considered a friend.

But who was it then? And why? The why bothered him more than the who. They'd find out the who sooner or later. He hoped the guy was still in the yard so he could find out tonight, no thanks to Frank Bruno. He shifted the gun to his left hand and wiped his right palm on the seat of his jeans. Crazy how his hand could be sweating so much when the air around him was freezing every other part of his body. Where the fuck was the bastard?

The eerie silence of the yard was suddenly shattered by the shrilling of police whistles and wild shouts. Alex couldn't make out what the voices were shouting; it sounded like howling gibberish to him. But the noise was coming closer. Damn! If the sniper was anywhere around, they'd scare him away and ruin the whole thing.

A voice out of the hubbub shouted, "Alex! Take cover! He's on top of the trains! We're coming!" It was Edie. But what did she think she was doing? Leading the Charge of the Light Brigade? They were supposed to stay put, out of the way and here they were, rushing into the yard with the graffiti writers blowing those damned police whistles that Blitz had handed out. If Edie didn't know better, Maldonado should.

He couldn't see where they were but he heard them running across the gravel and the unmistakable sound of a subway door opening and closing. Then everything went quiet again.

He slithered out from between the cars and looked up and down the long aisle between the trains. Nothing. But the shouts and whistles would have warned him. He'd be lying low, or he might try to make a break for it. If he tried to get away, he'd have to head for the fence. From the ground, Alex couldn't see the fence. But from the top of a car, he'd be able to see in all directions. He'd also be on view under the lights from every corner of the yard. But so would the sniper if he was up there.

Swiftly, he clambered up the end of one of the cars and hauled himself onto its roof. Lying flat on his stomach, he scanned the yard, first in the direction of the gate where he and Maldonado had entered, then in all directions, without seeing a sign of life. Lights blazed in the windows of the distant watchtower, but if there were guards in there, they might as well be asleep. There was no alarm, no sign that the gunshots or the police whistles had roused them. Alex stood up.

He knew he was making a target of himself, but if that was the only way to draw the guy's fire and find out where he was, it was worth the risk. He stood on top of the subway car and waited for a shot to ring out. But no shot came.

Instead, at the other end of the car on which he was standing, like a black sun rising out of a steely sea, a dark shape appeared. He watched it rise, silhouetted in the light from the worklamps, and grow from an amorphous heaving lump to the standing figure of a man. A big man, holding a rifle. Mello's description hadn't been far wrong. Alex couldn't make out the face, couldn't tell if the eyes were blazing red, but he didn't need to know that to be absolutely certain he was confronting the graffiti sniper across the roof of a subway car in a yard in the Bronx, alone.

He aimed his revolver in a two-handed grip, steadied himself, and shouted, "You're under arrest! Drop the gun!"

The man just stood there, the rifle hanging loosely at his side. Alex could see that he wore a bulky dark coat and a close-fitting black hat pulled down low over his face, and that his broad shoulders seemed to slump with weariness. He didn't drop the gun.

Alex repeated his command and began to walk toward the sniper. If it was Blitz . . . he was about the right size . . . if Blitz had somehow gotten out of jail and come here to . . . but he couldn't be sure . . . he couldn't see the man's face. And he still couldn't believe that Blitz was the sniper. He'd grown to like the overgrown hulk; he liked the way he tried to protect the younger writers while still allowing them the freedom to make their own mistakes. And yet, there was something familiar about the shape. He moved closer, trying to get a look at the face.

The man standing at the other end of the car uttered a sound, part desperate sigh, part savage growl, and slowly, deliberately, raised the rifle to firing position.

Alex stopped and tightened his grip on the revolver. Both of his hands were now slippery with sweat, but his body was chilled and shivering, whether from the freezing night air or from an icy core of dread deep within, he couldn't tell. He'd never killed a man, never even fired a gun except on the practice range, but now, if he wanted to live, he'd have to do it. His finger tightened on the trigger, but still he didn't shoot.

"You won't get away!" he shouted. "Give up now or I'll fire!"

The man might have been carved from stone. The rifle never wavered. Alex stared at the barrel aimed implacably at his head. His thoughts raced wildly. Should he shoot first, and try to disable the guy? Should he wait for the sniper to shoot first, and possibly miss, to justify his own shots? Should he jump down from the train and try to fire from cover? What would Bruno do?

Alex took two steps forward. The sniper stood his ground and uttered a hoarse cry, not a word but a warning sound. His voice sounded inhuman, like that of a wounded animal. Alex moved forward again, finger tight on the trigger. The man tensed.

Two distinct shots rang out, one after the other. Alex dropped to the roof of the car and cradled his head in his arms. When he looked up, the man had disappeared. Below, the shouts and whistles started up again, and the sound of many running feet made a confusion of noise. Edie's voice called out above it all, "Alex! Where are you? Are you all right?"

Alex consulted his body. Two shots, but apparently neither one had hit him. He found no blood, not even a hint of numbness that might turn out to be a wound. His knees ached from the hard landing, but that seemed to be all. He crawled to the edge of the roof and looked over. The first thing he saw was Edie standing there, hands on hips, looking official in her blues, her face, naked with concern for him, gleaming whitely in the glare of several high-powered flashlights.

"Can you come down by yourself?" she choked, close to tears. "Do you want some help?"

Maldonado stood beside her, grinning. "We got him, old buddy!" he exulted. "Well, not us exactly. But why didn't you tell me you had practically the whole NYPD staked out in the yard?"

"What!" Alex stared into the blinding flashlight beams and tried to see beyond them. There was a dense knot of intense activity surrounding an open space on the ground. A familiar figure broke out of the crowd and walked over to stand beside Edie and Maldonado. Frank Bruno, hatless and in a heavy leather jacket, gazed sorrowfully up at him.

"Come on down, son," he said. "There's something here that you should see."

Alex swung himself over the side of the car and dropped to the ground. He faced Bruno angrily and said, "I suppose I should be glad you're here, but it didn't have to happen this way at all. Edie could have been hurt."

"Alex, cool it," Edie chided. "I'm okay. And I got what I wanted, didn't I? A piece of the action."

"I don't blame you for being mad," said Bruno. "And you're probably going to be a lot madder. I haven't been completely straight with you. But before we get into that, come and take a good look at the graffiti sniper." Bruno took Alex's arm and began walking him toward the knot of men surrounding the open space on the ground. "You were pretty courageous to stand up to him like that. We would have got him anyway, but you grabbed his attention long enough for us to get into position. Did you know who he was when you went after him?"

"Blitz?" Alex asked. "I can't believe it."

"Somebody call my name?" said a deep voice nearby. "I didn't get to play decoy because some turkey beat me to it. But I kind of like this police action. Could be I'll sign up for some more." Blitz came out of the shadows and took Alex's other arm. "Let's go take a look at the gunslinger."

The knot of police officers parted at a word from Bruno. The man lay prone on the gravel, not moving. Alex stood at his feet, large feet in workingman's boots, and let his eyes travel up the splayed legs to the back of the heavy wool coat. One small hole showed where the bullet had entered.

"He got off a shot before I could fire. I'm glad he missed. I was sure you were a dead one."

Alex looked up. Larry Farley was standing at the head of the fallen sniper. Uncharacteristically, he seemed subdued and uneasy.

The man on the ground groaned and tried to raise himself on his hands. One of the officers knelt beside him and said, "Take it easy, sport. The medics'll be here any minute."

"Can you roll him over?" Bruno asked.

"If you really want me to," said the officer. "I don't think it'll hurt him any more than he is already."

"Do it," said Bruno.

The officer and several others gathered around to lift the man and turn him onto his back.

Alex looked questioningly into Bruno's face. There was something there he didn't understand. There was a whole lot he didn't understand, but why was Bruno, and Farley, for that matter, looking so sad? They ought to be jumping for joy that the sniper'd been stopped.

"Now look again," said Bruno, keeping his hand on Alex's arm.

Alex looked again at the sniper, his eyes drawn first to the terrible exit wound in the man's chest. The whole front of his coat was a bloody tattered mess with bits of flesh and bone caught in the frayed strands of cloth. Although the man was still breathing, he wouldn't be for long with a wound like that. Farley could certainly be proud of his marksmanship.

A sound came from the sniper's mouth, a weak echo of the animal growls he'd directed at Alex on top of the train. Alex looked at the man's face for the first time and felt his legs buckle beneath him. If Bruno and Blitz had not been holding his arms, he would have fallen.

"Easy, son," said Bruno. "There was no way I could have prepared you for this. Now you understand."

Alex gaped. He couldn't take his eyes off the sniper's face, a face he knew as well as his own. "Pop!" he whispered. Then he turned to Bruno. "How long have you known?"

"Long enough. I started getting the idea when that anonymous call came through. The voice sounded vaguely familiar even though he tried to disguise it. And he was trying to pin it on you. That didn't smell right to me. The phone company was very helpful. He didn't even bother to use a public phone. We've been trailing him ever since Mello got shot."

"Why didn't you tell me?" Alex demanded.

Bruno shrugged. "I couldn't take the chance. You might have done something crazy."

"But why?" Alex pleaded distractedly. "Why, why, why?"

"Only he knows that," said Bruno. "Maybe he'll live long enough to tell us."

Alex broke away and ran to kneel by Theo's side. He gazed down into the pallid face on which lines of disappointment and impotent rage had been deeply etched. Theo's eyes were closed, but his lips hung open and a trickle of blood inched slowly down his chin. "Pop," he whispered. "Can you talk to me?"

Theo's lips closed, then fell apart again.

"Pop," Alex persisted. "Did you know it was me up there on top of the train? Did you know it was Paulie?"

Theo's eyes flickered open and he smiled. "Alex? That you?" The words bubbled and bled from his lips.

"It's me, Pop. Tell me. I have to know."

"It's over, isn't it, Alex? I won't have to do it anymore." Theo gasped and strained for a breath. "Oh, God, it hurts."

"Tell me about Paulie. Why did you do it? Why, Pop? Tell me something I can tell Ma."

"Don't tell your mother." Theo's eyes widened, and he sounded more like his old domineering self. "I don't want her to know anything about this."

"Okay, Pop. I won't tell her." It was an easy lie. He had to get some answers.

Farley bent over him and said. "Better leave him alone.

The medics are here. Maybe they can do something to save him. You can talk later."

"You shot him," Alex blurted. "You shot to kill and you did a good job. Thanks a lot. Now, go away and leave us alone."

"Better him than you," said Farley, but he backed off and signaled the men with the stretcher to wait.

Alex hunched over Theo as if he could protect him from the ring of curious eyes that surrounded them. Theo, staring at the sky, struggled to speak.

"Yeah, Pop," Alex urged him. "I'm here. I'm listening."

"I never mean to hurt Paulie. I didn't even know it was him until after. All I ever wanted was for him to shape up. It was an accident. It wasn't my fault." Theo sighed and closed his eyes.

Alex waited. He took Theo's hand and held it. It was like holding the cold hand of a corpse.

Theo took a deep shuddering breath and spoke again. His voice was barely a whisper. Alex had to lean closer to hear what he said.

"The way he looked at me, Alex. I'll never forget that. My own son looking at me with such contempt. I wanted to help him, but he wouldn't let me. He cursed me and he crawled away and hid under a train. I got mad. I went away and left him there. I didn't think he was hurt that bad. I hadn't hit any of the other ones. I just wanted to scare them. I wanted to scare Paulie out of doing that graffiti, but I never wanted to hurt anybody. Am I dying, Alex? I don't want to die."

"No, Pop. We're just waiting until you're ready. Then we'll take you to the hospital."

"I hate hospitals. Tell your mother . . . tell your mother I got hit by a car."

Alex felt someone kneel beside him. He didn't look away

from Theo's face, but he knew that Edie was there. She put an arm around his shoulder, and her warmth reached and spread through him.

Theo gave a racking cough that shook his whole body. When the spasm was over, he lay gasping. But still he tried to talk, each word an effort. "I wanted to stop," he said, "but I couldn't. After Paulie was dead it was like I had to keep on and on. I drove all over the place, trying to stay away from it. But I kept winding up back at one of the yards. This one or Coney Island, back and forth, back and forth. I never went back to the place where Paulie . . ." His voice broke off and he let out one of those animal sounds.

Alex shuddered to hear it. Theo had gone off the deep end long before any of this had happened, and none of them had noticed. What had driven him? It couldn't have been simply Paulie's graffiti-writing. That might have been the thing he focused his fury on, but the fury was there already waiting to be let loose. There were so many things that had made Theo angry. His whole life was an excuse for the rage he could do nothing about. Alex wondered if it all had something to do with the secret of his own birth.

Theo clutched at Alex's hand. "Where's my gun?" he asked. "You thought you hid it on me, but you weren't so smart. I found it. Give it to me."

"No, Pop. No more guns. You don't need it anymore."

"Yeah. You're right. I knew it was you up there. I heard that girl call your name. I wanted to shoot you, but I couldn't. Why should you live when Paulie's dead? And you're not even my kid. You didn't know that, did you, wiseguy? Why should anybody's kid live when my kid is dead? But I lost my nerve. I couldn't do it. I shot up at the sky. Maybe I shot God. I hope I killed the bastard for all the good He's ever done for me. So that's the end of the story.

283

Get lost now. I don't want to talk to you anymore." He closed his eyes, and his breathing became slow and shallow.

Alex stood up and backed away. Edie went with him, holding his hand. He couldn't bear to look at her. He watched a team of paramedics move swiftly into action. Theo, as they lifted him onto the stretcher, seemed shrunken and pitiful, no longer the loud, bullying tyrant Alex had known all his life. He tried to make himself believe that if Farley hadn't shot first, they might be carrying him out of the yard instead of Theo, but he couldn't make it work that way. Not after what Theo had told him. All he could do was feel sorry. Revenge wasn't so sweet after all. It left him empty and sad, with no idea of what to do next.

He turned away from the scene and spotted Blitz talking to the four graffiti writers, who looked nervous and unhappy. Blitz motioned Alex closer and called out, "What say, brother of Dreemz? We turn them in or what?"

"Hey!" Juice protested. "We made a deal. Ask him."

"You, maybe," said Blitz, "but not me. I don't like what you turkeys did. You got some heavy explaining to do."

"He's right," said Alex, "but it's really up to Edie. She's the one they kidnapped."

Edie walked up to the four and gazed at them one by one. Then she turned to Blitz. "They're a pretty sorry sight," she said.

"Not sorry enough," said Blitz. "They're lucky they didn't get themselves killed."

"Please, lady," Juice pleaded. "We didn't hurt you none. We only wanted to get Blitz out of jail."

"I wasn't in jail," said Blitz.

"But I saw you get busted," said Juice. "I saw the cops take you away. I was hanging out across the street from your place, and I watched the whole thing."

"Yeah," said Temper. "He come and he tell us we got to

get you out. He say, 'They got one of us so we get one of them. Make a trade.'"

"Dumb," said Blitz, shaking his head. "You guys are just plain dumb. Did you think I'd just let myself get arrested like that? I went with them because I wanted to. It was supposed to be a decoy and I didn't want you kids messing things up."

"They may have been dumb," said Edie, "but you've got to admit they're loyal."

"They had me convinced," Alex added. "I thought Bruno'd pulled you in and shut me out. But why didn't he tell me what he was doing?"

"Do you really need to ask?" said Blitz. "He had a pretty good idea who the sniper was. He didn't want you to have to face it until it was all over. I've met up with a lot of cops in my day, but never one like him. The guy's real."

"So you say," said Alex. "But I'll never forgive him for what Edie went through."

"Why don't you let me worry about that?" said Edie.

"What about us?" Juice interrupted. "We gonna stand here all night while you make up your mind?"

"I hope I don't hear someone mouthing off at me," said Blitz, "'cause if I do, that mouth is gonna be missing some teeth."

"I wasn't talking to you," Juice protested. "I mean her. She gonna turn us in or not?"

Edie started to speak, but Blitz interrupted. "First, you apologize."

"Do what?"

"You heard me. Tell the lady you're sorry for what you did to her."

"Oh, I'm sorry!" Temper shouted. "I'm so sorry. Can I go now?"

Kraze stepped up to Edie and said, "I'm glad you're okay.

We never meant to hurt you. I was filming the whole thing. I'd like to show it to you sometime. And, um, I'm sorry."

Sham hung back and muttered.

"I can't hear you," Blitz prompted.

"I just wanna go home," he blurted. "This is all bullshit."

"I still can't hear you," said Blitz.

"Okay, okay. I'm sorry." He turned his back on them and kicked at the gravel underfoot.

Only Juice remained stubbornly mute, glaring at Blitz.

"Your turn," Blitz reminded him.

"I never apologized to nobody in my life. You the one should be apologizing, acting like you're some kind of cop yourself."

"That's right," said Blitz. "I'm gonna be looking into the possibilities. Time I did something besides babysit a bunch of bugged-out infants."

"I don't believe this!" Juice cried. "I thought we was friends." He turned to Edie. "Lady, you said it before. You said we was loyal. Now look what he's doing. He's going on the other side. What kind of a friend is that?"

"A good friend," said Edie. "He's trying to keep you guys out of trouble. Listen, everybody. If it's up to me, I say let's all go home. We've all got a lot to think about, and I'm too tired to do much serious thinking right now."

"You mean that?" said Juice. "And I don't have to apologize? And you won't grass on us?"

"I mean it," said Edie.

"Well, then, I'm sorry. You're okay, for a cop and a girl."

"Thanks," said Edie, smiling. "But don't ever think of doing anything like that again."

"No, ma'am," said Juice. "Tell you the truth, it was getting to be a pain having you around and trying to figure out what to do with you. Come on, you guys. Let's book on outta here before she changes her mind."

"Yow! Got the urge to write! Got to do it tonight!" shouted Temper, dancing around and waving his arms. "Anybody got some paint?"

"Go home!" Blitz roared. "Before I start knocking heads together."

The four graffiti writers ran off across the yard and disappeared into the shadows.

"What now, brother of Dreemz?" asked Blitz softly. "You got a hard road ahead of you."

"I don't know," said Alex. "I guess Edie's right. We should all go home and get some sleep. See how things look tomorrow."

"One thing's for sure," said Edie. "I don't think we need to worry about Richie dropping out of the Academy. Look at him." She pointed to Maldonado who was busily helping a group of police officers mark off the area where Theo had fallen. "I'm glad you brought him along," she added. "He really laid it on the line to those kids. Got them to think about what they were doing. They're not bad kids, you know. Just a little wild."

Blitz laughed. "Wild is right. And I don't want them ever to be completely tame. Just to count ten before they make their moves." He held out his hand to Alex. "Never thought I'd be shaking hands with a cop. Be seeing you around, brother of Dreemz."

"I hope so," said Alex, and he was surprised to realize that he meant it.

As they watched Blitz fade into the shadows of the yard, Alex put his arm around Edie's shoulder. "I hope I'll be seeing you around, too," he said.

"You could start by getting me out of here. I don't even know where we are."

"End of the line," said Alex. "Deep in the Bronx. We'll have to take the Number Two train."

"No, you won't." Bruno had walked up behind them and gripped Alex's arm. "I just happen to be going your way, Alex. I want to talk to your mother, tell her what's happened."

"That's my job," said Alex stiffly.

"Mine, too," said Bruno. "They've taken your father to Bronx Municipal, but it doesn't look too good for him. I'm going to get your mother and take her there if she wants to go."

"The hell you are!" said Alex. He knocked Bruno's hand off his arm and faced him angrily. "You leave my mother alone. She's seen enough of you. I'll take care of her."

"Look, son," said Bruno. "There's a lot you still don't understand, but there isn't time to explain it to you now. Your father was still alive when they took him out of here. I want to give your mother the chance to see him. You had your chance to talk to him, didn't you? What about her? Don't you think she deserves the same chance? But we have to move fast. He won't last too long."

"I'll take a taxi," said Alex stubbornly.

"Alex, be sensible," said Edie. "Where are you going to find a cab around here?"

Alex whirled on her. "Are you taking his side?"

"I'm not taking anybody's side. But if he's going, I'm going with him. You can do what you like."

"Come on, Alex," Bruno urged. "I know how you feel. But believe me, it's all going to look different to you very soon."

"You couldn't possibly know how I feel," said Alex.

"Alex," said Edie. "You're wasting time."

"All right. All right. We'll go with him. But I don't want to talk to him or listen to any more of his lies."

"It's a deal," said Bruno. "I won't say a word until we get there. Now, let's get a move on."

They followed Bruno out of the yard. The red Trans Am was parked on one of the side streets off Furman Avenue. Alex and Edie squeezed together into the back seat. Before they drove away, Bruno switched on the tape deck at top volume. Even Alex recognized the first strains of Beethoven's triumphant "Eroica" symphony. He whispered to Edie, "The son-of-a-bitch is feeling like a goddamned conquering hero."

They sped through the night with the music blazing the way as urgently as any police siren.

26

The porch lights were on and all the windows glowed with light when they drove up in front of the house and parked. Before Alex had climbed out of the car, his mother threw open the front door and ran down the steps.

"Alex! Alex!" she cried. "Thank God you're all right!"

"Of course I'm all right, Ma." He whipped off his down jacket and wrapped it around her trembling shoulders. "Don't you know any better than to come out in the cold without a coat?"

"Go ahead. Treat me like a baby." She smiled tremulously up at him, but tears brimmed in her eyes and began running down her cheeks. "I was so worried about you. Do you know how late it is? Theo's not home yet."

Frank Bruno finished locking his car and came over to them. "Let's go inside," he said. "We have to talk."

Dorothy Carlson looked at him and then at Edie. "What is this?" she asked. "What's going on?"

"Inside, Ma," said Alex. He guided her up the steps and through the front door, with Edie and Bruno following close behind.

Once inside the house, Bruno went straight to the telephone, motioning to Alex to take his mother on back to the kitchen.

"I'll make some coffee," Edie volunteered. "I could sure use some."

"It's Theo, isn't it?" Dorothy quavered. "Something's happened to him."

"Come on, Ma." Silently, Alex led her back to the kitchen and pulled out a chair for her at the round table where so many breakfasts had been eaten. The radio was playing softly, easy-listening music for night owls. Alex switched it off in case a sudden news bulletin broke in.

While Edie filled the coffee pot and turned it on, Alex sat down next to his mother and took both her hands in his. "Why do you think something's happened to Theo?" he asked.

"What else am I supposed to think when the police come to the house in the middle of the night? He's not here to bring me *good* news, is he? What is it, Alex? I'd rather have you tell me than a stranger."

"I'll tell you, Ma. But I want him to hear what I have to say. I've been thinking about it all the way home."

"All the way home from where?" Dorothy asked.

Edie pulled out a chair and sat down beside them, close to Dorothy. "I know it's hard to wait," she said, "but it'll only be a few minutes. He can't stay on the phone forever. And Alex wants to do this the right way."

"If there is a right way," said Alex bitterly.

When Bruno walked into the kitchen, he was met by three pairs of expectant eyes. He shook his head and said, "No point in going up there now. He came in DOA."

"You might as well sit down then," said Alex.

Bruno pulled out the armchair with the faded cushion on the seat, Theo's chair. Alex started to object, but then let the moment pass.

"Coffee's ready," said Edie. She got up and poured a cup for each of them, and then sat down again. "Go ahead, Alex," she murmured.

"I'll do it if you want me to," Bruno offered.

"No," said Alex. "It's my job."

"I know what DOA means," Dorothy whispered. "Dead on arrival. Is it Theo?"

"Yes, Ma. It's Theo. But there's more."

"Let me guess," said Dorothy. "Theo was the killer. He killed his own son and shot that other boy. God knows how many more he would have killed. Am I right?"

"How did you know?" Bruno asked. "How long have you known?"

Dorothy threw her head back and gazed at the ceiling. "How did I know?" she repeated. "Might as well ask how I remember to keep on breathing. I just knew. Oh, not in any way that would mean anything to the police. But do you think I could have lived with a man all those years and not known what was eating at him? I think I knew it from the way he couldn't look at Paulie there in the morgue. And I certainly knew it when he tried to shift the blame onto Alex."

"Why didn't you tell me?" Bruno asked.

"How could I?" Dorothy asked, looking him straight in the eyes. "He was my husband."

"Ma," said Alex, "you should have told *me*. Don't you think I deserved to know? He was crazy enough to have turned on you."

Dorothy picked up her coffee cup and took a sip. "Good coffee," she murmured. "Yes, I guess he could have. It didn't matter to me. I thought I had nothing left to live for. I wanted to die. I almost did, before Alex put some sense into my head. Alex, why do you think I asked you to get rid of the rifle? It wasn't because of Paulie. It was because of him. I was afraid he was going to stick it in his mouth one day and blow his brains out. I can't tell you how many times I begged him to go see a doctor. But he wouldn't. I

292

never thought he'd hurt Paulie, though. Anybody else, but not Paulie."

"He told me it was an accident, Ma," said Alex. "He said he didn't mean to kill anybody. He just wanted to scare Paulie out of doing graffiti. He didn't even know it was Paulie he was shooting at. It wasn't the first time he'd done it. Nobody got hurt before. I believed him. If you'd seen him, you would too."

"How could a thing like that be an accident?" Dorothy fixed her bleak eyes on Alex's face. "I'm glad he's dead," she said fiercely. "Did you kill him? I hope you did."

"Me? No!" Alex exclaimed, shocked at the truth that had finally found its way into the open. "I had my chance, and I blew it. One of the other cops did."

"Tell it all, Alex," said Bruno. "If Farley hadn't fired when he did, you wouldn't be sitting here right now."

"That's not what Theo told me. He said he lost his nerve and fired up into the sky. He knew he was dying. Why would he lie about it?"

"Enough," said Dorothy. "It's all over. I don't want to know any more. Who lied and who didn't lie, it really doesn't matter. What matters is it's almost morning, and I don't know what I'm going to do with the rest of my life." Tears ran down her cheeks again, but she went on talking, more to herself than to them. "Theo took up so much of my time and my mind. From the very beginning, he needed me. He needed more from me than I could ever give him, but he could never admit that he needed anyone. All of his shouting and bullying was just to cover up the scared little kid inside. There wasn't anything I could do about that. He wouldn't let me. He never gave himself a chance. I hope he's at peace with himself now." She dried her eyes on a paper napkin and gripped Alex's hand. "Don't hate him," she said.

"I'll try not to," said Alex. "But what about you? You shouldn't be alone. I'll give up my apartment. I'll come back and stay with you."

"Alex," said Edie cautiously, "do you think that's a good idea?"

"Wait," said Bruno. "Before anybody does anything, I want to hear what Alex plans to do. What about the Academy, Alex?"

"Good question. What about it?"

"Are you going to finish your training?"

"You must have been reading my mind. All the way home, I kept thinking I was too soft for police work, the way I froze on top of that train. Don't get me wrong. I'm glad it happened this time. But it could happen again. Even if it didn't, I'd always have the fear of it happening again. So, to answer your question, I don't know if I'm going to finish my training. Right now, I feel like dropping out."

"Will you give it a week before you decide?" Bruno asked. "Just one week?"

"I could do that," said Alex.

"And could you stand to have dinner at my mother's place next Sunday? All of you?"

"Dinner?" said Dorothy, incredulously.

"Well, you've got to eat, don't you?" said Bruno. "And my mother's a pretty fair cook. Ask Alex."

"She's a wonderful cook," said Alex. "But why?"

"Do I have to have a reason?" asked Bruno. "Let's just say I want to keep in touch." He stood up and held out a hand to Dorothy. "Mrs. Carlson, I'm sorry it turned out this way. If there's anything I can do. . . ."

"Thanks," said Dorothy, taking his hand. "I don't think so." She got up to walk with him to the front door. "I'll be going back to work in a few days. That'll help. And I'd like to come to dinner on Sunday. Maybe your mother can tell me a few things about having a cop for a son."

294

As Bruno and Dorothy left the kitchen, Edie said, "Alex, don't turn your back on Bruno. He's trying to help you."

"I know that," said Alex wearily. "I just don't know if I want his help. Shouldn't you be going home? Bruno could give you a lift."

"I don't want to leave you alone tonight. And I don't want to be alone. Would your mother mind if I stayed here?"

"I don't think so. She likes you. Oh, Edie, let's never have secrets from each other. None of this would have happened if there hadn't been so many secrets."

"I've got one secret I'm going to let you in on right now," said Edie.

"What's that?" said Alex, staring at her apprehensively. "You're not pregnant?"

"No." She reached across Dorothy's vacant chair and took Alex's face between her two hands. "It's just that I realized tonight, when you were up on top of that train and the shooting started, I realized how very much I love you. When I saw you fall, I thought you'd been shot. It was like being shot myself. If Farley hadn't done the job, I would have. And you know I wouldn't have missed."

"Sharpshooter," Alex murmured. "I guess I'd better not ever cross you up."

"Damn right," said Edie. "And now I think it's time we got some sleep before it's time to get up and go to the Academy."

When Dorothy returned to the kitchen, she heard their slow footsteps going up the back stairs and she smiled.